YOU MIGHT JUST MAKE IT OUT OF THIS ALIVE

I0524572

Garrett Cook

ERASERHEAD PRESS
PORTLAND, OREGON

ERASERHEAD PRESS
PO BOX 10065
PORTLAND, OR 97296

WWW.ERASERHEADPRESS.COM

ISBN: 978-1-62105-173-2

"Re-Mancipator" first appeared in *The Bizarro Starter Kit (Purple)*
"Beast with Two Backs" first appeared in *In Heaven, Everything is Fine*
"Dieselpig" first appeared in *The Magazine of Bizarro Fiction #11*
"Having Set Out to be Vanquished" first appeared in *Deepest, Darkest Eden*
"Brian's Girl" first appeared in *Exquisite Corpse, April 2008*

Cover art copyright © 2015 by Jim Agpalza
www.JIMAGPALZA.com

Printed in the USA.

Acknowledgments

To everyone who gave this shit a chance.

Jeff Burk, Andrei Codrescu, Cody Goodfellow, John Skipp, Cameron Pierce, Jonathan Moon, Kirsten Alene Pierce, and Edward Morris.

To everyone who gave me a chance.

John Robinson, Rose O' Keefe, Leza Cantoral, Matthew Winner, Lydia Fascia, Esther Wakefield,Sheryl Westeleigh, Wick Hill, Jennifer Robin, Nikki Guerlain, Chris Kelso, Nathan Carson, Lynn McSweeney, and all the clients whose faith in my skills have kept me alive

Thanks.

Eraserhead Press Books by Garrett Cook

Jimmy Plush, Teddy Bear Detective
Time Pimp

CONTENTS

Re-Mancipator

He pulled out of her and saw a smile that had seldom been real. It had been a smile for the milk fund and for movie magazines, a smile seldom shared in earnest and seldom a genuine postcoital gift.

"It should always be like this, Johnny Booth," said Norma Jean, whispering into his ear, contributing these words and a few small, affectionate bites at the same time, "it should be like this, forever."

John Booth's face, which was seconds ago the very picture of joy and serenity, turned into hard plastic.

"We can stay here," Norma Jean explained desperately, "we can stay here and we can survive and build a life."

Booth hated turning his back on her, but he wasn't going to be silent or pretend nothing was happening as men often did with women. He knew her history, the chances at happiness she had lost, the ones that weren't about happiness at all. Which is why it pained him to say what he was about to.

"Norma Jean, I could be happy with you anywhere. There isn't a world so awful that it wouldn't be brightened by wakin' up next you for the rest of my life. But, baby, I fucked up the world and I've gotta go out there and unfuck it. There's no way around it."

A lot of things could be said about the girl and her acting skills, stiff, naive, inhuman, awkward but there was something she could do that few actresses could do like she could, and that was cry. Besides pills and disappointments, she had tears to spare and when he said that he was goin' out to unfuck the world, she proved it.

"You can't go out there, Johnny. You gave me another chance, made me happy for the first time. There's never been a man who made me happy and meant if before, Johnny Booth and you know it. What about me?"

He answered the question by grabbing her face and kissing her. It was rough, it was aesthetic, it was a celluloid kiss from a real man's lips, it insisted on being filmed, but still it was just for them. She dried her tears. She understood.

"So it's like that, Johnny?"

"It's like that, Norma Jean."

She smiled and crawled under the bed, giving him a view of one of the finest asses to grace the silver screen as she did. If things weren't so emotional and he didn't have to go, he'd have wanted another go at her. When she emerged, she had the flamberge. She knelt before him and presented it. He felt his legend crackle, he felt the story the image could build, the power and the beauty of being handed a magic sword by Marilyn Monroe.

"May you kill many Lincolns," said Norma Jean solemnly.

"You know I will, Norma Jean," John Booth replied and they left the bedroom together.

Musashi was in the hallway. It wasn't surprising. He never slept.

"You're going now," he said. Many of Musashi's statements sounded like questions and many of Musashi's questions sounded like statements.

"Yes, I'm going."

"Good?" it sounded like a statement but Booth could tell he was asking him.

"It will have to be."

"Good."

"Yeah."

"Remember what I taught you."

Booth laughed.

"How could I forget? You're Musashi Miyamoto."

In the kitchen, Homer was blowing smoke from his hookah at Herodotus. Although blind, he could tell about where the historian was. Herodotus wished he could use the hookah but couldn't, being a cat and all. Homer stopped when he heard footsteps.

"That you?"he asked as Booth and Norma Jean entered the kitchen.

"No, it's seven Lincolns," said Herodotus, holding back a snicker.

Homer jumped to his feet.

"Shit! This is what I've been practicing for. Get my sniper rifle, cat, it ends tonight!"

The cat rolled his eyes. Homer, being blind of course did not see this.

"Of course it's Booth, you crazy blind bastard. And that's not a sniper rifle. It's a saxophone. I've been fuckin' with you because you ate my good cheese."

Homer blew smoke in the cat's face again, this time it was not out of generosity but malice.

"Asshole."

Booth hugged the blind bard.

"Thanks for everything."

"It was nothing, If anything I ought to thank you for the story you've given me. They're a hell of a commodity for bards."

Booth rubbed Herodotus behind the ears.

"And thanks for what you've done. You've been a hell of a sport, too."

Herodotus purred.

"It wasn't all that bad, Booth. I'm honored to know a man who's as willing to right a mistake as you are. Good luck. Give 'em hell."

Booth nodded.

"I will kill many Lincolns."

And at that, John Booth stepped outside, flamberge in hand into a hell of his own making, a nightmare world built on a foundation of lies to do what any good man with access to a big sharp blade ought to do: to make history.

II.

Noctys Blakblud, Gothrocker General of Washington, DC tossed a sack of Marilyn Monroe parts at John Hbooth's door instead of knocking. He figured it would be louder and a more rockin' kind of thing to do. Hbooth did not respond on the first toss, so he tossed it again. The noise was squishier this time. Hbooth heard the first toss but since it was 4 am and he'd worked until 2:47 creating Marilyn from soulstuff and Historion particles, Hbooth was slow to rise. He heard the second toss and had a good idea why it sounded squishier. Sack of body parts. Again. Hbooth ran for the door like a bat out of hell before a third . Sure enough, an angry Noctys was holding a bloody sack.

"My liege, it's four am…"

Noctys took a swig from a bottle of rubbing alcohol.

" I've done a shitload of coke, Hbooth!"

"I take it Marilyn is in that bag."

"Yes," snarled Noctys, "your shittyass Marilyn Monroe is in this sack."

This instantly made Hbooth defensive. He took pride in the fruits of his candyman talents.

"You realize that wasn't a clone or anything, that was Marilyn Monroe. So, my Marilyn Monroe was not shitty, but perfect.. And it seems you have killed her."

Noctys flipped Hbooth the bird.

"Perfect, my ass! This Marilyn couldn't sword fight worth shit!"

Hbooth rubbed his temples with two fingers. His brain was starting to ache.

"I brought Marilyn Monroe back to life, constructed this flawless copy of her body and you got in a sword fight with her?"

"A flamberge fight to be precise. What did you think I was going to do with her?"

Put his dirty, rockstar hands all over her large, round wonderful breasts, breathe all over her shining alabaster skin, stick his syphilitic prick into her...Hbooth was almost kind of relieved that it had come down to a flamberge fight. Feeling her soul as he reconstructed her with candyman's gift and Historions, he experienced her poetry, her despair and he longed for her, wished he didn't have to do what Noctys told him, wished he could have run away with her and not left her in the care of this rockstar creep.

"Did somebody tell you Marilyn Monroe was good at sword fighting?"

"It was a fantasy of mine. You work for me and you make these fantasies happen with your dead people powers. The candy man can!"

Hbooth was a candy man and that was what he could do, so Noctys was right. He just wished he didn't have to.

"You didn't need to bring me the corpse. I don't reanimate corpses. I use my talents and gather Historions and soulstuff to..."

Noctys tossed the sack at Hbooth. It hit him in the chest, knocking him to the ground.

"Boring! Make her again! Make two so I can race 'em!"

Hbooth sighed. Rockstars would never understand the concept of candymen. The candyman could, but there was only one thing any candyman could do.

"You'll have to talk to Juanita. She's the one who can duplicate things."

"You're stupid and boring, Hbooth. You're totally like that ancestor of yours that killed Lincoln and ruined society. Thanks to your piece of shit ancestor, rockstars will always rule!"

Noctys got on his dragon-shaped motorcycle and sped off, laughing and chugging rubbing alcohol. Hbooth wished he had some to chug. Noctys was right. When his ancestor (who shamed the family so much that they put a silent h in the front of their names) killed Lincoln, he had doomed America to centuries of rule by idiots and eventually rockstars. The new president, Amber Honeylove could use a bullet in her head, if she didn't have a candyman that could make people bulletproof on her staff. If only there were still men like Lincoln, men who could stand up to the rockstars and lead America to freedom. If only…who can take the sunshine, sprinkle it with dew, cover it in chocolate and a miracle or two…the candy man can.

III.

'History," said Herodotus the cat, "is bullshit. The sooner people realize this, the easier the world will be to fix. It is easily manipulated, vulnerable to the machinations of evil men. You'll get more truth out of those yarns that Blind Fuckin' Willie Mc Tell over there spun for wine money."

"But history's the only true thing. By its definition, it has to be the only true thing."

"He's right," the bard chimed in, "it's bullshit. Anybody can make it, anybody can break it."

IV.

The words were not "Sic Semper Tyrannis." "He's sick, he's mental, it's rabies!" said John Wilkes Booth as he pulled the trigger, knowing what the lizard worshipers at Bohemian Grove had put into the negroloving Yankee president. He had used his skills as an actor to infiltrate the grove and find out why nobody had stopped him from trying to free the slaves and what he had seen, the orgies, the giant owl, the talking reptile statues…too much for most men's sanity to bear. But he was stronger than most men, strong enough to pull the trigger on a sick president, no matter what it would take.

V.

"Our boy's gonna kick her ass," said Noctys, beaming with pride.

"Yup, this debate's a lock."

Amber Honeylove had taken off her clothes and was violently humping the microphone. This was how her debates usually ran; lewd, naked and showered with candy, dollar bills and applause. Hbooth was worried about Abe. He looked green and sickly, like he might not make it. Was his patch job flawed? Couldn't be. He recited the mantra to himself.

"Who can take the sunrise, sprinkle it with dew…"

"…cover it in chocolate and a miracle or two," replied the Voice of Wisdom, "the candyman can."

Hbooth inhaled and exhaled repeatedly to calm himself.

"I didn't fail, I didn't fail, I didn't fail….the candyman can."

And indeed he could. But he did not know about his ancestor or the fatcat plot or what was called Abies by the fatcats as they sipped panda sperm at Bohemian Grove. He did not know that bringing back Lincoln intact brought back one scary motherfucker. He also did not know that Lincoln's first impulse when losing a debate was to bite his opponent on the arm. Which he did. Blood gushed from Amber's butterfly-tattooed arm as he took a good chunk out of it.

"Give 'em Hell, Abe!" shouted Noctys from the third row as he carved an inverted crucifix on his bare chest.

Hbooth shook his head.

"Noctys, I think something's wrong."

Noctys slapped Hbooth in the face.

"I don't fucking pay you to think!"

Amber should have called in her secret service goons to put an end to the feral president but biting was one of Amber's hundreds of fetishes. She pounced on Lincoln, ready to return the favor. Lincoln did not particularly know what to make of this, only that he wanted to eat her, so kept biting. And as he tore off bits of excessively tanned smooth teenage girl flesh, she began to change. Her head was expanding, becoming longer, more angular, more like his. Tufts of hair were appearing on her face and her bones were cracking and reknitting themselves. Her thick teen popstar legs were becoming long, spindly and stilt like. In short, she was turning into a tanned, large breasted Abraham Lincoln, complete with a fleshy pink stovepipe hat growing out of the top of her head like a tumor. Lincoln's eyes widened. He cackled maniacally. He embraced his pornographic teenieboppelganger.

"Lincoln loves only Lincoln!" he screamed before shoving his tongue down her throat.

For the first time in several years, Noctys was legitimately concerned.

"Hbooth, I shouldn't have ordered you to bring Lincoln back to life."

Hbooth slapped himself in the forehead.

"And I shouldn't have brought Baudelaire back to life so you could get syphilis from him. I also shouldn't have told you what Baudelaire and syphilis were."

"I quire agree. You should be punished. I could fuck you and give you syphilis."

"Uh…that would be REWARDING me." It was a lie but Noctys would certainly believe it.

The tall spindly Lincoln monster that had once been Amber Honeylove disengaged from Lincoln, feeling a greater urge for carnage than carnality. Surprisingly fast for such a gangly, addled creature she lunged at one of the secret service agents, dragged him to her with her Lincoln long arms and began chewing on his face. As she chewed, his bones broke and knitted as they had in her, and the big pink stovepipe of flesh grew out of his skull. She and Lincoln laughed together.

"Lincoln loves only Lincoln!"

The secret service man bit another secret service man who bit a cameraman who bit another cameraman, who bit another cameraman who bit a girl in the first row who bit the girl next to her who bit another that bit another in an orgy of biting and Lincolning. The audience was applauding.

"Lincoln! Lincoln!"

"Bite 'em all, Abes!"

"I want a beard like that!"

"I want to be tall!"

"I want to be a hero!"

"Anyone can be president! Even a woman!"

This would have been an excellent time for everyone to flee in terror and evacuate the auditorium but it was America and in America, you can't be afraid of Abraham Lincoln and the approval of their peers, rabid Lincoln monsters or not told the audience that everything was cool and there was nothing better to be than Abraham Lincoln.

Noctys joined the crowd rushing the crowd of Lincolns that was rushing the crowd.

"Make me president! Make me president!"

"Noctys, he's a monster!" Hbooth protested.

Noctys flipped Hbooth two birds.

"So am I! So are all of us!"

Hbooth decided to rush the exit instead of arguing with Noctys, who, sadly enough would probably be better off as a Lincoln monster. As the only person fleeing, it was not very difficult to reach the exit. What would be difficult was to figure out where the hell to go next. He hopped on Noctys' dragon-shaped motorcycle and got to thinking. He only got to think for about a block before his thoughts were interrupted

Turned out that enroute to the debate, Lincoln had already bitten several people and those people had been rampaging through town claiming other victims for an hour.. For rabid undead Lincolns, a one hour head start was plenty.

V.

Hbooth took off the blindfold. Five. Wasn't bad. Wasn't good either. Five hatless mannequins did not mean hope for the future by any stretch of the imagination. Musashi grunted. Hbooth was taken aback to discover that it was Musashi's approval grunt.

"Doing better."

"Thank you, Musashi."

Musashi punched Hbooth in the gut. His feast was like a meat tenderizer.

"Only the weak man accepts compliments!"

"I am sorry…"

Musashi punched him again.

"Only the weak man apologizes!"

"O-okay…"

Another punch.

"Only the weak man stutters!"

Hbooth put the blindfold back on and readied the katana. Musashi started the stopwatch. Slice, slice, slice, slice, slice, slice, slice, slice, slice, beep. Hbooth removed the blindfold. Seven sliced hats, one mannequin nicked on the shoulder. Musashi grunted a slightly nicer grunt.

"Better."

"No, still bad."

"Good! You start to get it!" Musashi smiled and killed the bottle of rice wine he'd been chugging.

"Thanks, I thought I was doing…"

Musashi smashed the bottle over Hbooth's head. It didn't hurt much. Noctys had broken a lot of bottles over his head in his day.

"Everything okay?" asked Homer, having heard the sound of the broken bottle and rushing to find out if all was well. Herodotus was on his shoulder.

"Hrmmm," Musashi grunted.

16

"Oh, good. How many dead mannequins?"

"Seven," said Hbooth, "but it's not good enough."

"I agree," said Herodotus, jumping down from Homer's shoulder and lying on the floor to clean his genitals, "especially for a man descended from a man who was famous only for killing Lincoln. You should be a genius at killing Lincoln."

Homer raised an eyebrow.

"In Ancient Greek, there is no H. It's just a rough breathing."

V.

Stovepipe heads as far as the eye could see, skinny-tall wobbly unmen biting, clawing, homogenizing, making everybody the man that history had loved so dear, the rabid lunatic slain by the hanged patriot, secret weapon of the fatcats of Bohemian Grove who passed the Holy Grail around and drank to the end of mankind, to a world where everyone was one rabid monster president that could be easily controlled with reptile mind control techniques. They kissed a photo of John Hbooth, praising his mistake and themselves for their centuries of fake history. They knew if they made a hero out of Lincoln and a monster out of Hbooth somebody would bring back Lincoln and the Historions would duplicate the disease exactly.

A Lincoln walked onto a city bus, sat down beside an Asian male to female transsexual. Took a bite out of her arm. Took a bite out of her neck and her bared thigh. Made her greenish, made her lanky, made her head extend. The Lincoln moved crossed the aisle moving onto the next seat, as the greenish, bearded miniskirted Asian tranny Lincoln stood up to take the bus by surprise. One armed Vietnam vet en route to the welfare office got bitten. The Abies gave him back his arm, to choke, grab and scrape, to drag the fleeing screaming Elvis impersonators en route to the Council of Elvises meeting by their throat, bring them to his sharp toothed mouth, and make them like him. The courageous driver tried to crash the bus, martyr himself before the illness could spread, but trannies, grannies, Elvises and Vietnam vets with Lincolnized faces wouldn't let it happen. Instead, the bus careened into a group of nuns on a walk with some children in wheelchairs, kept going and then crashed.

Fire and impact were not enough, burned though they were, scarred though they were, the Abies reknit their bones and reminded them of their thirst for flesh and their desire to homogenize the world and make it Lincoln. Nun corpses, crippled children corpses, granted the breath of life by disease, malice, egocentricity. Child Lincolns on stunted long Lincoln legs and Lincolns in torn nuns habits joined the band of burned monstrosities to find more to rend and rip and reconstruct.

Ragtag street people armed with makeshift spears and flaming Old Granddad molotovs tried to fight back to little avail. The Lincolns were hungry for their selfhood, hungry for the taste of Lincolnfree flesh in their mouths and the thrill of knowing that there would be one more of them. Lincoln loved only Lincoln and that was that. They weren't doing so hot until Charlie Battleaxe showed up.

Before the Lincolns came, Charlie Battleaxe was an urban legend, something homeless parents used to remind their kids not to talk to heavymetal hasbeens. Before Noctys Blakblud took over, Gothrocker General wasn't a job. The furthest a Gothrocker could progress in the government was District Gothrock supervisor and DC was a town run on Metal. But, Noctys was louder, dumber and more willing to cut himself to entertain voters and Charlie was reduced to living alone in his trillion dollar fortress of a mansion without butlers, maids, prostitutes or candymen. So, in his loneliness, he roamed the streets killing homeless people with a battleaxe. It wasn't out of malice or contempt, he just couldn't come up with a better way of reaching people.

Charlie Battleaxe didn't want anybody horning in on his murder and the Lincolns seemed like they would do just that.

So, the fat, red-bearded tattooed metal has-been and Viking manqué took up his axe for the people. He rushed into the fray, eyes afire, heart full of anger and sorrow and started taking heads. Smiling, awash in arterial spray, he screamed out.

"Thank you, Minot!" was all he he could think to scream. The feeling of pride left him momentarily thinking he was back at the Minot, North Dakota Civic Auditorium opening for Quiet Riot again. The delusion vanished when he realized that at the Minot North Dakota Civic Auditorium six and a half foot tall Japanese tourists with stovepipey flesh growths didn't try to throw the snapping severed heads of bearded housewives at him. He decapitated the bearded Lincolnized Japanese tourist only to find that its head was rolling around on the ground trying to bite his foot. Since he was wearing sandals, he didn't dare kick it, but since he had a battleaxe, he buried it in its stovepipey growth.

"Lincoln loves only Lincoln!" it screamed, unable to articulate its pain in any other way. He brought down the axe again, splitting open the growth.

"Thank you, Minot!" Charlie Battleaxe was hoping more blood would spray out. It did not. What did, however crawl out were a bunch of tiny lizards with Abraham Lincoln faces who were foaming green stuff at the mouth.

"Lincoln loves only Lincoln!" they squeaked before melting into a puddle of green, foamy lizard goo.

"Thank you, Minot!" he screamed in reply, slicing another Lincoln's stovepipey growth in half. Lincoln lizards, green stuff and goo yet again. The homeless survivors took shelter behind trash cans, rooting for Charlie Battleaxe but still too frightened to help him out. The Lincolns grew more zealous, gathering in a bigger, tighter knit group, ten at a time. But Charlie Battleaxe wasn't standing for it, Charlie Battleaxe was a creature of heavy metal psychosis, wanton violence, deep-seated, misplaced wet brain rage, something a man from the 1860's couldn't understand, even as a rabies inducing zombie juggernaut.

VII.

"Be careful," warned the statue of Herpetarch Slyxx'ks'h, "she is a phenomenal swordsman and very familiar with the works of Musashi."

"Panic not," said Kennedy's fatcat clone assassin, "I've made several phone calls as the president. She is demoralized, she's been doing too many pills. Jackie and I can easily defeat her."

Jackie sipped her strength-enhancing panda sperm reptile cocktail.

"That little blonde bitch is good as dead."

The fatcats laughed as they invented crack to spread through the ghettos and injected monkeys with Anthropoid Infecting Dark Sorcery, an acronym which they would later claim meant something else.

"Your confidence pleases me. Let us only hope that her skills never fall into the hands of the Booth family."

The fatcats laughed again.

"Forgive me, Herpetarch," said Frank Sinatra, "but there's no way. Marilyn dies tonight and we'll make it look like an accident. I've already gotten her addicted to sleeping pills through the mob psychiatrist I had taking care of her."

The fatcats laughed again.

As night fell, Kennedy's fatcat clone came to the door.

"Johnny? Is that you?"

"It is in fact me."

Through her sleeping pill haze she could have sworn he didn't have his Boston accent. He hadn't been using his accent much. Probably because that cunt Jackie made fun of him for it . She had always thought something was up with Jackie, but Frank had said it was just jealousy and Frank was a smart guy. Frank knew people. Frank could be trusted.

"Johnny, I'm sad. I'm lonely, Johnny."

"It is beautiful and ironic that in your loneliness, you are not alone."

"Oh, Johnny, you always know what to say."

The Kennedy clone from Bohemian Grove was in, Marilyn's nightgown hit the floor and a champagne bottle was uncorked. .All was going according to plan for the reptiles.

IX.

"We need a war council," Marilyn suggested as she swung the sword at a Lincolncougar.

"A war council? How are we going to get a war council?"

"You could make one."

Hbooth wasn't too sure about the idea.

"What if all the people on the war council have egocentric zombie rabies?"

Marilyn took a moment to respond, since she was narrowly avoiding the Lincolncougar's teeth.

"I don't think that's going to happen, Johnny."

X.

Hbooth hit the gas hard on the dragon-shaped motorcycle, wondering what the hell there was to do beyond dodging Lincolns and getting someplace safe so he could maybe think of a way to undo the mess he'd caused out of hatred for rockstars and love for Marilyn. Sweet little Marilyn would certainly not approve, sweet little Marilyn would say…she'd say…shit. Shit! This was no good. Marilyn was at Noctys' mansion, a mansion whose door Noctys had just driven through on his motorcycle. A mansion with a mural of Jefferson Davis painted on its side, which would surely irritate the Lincolns. Hbooth found himself wishing he was one of those candymen who could go from one place to another just by thinking of it. Instead of one of those candymen whose ability to resurrect the dead doomed civilization. At least there was only of those. Too bad that one was him.

A group of Deadheads had just been bitten by some hip-hop loving Tommy Hilfigger'd suburban poseurs whose stovepipes had torn apart the black winter hats they had previously used to show how cool they were. Now they were much cooler and had much bigger hats. Now they were like most of the people they admired, now they were like almost everybody. Hopefully not almost everybody. How fast could this have spread? Hbooth discarded his thoughts of epidemiology and resumed motorcycle survival thoughts. Unlikely motorcycle survival thoughts.

"Lincoln loves only Lincoln!" he screamed.

"Lincoln loves only Lincoln!" one of the Deadheads shouted as the Lincolnizing process finished up.

"Lincoln loves only Lincoln!"

"Lincoln loves only Lincoln!"

The hiphop and Deadhead Lincolns were fooled by this simple gesture. If he could try it on every other Lincoln between there and Noctys' mansion, it would be fine. If it worked. These Lincolns caught on a few seconds too late, started their stilty shambling toward him when he was already out of sight and all he needed do was take a short cut down an alleyway to make them forget he had existed. He hoped it would continue to be this easy. He zoomed down another busy street, trying the mantra on a Lincolnized prostitute and a recently Lincolnized cop who must have been stupid enough to try to arrest her for Lincolnizing a gawky, Lincolnheaded French poodle that barked hungrily for flesh.

"Lincoln loves only Lincoln!" the prostitute shouted back.

"Lincoln loves only Lincoln!" the cop shouted.

The French poodle was not convinced. With his beast sharp nose he knew what Lincoln smelled like and what Lincoln did not and what Lincoln didn't smell like smelled like food zooming by on a motorcycle. Luckilfor Hbooth a six foot high French poodle on Lincoln legs was not much of a runner, unluckily for Hbooth, the French poodle had already bitten an Irish wolfhound and a Chihuahua that were sniffing around for survivors not far from him. On its long new legs, the Irish wolfhound was almost as fast a motorcycle, and the Chihuahua, its skinny, tiny body skittering like a spider on bony Lincoln limbs actually was.

Though the jump was awkward, the Chihuahua made it, clinging to the back of the motorcycle to get at Hbooth, who had to drive with one hand as he punched it in the face. Hbooth was distracted, driving slower, potential prey not for just for the wolfhound and the Chihuahua, but for a mass of Lincolns down the street that heard the motorcycle and knew that it meant people. By the time, he managed to gouge out the Lincoln chihuahua's eyes and toss it off the motorcycle, it was the least of his problems.

If Hbooth had been listening for it, he could have heard Charlie Battleaxe calling out "come back!" Charlie had been dispatching Lincolns for several minutes (a pretty long time considering the Lincoln attacks had only been going on for about an hour and a half) and he showed no signs of tiring and stopping. Lizards and goo everywhere, homeless people applauding him (though still wanting nothing to do with the fight). Life was good and now the bastards were running. After the sound of a motorcycle. He ran after them, axe held aloft to see what it was they were chasing after and chase them in turn.

This is how Hbooth and Charlie Battleaxe met up. Hbooth was trapped between the hungry Lincolns Charlie had been fighting off and the Lincoln dogs that had been chasing him. He figured he was good as dead or good as Abe. But, Charlie Battleaxe had no problem with splitting a couple stovepipes from behind so he could see what they were after. And when he did, he was happier to split a lot more.

"Blakblud! Blakblud!" he growled as he split two stovepipes in one wide battle axe arc.

Noctys' dragon-shaped motorcycle had at one point been Charlie Battleaxe's most prized possession, a badge of authority and metal supremacy. But, during the election Charlie had been so sure of his rock supremacy over Noctys that he bet his motorcycle. He lost that bet and lost the cycle and it was many of the factors leading to his downward spiral into homeless axe murder.

"Blakblud, you bastard, you're mine!" Lincoln after Lincoln fell at Charlie's axe, so many that the Irish wolfhound ignored the motorcycle to pounce on Charlie. It made a more valiant attempt than any Lincoln yet, actually using its mass and bestial fury to bring him to the ground and prep him for a bite. Still, even a monster dog couldn't get between the crazed metalhead and his custom motorcycle. Charlie found the strength to split the dog's stovepipe roll it off and jump at the motorcycle.

Hbooth rolled out of the way just in time, leaving Charlie flat on the pavement, prey for more advancing Lincolns, who'd been converting homeless people as Charlie dismembered their brethren. As he gunned it toward the mansion, Hbooth hoped the metalhead would stay down, though he was frightened at the thought of such a fierce man being converted into a Lincoln. He didn't know what to feel when the fierce metalhead stood up again, pursuing the motorcycle, forgetting how much faster it could go than he could.

Hbooth idled the bike and got off. It occurred to him who this was and why he was chasing him.

"I'm not Noctys, Charlie. I'm his candyman. And I need to get back to his house safely. When you get there, you can break anything you want , you can piss all over his collection of original Goya paintings, you can make sexually explicit phone calls to his mother. Whatever. I hate the bastard and he's probably a Lincoln by now anyway. I'll even give you the bike if you let a friend and I hide out at your place."

Through street-crazy and slaughter-fogged, Charlie saw reality once more, head jerking into alertness with a gesture appropriate for a stalking Michael Myers. He remembered that Noctys usually did not wear a shirt, was usually covered in cuts and meaningless tattoos and was usually very quick to proclaim that he was Noctys, while this guy was quick to deny it. Noctys also wasn't afraid of most sharp things, so wouldn't have tried to flee. Wasn't Noctys. It was Noctys' poor, long suffering candyman. Damn good candyman. He'd always wanted this guy instead of his candyman, who had the power to turn diamonds into cheese and vice versa.

"Damn, I know you. You ain't Noctys at all. Good for you. Goth rocker general or not, I still got a feelin' like it would suck being that guy."

"I think so too. But not to worry, he's a Lincoln now."

"Good. It ain't like I ever needed an excuse for killin' but damned if it ain't nice to have one every once awhile, besides, you know, that I'm out of my fucking mind."

"You might be out of your fuckin' mind, but you figured out how to kill Lincolns."

Charlie shrugged.

"I just didn't like those damn arrogant foofy skinhats. They make me real mad."

Hbooth surveyed the devastation. There were more corpses than he could count.

"Shit, Charlie, I can see that."

"I wouldn't have voted for that cocksucker that's for sure. You and me got a lot in common, John Wilkes Booth, you come from a family of Lincoln killers and I'm a damn good Lincoln killer." The hairs on the back of Hbooth's neck stood up on end. He still didn't want to be thought of as a descendant of John Wilkes Booth.

"Different Booth. I'm Hbooth with an H."

"Suit yourself," said Charlie, "then you drive and I kill."

XI.

"That sounds awfully simplistic."

"Not to me," Homer chimed in, "it makes a lot of sense."

Musashi grunted. Possibly in agreement.

Marilyn poured another glass of champagne with vodka.

"He's not just any cat, Johnny. He's Herodotus."

"But…"

"Just go to the theater," the cat said slowly in a tone that five years old would have found patronizing, "and do what you do, but backwards."

"I don't see how I could travel in time."

"Just revise history," said Homer, "it's easy. I did it all the time."

"That doesn't make any sense."

"That's because it's bullshit, time travel, raising the dead, history, it's bullshit."

XII.

"Who can take the sunshine, sprinkle it with dew…"

"Cover it in chocolate and a miracle or two," replied the Voice of Wisdom as Hbooth carefully wove together the Historions that made up Marilyn. It felt nice feeling her soul and the contents of her life coming together. He felt a creepy urge to lick it since he thought it would taste good, in spite of the sourness and the bittersweet quality of it all. It certainly smelled nice enough. She certainly smelled nice enough. He picked up some things he had missed as he examined and joined with her soul the night before. Such as her passion for samurai culture and swordsmanship. Noctys had been right. Must have been a coincidence, one of his many misfiring neurons misfiring correctly. Well done, Hamletmonkey. Too bad it had ended so badly. She didn't like the cuts at all, didn't like…when Noctys snuck up, tasered her, impaled her on his sword and then put a sword in her hand when she was down to make it look like he won. Durable soul in spite out of all the times it had succumbed to despair, wasn't feeling "oh, the misery of being impaled!" but rather "I could've beaten that bastard, I'm sure his technique was inferior."

She stepped out of history shimmering in one of her gowns from Some Like it Hot and kissed Hbooht on the cheek.

"Oh, it's you, you wonderful boy!"

He blushed.

"Hi, Marilyn."

"That wasn't as long as the last time."

Hbooth tried not to laugh. It would've been at the ingenuousness of the statement not at the stupidity if he had, though.

"No, it certainly wasn't. He wanted you back."

She smiled. Her eyebrows fluttered.

"Really? He wanted me back?"

"Well, you know…"

She hanged her head. Her smile disappeared and she commenced searching Hbooth's nightstand for champagne. Hbooth had anticipated this and had purchased some.

Marilyn slapped him. She placed a hand on her chest.

"My goodness! What kind of a man keeps champagne in his nightstand all the time."

Hbooth was shocked. He couldn't find a reply. She shocked him again, when she started to giggle.

"I'm just pulling your leg, Johnny. Why don't you get some ice?"

He smiled and nodded, still tongue tied by love. He went to the kitchen and got a bucket of ice. Hbooth kept lots of buckets in his house for when Noctys would drop in. Seemed like that man couldn't go five minutes without excreting something. He was relieved that he could find one that hadn't been used yet.

Marilyn applauded his return.

"My goodness, champagne in your dresser, ice buckets in your kitchen. You're like the Ritz, Johnny."

He poured her half a glass with some ice. He anticipated her next question.

"Vodka?"

"Next drawer down."

"Incredible."

When she poured the vodka, it was oddly dainty, hitting the rim exactly.

"I'm such a hypocrite, sometimes, Johnny," she said, with a tinge of melancholia, "I study Bushido and I can't stop drinking. Then again, how do you stop drinking when you spend your time with Sinatra and the Kennedys? Hmm? It's difficult, Johnny, it really is. Actress, woman, lush, samurai. What's a gal to do?"

Again, Hbooth could not find an answer. Marilyn giggled.

"You're quiet, Johnny, I like that. Not often that a man will just sit and let a girl talk like that. Except for when he doesn't care what she's saying. But you care, don't you?"

"Yes."

"Well, there's one word. You drinking?"

"I…"

"She poured him a glass of champagne. He took it. He could use one.

"Thank you."

She touched his face.

"No, thank you. Not every day a guy brings you back to life, even if it's his job."

He leaned in closer.

"I'd do it even if it wasn't my job."

"I know you would."

A big fat, awkward silence sat down between them with crossed arms, shaking its head disapprovingly. It couldn't be seen but they knew it was there. Hbooth backed up.

"Noctys should be here in a couple of hours to pick you up."

Marilyn poured and down a drink in one move.

"Well, somebody thinks highly of his prowess in bed."

"Marilyn, I…"

She silenced him with a kiss. He felt like his heart was

28

going to implode. He leaned back in and put his hand on her thigh. Then she shocked him again by breaking the kiss and standing up.

'"John Hbooth, you are a coward. You're a chickenshit slave to a rock and roll idiot and I will have nothing to do with you. You have a fantastic gift and you don't use it for anything but serving that sword swinging psychopath."

She locked herself in the bathroom and cried. He pounded on the door, trying to reason with her as a courtesy, not because he thought it would work.

"Marilyn, I'm sorry. I can't do anything with you. I've brought you back for Noctys and while he's still in charge of me, I can't be with you."

"Well, why's he in charge? Can he bring back the dead? Is he smart? Is he useful? Is he amazing? Why's he in charge?" she shouted through the door.

"Because he's a rockstar and rockstars are in charge."

She opened the door.

"I bet his music's terrible," she said, pouring herself another glass of champagne.

Hbooth laughed as he poured himself one.

"He has a song called Niggersperm Magic Machine."

"Jesus. Why couldn't jazzmen run the country?"

"Not popular enough."

"I know, but most of them don't do anything worse than reefer."

"I suppose they don't."

They lay together, thinking Noctys and how when he came they were going to be separated, until he broke her yet again. He didn't want to see her brought to him in parts. There had to be something else that could be done. But what? He was bound to serve his rockstar master and while his rockstar master still lived, he couldn't violate the candyman's oath and use his power for himself. Not while Noctys lived…or not while Noctys was his rockstar liege. He'd been thinking before about how he was a candyman, how he could make the dead come back to life and how the world would be better if rockstars no longer ruled. As the plan materialized completely, a smile devoured half of Hbooth's face, just as his next decision would devour the world.

When Noctys arrived, Hbooth didn't hesitate to present the idea.

"My liege, before you go, I've got a candidate who can beat that bitch, Amber good."

Noctys did something he seldom did in his loud, stupid rockstar life: he listened to the proposition.

XIII.

"He's sick, he's mental, it's…"

The scream and the shooting did not occur. The death and historical canonization of Abraham Lincoln and the demonization of John Wilkes Booth did not occur. Before Booth the much elder's pistol fired, Booth the much younger got the drop on him with his Historion gun. Firing rapidly accelerated Historions with the consent of existence, Booth repented for something that was one hundred fifty years from being his fault in order to make sure his own sins would not be committed at all. He turned a villain who should have been a folk hero into fading particles of myth, a story nobody would ever think to tell or to retell, a name that would show up instinctively on tips of tongues when people would talk of history's villains and disappear because it wasn't the right one. Hero or villain, there was nothing left of him.

Booth the younger shuddered as the Historions undid his ancestor, knowing that only moments later, he would start to come apart in incomprehensible ways. There couldn't have been a John Booth, could there? There wasn't a man descended from another man who should have been but wasn't, there wasn't a man that destroyed that man since there was no man to destroy. Claws and rending hooks of bullshit history, bullshit physics, bullshit myth, bullshit fictions were yanking on him hard. Eating every scrap like dogs by the dinner table, they left only a sense of profound emptiness that filled the theater, an emptiness that nobody could explain but everybody felt.

"Don't mourn me," Lincoln said to the theater, "don't mourn me, because I think I have rabies of some kind and I feel violent and stupid and empty, the world feels emptier somehow. Lincoln loves you, America, so forget Lincoln, forget him!"

Lincoln jumped off the balcony onto the stage, hoping to finish himself off in a dignified but flamboyant manner. He did not. As John Wilkes Booth had after jumping down from the balcony, Lincoln only broke his leg. But, he had publicly proclaimed he was rabid and looking to die a hero's death to a crowded theater. The consequences of yelling "fire" would have been mild in comparison. Cast and theatergoers descended upon the president, beating, kicking, biting and rending him. Knowing somehow that it was for the better, Lincoln died with a beatific smile on his face, even as the patrons of Ford's Theater beat, molested and mangled him, pounding his head against the stage until it burst open and hundreds of little lizards crawled out.

XIV

"I'm starting to get exhausted," Charlie complained as he punched a Lincolnized pony in the face, "Most days I only kill five or six things with an axe. Today, I've killed like ten!"

"I think it's more like a few hundred, Charlie. You're very good at killing things with an axe."

"Yeah, it's just that and Metal. When we get to Noctys' house can I do some Metal?"

Hbooth hoped he wouldn't.

"Sure, Charlie, you can do all the Metal you want."

"Good, because I fuckin' love Metal! Even more than I

love killin' things with an axe!"

The pony's stovepipe was thick. It didn't snap so quickly as a human's, which didn't look good for Charlie. To make matters worse, a twelve year old anorexic Lincoln in a pink party dress sat down on the pony's back and began grabbing at and trying to bite Charlie. With one hand, he punched the pony in the face, with the other he hacked at the stovepipe.

"Can't you drive this any faster?" Charlie shouted at Hbooth.

"Not faster than a Lincolnpony."

"I hate when these things are animals!" As a chop from Charlie left the pony's stovepipe hanging by a thread, the pink party dress girl caught ahold of the metalhead's face punching arm and prepared to take a bite. Time slowed down to a crawl as she prepared to clamp down her jaws on him and the axe prepared to disconnect the pony from its pipe. A fang grazing skin, a flap of stovepipe flying, screams of tiny lizards, a startled twelve year old letting go as the pony beneath her crumpled and died. A metalhead's eyes widening in terror as he realized how close he'd come to becoming one of them. The motorcycle finally creating some distance from the wandering Lincolns. It was a tense few seconds.

A tense few seconds that got tenser when they reached Noctys' ill protected mansion. Tenser because Marilyn was inside and the place didn't even have a door, tenser because while Lincolns tended to go after other food when prey was out of sight for more than a few seconds, they weren't too far away to be found and tenser because Charlie was growing tired. His muscles were tense, he'd nearly been Lincolnized and the deep reservoir of violence in his heart was starting to dry up. As soon as Hbooth idled the motorcycle Charlie held out the battle axe.

"Hbooth, I can't fight anymore. You're going to have to be the one who kills Lincolns."

"I don't know if I can do that."

"You want to save your girl?"

"Yeah."

"Do you feel bad about making all those damn Lincolns?"

"I only made one."

Charlie glared at him. Hbooth did not object to the glaring since he knew it was quite justified.

"Fine, I'll take it," said Hbooth.

Hbooth took the battle axe, not too sure if he could even swing it but pretty sure he might have to. Surer when he noticed Noctys' pet polar bear, now several inches taller, teetering on undersized skinny legs and sporting a goatee, a Lincoln face and a stovepipe hat. Hbooth wet himself. Most people would have. Polar bears are gigantic. Lincolnized polar bears were colossal abominations against nature. The battle axe felt woefully insufficient. Hbooth himself felt woefully insufficient. His whole life he had been mocked for being descended from the man that killed Lincoln and now, he was in a position where he was responsible for returning Lincoln to the world and would have to kill him several times. Hbooth briefly contemplated suicide. The contemplation was very brief as the only thing he could commit suicide with would be the battle axe, which was not very good for suicide at all.

He held the battle axe over his head, telling his body to go in there and charge, to prevent Charlie from being eaten or Lincolnized by the furry, white death god. Hbooth had known that sooner or later working for the kind of asshole that thinks he needs a pet polar bear would cause problems and he was proven right. All that could be done was to charge the bear… the beloved sixteenth president bear. To charge the bear like an endangered species killing presidential assassin. Hbooth did not charge. He quivered, then froze. His eyes widened as he watched Charlie Battleaxe's head bitten off by the Lincoln bear. Then he fainted dead away when Charlie Hatbox's head grew back, albeit elongated, stovepiped and equipped with a very familiar goatee.

In what might have been a faint based hallucination, Hbooth met the Greek poet Homer on the steps of the Lincoln

Memorial. He fainted again at the sight of a gigantic bronze Lincoln. He awakened once more at the Lincoln Memorial and fainted once more. The process repeated itself six times before Hbooth gained his bearings and realized that he was probably in a faint based hallucination and even if he wasn't Lincolns couldn't Lincolnize statues.

"Hi," said Homer, "are you John Hbooth? I'm blind, so you could be anybody."

"Yes," said Hbooth.

"You've fainted eight times in the past five minutes."

Hbooth was grateful Homer couldn't see his face turning scarlet. He was already embarrassed enough that he'd fainted seven times in front of the author of the Odyssey.

"Sorry."

"You should be."

"I am."

"Good."

"Good."

Homer produced a joint out of thin air and lit it.

"I've been sent here by the Voice of Wisdom. You fucked up. But, there is hope, yet. There's always hope, although the Voice of Wisdom likes to hide it in the damnedest places. Like zombie-ridden wastelands."

"So what should I do?"

Homer offered Hbooth a toke. Hbooth declined. Homer shrugged.

"Well, you need to assemble a war cabinet using your Historion powers. The cabinet must include me, Miyamoto Musashi and Herodotus. But, the Voice of Wisdom will only give you enough soulstuff to make Herodotus into a cat. Probably because it's funny."

"And this will resolve the Lincoln problem?"

Homer shrugged.

"Hell if I know. But you've got a lot to learn about history and heroism and they're the people to teach you."

Hbooth's eyes opened and he found himself on the back of the dragon-shaped motorcycle. Marilyn was driving.

"Marilyn?"

Marilyn did not confirm it was her, she was busy cutting the stovepipe off a Lincolnized panther with her flamberge.

"How the hell did you survive?"

Marilyn did not answer again because two Lincolnized gorillas were meeting their doom at the edge of Marilyn's keen blade.

"Oh."

Marilyn giggled.

"What, you didn't know I'm one of the greatest swordsmen in history? I'm no Musashi, but I've read the Book of Five Rings so many times…"

"If we survive, you might get to meet him."

Marilyn made the face Marilyn Monroe made when she got surprised.

"Really, Johnny?"

"Sure thing. We've got to get somewhere safe."

"Well, I stole some house keys off a dead Viking. Will those help?"

A tiny snowflake of hope dropped on Hbooth's tongue. It tasted of pollution, Ash and carcass but it was a start.

"Yes, turn right here."

Marilyn turned right, slicing through a girl scout troop and a freakishly tall Abeheaded pangolin and as they rounded the corner, they both caught sight of Charlie's veritable bunker of a mansion, built from thousands of electric guitars magnetized to steel walls. Swinging pendulum blades hung from the trees and half buried land mines promised death to all intruders. It might not have been possible to be completely safe from Lincolns, but at Charlie's house, they'd be pretty close. Here, they'd be able to relax, build the war council Homer had told them to and hopefully find some way to clean up this mess.

XVI.

The Bohemian Grove fatcats almost choked on their panda sperm when they saw what the spy satellite orbiting Charlie Battleaxe's house was recording. They embraced each other, crying and screaming and begging the Herpetarch for answers. and salvation.]

"You have failed me," said the Herpetarch,"you have failed yourselves and reptilekind alike. You sicken me, you sniveling bastards."

"Please, oh godking of lizards," said Frank Sinatra, who was of course not dead at all, "you must help us! He's going to ruin everything."

"No," the Herpetarch replied, his tone quite firm, "you've failed and you can fuck up society for yourselves. If there's anything you can do it's that."

Sinatra shook his fists and began to cry.

"We're fucked! We're fucked! It's the end."

"Relax," said Mykle Hansen, placing a hand on his old friend's shoulder, "it's not over yet. All we have to worry about is John Booth. The guy's got nothing going for him but a magic sword and some kind of hoodoo pistol."

Madonna wagged a bony finger at the world famous author. The two had never gotten along. Yes, Hansen had invented Twitter, allowing the fatcats to spread cancer faster than ever but he often overlooked the bigger picture and seemed to be in it more for the panda sperm and slaves than for the reptiles. Madonna was always in it for the reptiles.

"Again, you miss the point, Hansen! John Booth is a candyman capable of manipulating Historions to bring back the dead. If he reverses the process using a Historion pistol, the history we've created is going to be fucked up for good!"

Hansen waved Madonna's wild theory away, although he secretly knew that her knowledge of Arcanoscience was far greater than his and she was probably right.

"Ha! That's a good one. There's no way he could come up with that. It's too crazy by half!"

Hansen and Madonna were both right. While it was certainly true that nobody was nearly as crazy as Madonna, Hansen was wrong in that Booth had discovered that by reversing his Historion reconstruction process, he could destroy the history the lizards had fucked up...for good. Hansen was right to point out that Booth had nothing but a magic sword and some kind of hoodoo pistol to take on every Lincoln between Noctys' house and Ford's Theater. Watching Booth step out of the mansion into a city overrun by hungry Lincolns, Mykle Hansen looked pretty damn smart for being so cynical.

Booth was at once terrified and dead calm, his faith in himself unwavering, though perhaps devoid of context. I am invincible for some reason. I am a hero for some reason. I am a hero because I have decided to be one and heroism is bullshit. I will make history because I can and history is bullshit. Herodotus the cat told me so. He breathed deep, readied the sword and tried not to count, tried not to think that it was his fault. Tried to be nothing but a man swinging a sword above his head to open up several disgusting growths and let loose the hideous lizards inside of them. The seven year old girls who had become Lincolns were not in his mind innocent children he had fucked up by reviving a rabid president, they were pink tubes full of lizards, the grandmothers were bearded old ladies with lizards in their heads, the wheelchair bound veterans were monster presidents on wheels that could not be suffered to live.

Hansen and Madonna looked on in shock, through the cameras to see the bringer of Armageddon transformed into a knight of redemption as had been written in books of The Lizard Scriptures that the Herpetarch had insisted were Apocrypha and therefore none of anybody's concern. The Herpetarch lacked the perspective of a Greek historian in a cat's body, a historian that would have reminded him that Apocrypha means bullshit and history is bullshit, so...

"Dino, Sammy, I'm comin', I'm comin'!" screamed a desperate Sinatra as he shot himself in the face. As a woman with no loyalties who could not resist fresh blood, a hungry Madonna stopped panicking about Booth while she slurped up the mess that used to be the chairman. His face bits tasted like victory, for she had been cochairman for all this time. Hansen shrugged, taking Madonna's seat and summoning more slaves to top off his panda sperm and add a few shots of Secret Reptile Spacevodka. Maybe the Lincoln plan had fallen apart, but at least he'd earned a promotion.

Ironically, as Madonna was ingesting the vital fluids of her former boss, Booth had come face to face with a familiar figure. This Lincoln had wandered a fair distance from the Civic Debatodome and had, as Booth had figured before, been better off as a Lincoln. As a rockstar and a politician, Noctys Blakbludd had not been especially efficient, but his biting and Lincolnlove had led to over a thousand converts including a Galopagos tortoise that had escaped the zoo. Booth really enjoyed killing this particular Lincoln. He wished he could kill him twice. But a hundred Lincolns into the Lincoln phalanx was an opportunity just as good.

A hat! An actual hat. And a real stovepipe hat meant he had found the cause of many his sorrows…at least the cause of his sorrows that was not himself. As he brought down the magical flamberge to do what Booths did best, he thought of the film The Lost Boys and how killing the head vampire turned everybody back into people. That would have been really great. It's a shame Lincoln had become a rabid zombie thing instead of a vampire. If The Lost Boys had gotten it right. Lincoln crumpled and died and the world was still mostly Lincolnized. People were still empty, rabid abominations gnawing on everything that wasn't like them. There was a long, cylindrical tube on everybody's head still and inside it there were still lizards.

If Ford's Theater weren't in sight, Booth would have been pretty depressed.

XVI.

Marilyn parted grave dirt and history as she angrily dug her way to the surface. She was going to make the fake JFK pay for leaving her for dead and replacing her lover. She'd make Jackie pay too. The Voice of Wisdom speaking in falling leaves and tiny fluctuations in temperature told her to get a rifle and go to Dallas. The Voice of Wisdom often told people to get a rifle and kill the president, yet most of them and most of their doctors and family members always said it was a bad idea. Lucky for the Voice of Wisdom and history at large that Marilyn was pissed off that she'd been left for dead by a fake president and his fatcat bride.

Even having just crawled from the grave, it was not difficult to find somebody who would pick up a hitchhiking Marilyn Monroe. If it weren't for the grave dirt, she'd have been able to leave the trucker starstruck and unable to make her pay for the ride with a blowjob. It wasn't too bad. She didn't swallow and a presidential assassination was more than worth the taste of sperm on her breath. The trucker's name was Oswald and he was very happy to save Marilyn some trouble and let her borrow his rifle. He was going to the book depository to find a book on how to best adjust the scope on his other identical rifle.

She lay down on a nice grassy knoll where she could get a good view of the fake president's car, took aim and made history. History omitted the greenish lizard goo that came out of the head wound and that the president was actually an impostor, but other than this, Marilyn's lucky shot made a pretty big splash. She rose to her feet, ready to flee the scene only to find the president standing behind her. She didn't mind that this was probably the end. At least she'd killed one impostor. It was disconcerting that there were so many of them, but she didn't have a hell of a lot to live for anyway and if this was one was going to finish her, then there wasn't a lot that she could do.

"Norma Jean," said Jack Kennedy, "I don't know if I can

explain it, but somewhere else I was somebody else who loved you and suddenly I wasn't this person. But I can feel the love and I can feel that we've got great things ahead of us."

They joined hands and began a grueling odyssey to find someplace safe. History said neither of the two dead American heroes were ever seen again, but history, as Herodotus the cat said, is bullshit. Love isn't.

Assorted Salesmen
at the Birth
of the Antichrist

Phyllis Trotsky of Trotsky Chevrolet says:

It was cold in the suburb of Hell, not like they say it is. I came to him bearing a free calendar and it seemed to make him happy. It rained semen for days after that. I had never been able to conceive with my husband but next week I found out I was pregnant with quints!

Hieronymous Glasscock of Hieronymous Glasscock and Sons Aluminum Siding says:

He looked at me through his eyeless sockets, hoping I had brought something nice. He stuck the Hotwheels ambulance I'd given him into his left hole and damned if it didn't look like he could see through it! Next morning I woke up and I had no legs. I can't keep the chicks away from me!

Martin Fisting of Quality Pizza Accessories says: I thought he would be bigger.

Hector Caswell of Caswell Glove Compartments says: How bad could it be? It's a baby!

Lucien Balderston Rhys Meyers of Balderston Rhys Meyers Lubricants says:

It was better the first time. Less commercial. Like Woodstock.

The Adventures of Blackmetal Bjorn and Accomplice Boys ...In Technicolor!

Gym class. January 25th

Redporsche Richfag fights at the edge of the mat to grind our hero's eyelinered face into hardwood. Aglow with patrician arrogance and bloodthirsty as beleaguered protagonist squirms beneath him head buzzing, mouthing silent prayers to Odin. Odin does not answer. Odin favors fighters. There is no fighting happening now. There is a guylinered invertebrate suffering and waiting for the bell to ring. As bully bait Dustin, the pale alterego of Accomplice Boy he can do little. If he had his mask, if he had his mentor, if he had...

What he has is a bloody lip, a cut face and an erection rubbing against him. And the shame and the knowledge that he has been bested by a Christian. The lovegod shames the old gods with a series of taunting thrusts that he knows Coach Hargreaves has to see. Hargreaves is a servant of the love, the faggot and the peace god. Does a part of him know deep down that pale, skinny Dustin is what he is becoming? Does he know the secret of Accomplice Boy?

Dustin wonders and waits, face stinging, head spinning. Odin does not help the weak. Odin does not help the ones who acquiesce to Christian beatings. He spits blood, staining the hardwood floor. He endures the laughter, each giggle a bullet, of cheerleaders eager to see that the captain of the wrestling team is better at wrestling than a boy forty pounds lighter than him who never wrestles at all, except when he is forced to in gym class. Ha ha ha bang bang bang thrust thrust...

Dustin can barely breathe. His limbs ache. His lip is cut, his eye makeup smudged. Redporsche richfag lets out triumphant roar. He, a mighty predator, Dustin pathetic worm. Silently praying to the old gods who will not answer out of shame, waiting for the bell. The prayers will not be answered, but the time will pass. Redporsche richfag twists his arm. He doesn't scream. At least he has that going for him. At least he didn't scream.

The bell rings. Wounded Dustin gets on the bus, doing his best to ignore the whispers and the insults and the laughter, the flying painpellets of laughter cutting through paper-thin skin of the unmasked weakling. It is like this every day. It will be like this every day. Every day he meekly waits until he gets home, enduring the taunts and the misery and the laughter. It will not get better. Not until he makes it better.

He walks into his house and finds Blackmetal Bjorn is already there. Seven feet high, a shirtless tower of muscle with runes and swastikas carved all over his arms and bare chest. Dustin stares into the symbols, knowing well the disapproval of the old gods and the disapproval of the mighty hero who has become his mentor. Blackmetal Bjorn punches Dustin in the stomach. The warrior's Viking strength , combined with the pain and the misery and the humiliation of wrestling are enough to make him throw up. Lasagna and blood, red with chunks of white, lumpy, stinking. Bjorn rubs his face in it, like the bad dog he is. Like the little bitch he is.

"Clean it up!" Bjorn screams. Thankfully, Dustin is permitted a towel. And Blackmetal Bjorn puts on his third album, so Dustin can enjoy his thundering hymns to the gods of the old and the old perfect world.

"Be quick, Accomplice Boy, for there is much to be done!"

Norway. A Prison Cell. March 16th
He didn't seem that big. The name, the reputation, the swastika and runic tattoos made him big, but Agent Caswell took him for about five foot seven, starved down to about 125 pounds.

43

The kind of guy his mother would say "a good stiff wind could knock him over." Yet in the bright, polished steel of his eyes you could see a man that would simply not allow it. Nothing is permitted that I do not permit. The extra wrong kind of a man to interview.

"So, mister…" Caswell couldn't say the name. He knew it wasn't the guy's birth name, but he also knew he wouldn't answer to any other. He didn't like having to play this game. Caswell looked at Soames, who shook his head. If Caswell, wasn't gonna say it, Soames sure as hell wouldn't.

"Mister…"

Soames didn't say it. But the Norwegian did.

"Cunthammer." The word was as heavy, filthy and absurd as whatever it was supposed to represent. Caswell tried to look unperturbed. It didn't work very well.

"Yes. We have some questions…"

"Cunthammer."

"Excuse me?"

"Cunt-ham-mer."

"Yes, I'm aware of your name."

The Norwegian leaned forward. The look in his icy blue eyes suggested that he did so to bite their faces clean off.

"I will be addressed as Cunthammer because Cunthammer is my name. Cunthammer is my name because Cunthammer is what I am. If you will not address me as Cunthammer, then you can get the fuck out of here and tell your cocksucking nigger president that Bjorn Cunthammer will eat his heart."

Agent Soames got in Cunthammer's face. He was the one whose calling it was to get in people's faces.

"I'm not going to sit here and listen to you threaten the president. If you cooperate…"

Cunthammer laughed. He chuckled, then roared with laughter.

"If I cooperate, I get what? I get time off my fucking sentence? I don't give a fuck about that. A man called

44

Cunthammer is not afraid of prison. Prison fears me. It has swallowed me and it wishes to excrete me."

Soames and Caswell had been warned. And indeed, they should have known that a man who called himself Cunthammer would be hard to bargain with. They had come to Norway seeking answers though, seeking the last piece of a skull fragment lip gloss jockstrap puzzle and could not leave without knowing what they had to find out, though.

"Mr. Cunthammer," said Caswell clearly and shamelessly, "we just want to know if you have ever corresponded with a Dustin Lunquist."

Cunthammer mimed pondering the subject deeply.

"Hmmm...you know, I think..."

Caswell trembled a bit. Soames backed off.

"I might have. I don't know."

Cunthammer started to laugh again, each laugh a hard right jab, each laugh a "fuck you pigs!" Each laugh another powerful strike from the mighty Cunthammer.

Passing Period. March 5th

Blackmetal Bjorn lets fly one of his axes and splits a cruel, patrician skull in the name of the old gods. The bitch dared wear the sign of the cocksucking carpenter in the presence of the mighty Cunthammer. Accomplice Boy's sacred Tec-9 sprays draconic at richfag after richfag in the hall. The old gods move through Accomplice Boy, trained in stealth and the arts of war by the mighty Viking hero and he sprays the blood of weaklings where he goes. Five dead at the hands of our heroes! Who Accomplice Boy wishes dead ends up dead. The wrestling team emerges from the remedial math room to see the cause of the ruckus and the noise and to prove this. Red Porsche Richfag locks eyes with Accomplice Boy and furrows his Neanderthal brow, trying to remember where he has seen that hateful gaze before. But Accomplice Boy's identity is safe.

Try as they might with all their might, the wrestling team

45

cannot stop Accomplice Boy. Though they have pumped iron day in day out stacking bicep upon bicep until they look like they have small footballs under their skin. Small footballs and hard pecs and steroidal fury are not enough to take down the boy vigilante. They turn tail and run at the sight of him, cowardly closet cases they are! Three days ago, they'd made him wear a cheerleader uniform and do a little dance for them because he had failed to climb the rope fast enough. Spattered essences joins rust spots to paint green metal lockers a deeper red.

Blackmetal Bjorn shakes the magic Cunthammer with excitement. The runes on the ancient mystic warhammer glow with Odin's approval.

"You fight well, Accomplice Boy! History will know us as mighty heroes!"

Some are crying, some fleeing for classrooms. Some paralyzed with fear, unreliable legs wobbling at the sight of such power. They had not expected mild-mannered puny bullybait Dustin to become the whirlwind of justice that is Accomplice Boy. Who is that masked man? Who is his giant Viking friend? They know not that Accomplice Boy is Goldwater High's one chance at equality! Faggot jocks snooty bitches watch out. Accomplice Boy's guns are ablazin and it will not be the same. It will never be the same.

Gym Class. February 10th

Dustin fails to climb the rope fast enough. Somehow, even with the training from Blackmetal Bjorn, Dustin fails to be the warrior he needs to be. If Accomplice Boy were there, he would have been able to scamper up the rope in a matter of seconds. Then would have descended and with a series of thundering jabs, lain low the jocks with his berserker rage. But this is Dustin and not Accomplice Boy. He is not fast enough. He is not strong enough. Could this milky invertebrate endure the gym coaches and the hateful wrestlers and the giggling gangs of girls?

No. He must suffer the pointing and the flying pellets of laughter. Accomplice Boy will give one back for every one spent. The plan is in motion. The work is being done. Laugh now while you can, bullies and conformists, comeuppance is coming up! Coach Hargreaves brings a cheerleader uniform, forces Dustin the milky invertebrate to put it on like the little sissy he is and shake it like he means it. The conformists, Christians, faggots and jocks point and laugh. Ha ha ha bang bang bang ha ha ha bang bang bang. He will give back one for each one spent sign the yearbook in lead.

When it's all over, he goes home, met at the door by a punch in the stomach from his mentor and master.

"Get stronger!" Blackmetal Bjorn barks at the would be Accomplice Boy.

Push-ups. Shooting at cans. Going over the floor plan again and again and again. Life is not easy for Accomplice Boy. But it will be worth it.

Passing Period

Axes, bullets fly into the heads of foes. Into faggot faces and into taunting slut-tits overflowing from too little tank tops screaming suck me, bite me cum on me to everybody...but not to Dustin and not to Accomplice Boy, nosirree. Bite me football fag cum on me gangsta wigger wannabe fuckstick look at me plastic smile class president asshole! Accomplice Boy might have hesitated, but Blackmetal Bjorn, The Cunthammer, the divine punisher will not be swayed by the corn-fed teets of Midwestern mediocrity.

"In Valhalla, we will drink mead from the bosoms of the Valkyrie," Accomplice Boy whispers to himself. He blasts a panicking goth chick, superficially his sister, superficial inside and out, as she rushes to alert the conformity-mongers and the slave drivers that someone has come to liberate Goldwater High. A flawless shot! Straight through and she's done for! Her fat stupid eyelinered slut friend turns around to beg Accomplice

47

Boy for mercy to buy time for the bastards and bullies to show up and undo his labors.

Will Accomplice Boy be fooled? Will he grant clemency to one who looked on while a man who should have been her brother endured suffering and humiliations and depraved faggoty tortures? He hesitates, listening to the whiny, hissing, buzzing inhuman noise coming out of her stupid fat mouth. Accomplice Boy is a hero! Accomplice Boy is a fucking Viking trained in the Viking arts by Bjorn fucking Cunthammer! In Valhalla, they will drink mead from the bosoms of Valkyries. She does not fool Accomplice Boy.

He makes her fat face less of a face and more of a meat sculpture. Beware deceivers and traitors! Accomplice Boy knows your secrets and will not fall for your lies! He does not hesitate or stop and reflect on what he has done. There is still work to do in the hallways. They have not yet been cleared of liars and bullies and faggots and kikes and conformists and Christian hypocrites.

Their false Messiah has tried to supplant the Old Gods and tried to spread his message of both love and judgment and Accomplice Boy is not tricked. A bullet or ten for every shiny gold cross, for everyone who saw the Hammer of Thor around his neck and told him that he was a blasphemer and needed to find Jesus and ask for forgiveness. Accomplice Boy does not need the approval of Jesus Christ! Higher truer authorities guide his hands as bullets and throwing knives fly, as Black Metal Bjorn shakes the Cunthammer and screams for more and more and more!

Accomplice Boy approaches his mentor, pulls off the ski mask, eyes agleam with tears of joy and he kisses him full on the lips. Accomplice Boy does not know why this has happened. He is no faggot, but he is overtaken by the moment and the glory and the righteous brotherhood of war. It is the kiss of a son to a surrogate father who has taught him well how to vanquish the wicked ones and make Goldwater High a safe place for future generations. He is overtaken by the sight of panicked classmates tripping over the corpses of their cherished student council officers, of the teachers that tried to shield them from flying bullets and of their god's surprisingly weak champions.

Blackmetal Bjorn, he loves you, your music, your soul, your strength. Blackmetal Bjorn, don't reject him. Don't leave him alone in this chaos and loud and loud loud loud. Without you he is only Dustin. Bullybait pale faggot weak worm deprived...without you he is the victim and with you, the hero.

Will Blackmetal Bjorn accept the love of his sidekick and progeny in the heat of war? Bjorn is no faggot. Bjorn looks at Dustin in disgust...yes, Dustin. He has taken off his mask and he is no longer Accomplice Boy. What is he now but confused? What is he now but weak? Bjorn breaks off the kiss. He slaps the boy across the face with the mighty Cunthammer! It is only Bjorn's own training and beatings and abuse and declarations of resolve that prevent Dustin from losing his tender dodgeball scarred head.

Dustin hits the floor. He begins to cry like a little pussy who has been pelted with dodgeballs by warrior closet cases with nothing better to do. But he has been hit so much harder. Unmasked and confused about everything he is, he reaches for the magnum.

"In Valhalla," Bjorn lectures, "you will drink mead from the bosoms of Valkyries. You have carved your name in lead and you fought admirably but you bring shame to yourself. You challenge my teachings and you show me queerlove like a faggot, like a pussy! Redeem yourself!"

Accomplice Boy now Dustin puts the righteous firearm up to his head, reciting loudly a litany to the Old Gods, begging them and Blackmetal Bjorn for forgiveness for embracing weakness and seeking the petty tenderness that The Christ would have offered. Dustin can only redeem himself one way. But will he make it? Will he squeeze the trigger on time and gain freedom from his weakness?

A Prison Cell in Norway. March 16
"Lunquist had all your albums."

"He had good taste."

"His journals say you met."

Cunthammer pantomimes pondering.

"Lunquist, Lunquist, yes...yes, I think I..."

The FBI agents are prepared for disappointment. Cunthammer has been stringing them along for awhile. They are not surprised that the next remark is not a productive one.

"I played his junior prom. They released me from the dull monotony of prison life so that I could teach Americans how they rock in Norway. We hung out after the show, had a couple of beers and I taught him how to kill twenty nine of his classmates. I hope I don't get my sentence extended for being a party to underage drinking."

Soames feels tempted to hit the Norwegian. He knows this guy would like it. It's been awhile since Cunthammer experienced pain. And pain would make him feel so much more alive. So he holds back. He lets his partner do the talking. Cunthammer almost seems to like the guy anyway. Soames showed up with bluster he could not back up and Caswell came humble, but willing to stand up for himself.

"Did you correspond with Dustin Lunquist?"

Cunthammer doesn't feign deep thought. He doesn't hesitate to answer Caswell.

"Do you think I'd fucking remember? Do you know how many letters I write to crazy people or how many crazy people write me letters? You can't expect me to remember one name. I am a famous rock musician and a visionary philosopher and a priest of a resurgent faith. I cannot say if I knew him."

"What if I said I didn't believe that?" Soames asked.

"You are welcome to say it. And you are welcome to believe it. And you are justified in asking it. I might be lying to you, I might be insane. I killed a man. I burned churches. I made young men into Nazis. I have no reason to tell you the truth. You might have no reason to be here."

Caswell examined Cunthammer's face. There were signs of pressure, signs of agony.

"I don't think you knew each other. I think we're wasting our time here. And you know that."

Cunthammer rocks slightly in his chair. His still blue eyes dart between the FBI agents. His mouth opens and no words come out. Bjorn Cunthammer is hurting. Soames is not sure why, but Caswell knows, bringing down a bludgeon of his own, one that might just be a match for the Cunthammer.

"You have never spoken to or met Dustin Lunquist. You have nothing to do with what he did. You have never corresponded with him. The Bjorn Cunthammer he met and interacted with is most certainly a figment of his imagination. All of our time has been wasted, but at least we know."

Bjorn Cunthammer chokes somewhat.

"Maybe," he says, "maybe you're right."

***

Valhalla?...

Accomplice Boy has pressed the gun against the side of his head. He is ready to leave this world behind and let his soul move onto the great mead hall in the sky! He hath slain many dragons and now wishes to dispel his final shame. Will Accomplice Boy find glory in the afterlife? Will his actions earn the forgiveness of the mighty Bjorn Cunthammer? Dead mangled faces of classmates look on waiting, heavily invested in Accomplice Boy's next and possibly last moments...

But what? What is that noise? The door bursts open. Accomplice Boy turns around. The police have arrived. Blue devils here not to reward him for cleaning up the traitorous and the jocks and the gym coach, but to punish him in the name of America and the pussygod Jesus Christ. He aims the Tec-9, squeezes the trigger, silently praying to Odin that he will not die in this confrontation with the forces of the puny faggot carpenter of Jerusalem!

Surely they cannot stand up to the Cunthammer! Surely they cannot stand up to the mighty throwing axes of Black Metal Bjorn! And the skillful marksmanship of Accomplice Boy! But wait...what's this? Blackmetal Bjorn tosses no axes. Black Metal Bjorn shouts no praise and does not shake the Cunthammer in excitement. Blackmetal Bjorn has gone. Dustin doesn't hit a single police officer. Their gods make their bullets fly true. Fill the boy with holes. He does not see the light of Valhalla. He has not been granted the blessings of Blackmetal. The victim is another victim.

In a Prison Cell in Norway. March 16th
"Thank you for your time, Mr. Cunthammer. I'm sorry we wasted so much of it. But we needed to know. We didn't think a teenage kid could commit 29 murders with an accomplice that only existed in his head the whole time. Stranger things have happened, though."

The FBI agents leave and Bjorn Cunthammer sits alone in his cell. During his youth, he burned churches, he incited riots and made music in praise of the Nazis and the Old Gods and Aryan viking triumph. He talked of revolution and razing the new, glossy Christian world and blazing forth in the name of Thor and Odin and the Reich. He sang of terrorism and victory. He sang of never being victims again and burning the faggots at stakes. He murdered a man in a bar fight.

And he is nothing compared to the wild imagining of a sixteen year old American homosexual who he bet Odin loved a hundred times more than him.

An Author is a Beagle As a Flying Ace

Julie Newmar walks into my office. She doesn't know that I know who she is. Because she's wearing her costume.

"Can I help you?" I ask, though I'm afraid I can't.

"There's been a murder," she tells me.

"It'll cost you," I tell her, though it's a lie.

She stands up, and improvises and awkward, but sensual dance. Outside it's raining, but I'm not concerned. Julie Newmar is dancing.

"I'll take the case," I tell her and it brings me to Morocco. There's a hot tip at The Blue Parrot. Turns out I'm a cartoon dog with a vivid imagination.

A Girl in a Girl Mask Three Sizes Too Small

Julie Newmar walks into my office. But I know that this time it isn't her. Because her girl mask is three sizes too small.

"Aha!" I shout, pointing my gun in the face of Kali.

Kali pulls off her Kali mask and underneath it Julie Newmar.

"Aha!" she says, pointing a gun in my face.

She pulls off my detective mask and underneath is Jackie Gleason.

She cries. Rips open her Catwoman suit. Rips open the skin underneath. I take a bite from her chocolate heart. I cry. Julie Newmar is a woman like other women.

"Baby, you're the greatest!"

Apotheosis J

I am chasing Julie Newmar through the jungle. This is a new thing for us. I am caught by feral businessmen.

"Actualize yourself!" they scream.

"Branding is important!"

"Leverage!"

"Build your business development!"

"What the fuck does that even mean?" I shout.

They begin to cry. They pound the ground with their tiny business fists.

"We don't know!" they weep.

"Gold ticket inner circle audience!" one ventures.

Gold chains appear on my neck. I spit jargon at the speed of light. They eat each other. I don't want them to. I want them to. Wherever she is, Julie Newmar is sopping.

The Manchurian Can't-i-date

Julie Newmar is running for president. She has an assassination fetish. I'm curare'd up and standing on a building. She is giving a speech on how assassins are pussies. A man dressed like me has a question. Turns out it's me. Which is odd because I'm standing on that building.

"Will you marry me?"

"Yes," she says, looking up at that building.

I am confused. Do I kill her? Do I marry her? Do I fuck her? This game is hard.

The crowd disperses. Julie Newmar clutches her neck. She falls down.

"Avenge me," she says. "Marry me."

We do.

Hit and Fun

I.
The Locals

The Slashcats are real fuckin' gone! Don't you say nothin' bad about the Slashcats! The Slashcats make your kid sister wet. They make her explode juice like a geyser, like a man explodes, like you gotta pay a lot to see a woman explode like. They do that to your kid sister, they'll do it to your mama, so don't you fuckin' talk shit about the Slashcats! If you ain't from around here, which it looks like you ain't, I'll let you in on it. It'll cost you five dollars. Fine, three dollars. Well, okay then, asshead I'll tell ya.

The Slashcats are free spirits. Ronnie Ray's a cowboy, asshead! He's a real cowboy, not like you with your tin sheriff badge and floppy ten gallon and assless chaps. Fuck your bare white greenhorn bottom and not in the way you like it you cowboy wanna be fuckpig asshead. His 57 Chevy's rigged up to run on pussy juice and it's a lucky lady to run into Ronny Ray and the Slashcats when he's run out of gas. He'll pop open a Steel Reserve, take out his guitar and sing a song about how he's sensitive on the inside. And then he does his business, and when he's done the car's goin' again. It won't stop for days.

The Slashcats like to drive around and look for drunken teenage girls who are staggering down the road, the ones who look they're just about to topple over. Then Ronnie Ray pulls up to one and offers her a ride. Then when she's about to get in, they drive off and when they get about half a mile up the road, and then they pull over and wait for her to get there.

When she does, that's when the real fun begins. They take

turns running her down with their souped up hot rods, then when she's good and dead, they eat her flattened heart, lungs, uterus, kidneys, anything that survives being hit by eight cars and they draw a pentagram on the ground and chant "hail Satan" and they have a righteous orgy that's not gay at all because they're butch hotrod cowboys. The Slashcats are the real thing and they're real gone! Don't you forget it, tenderfoot! Hail Satan. God bless the fuckin' U S A! I love you Ronny Ray!

II.
Green Eye

In the library of Xerath, the seers drink souldust together and tremble. There will come a time when the Auspicians will be no more. Long have they sat and watched the fall of leaves and seen in them the proper course, long have the stars told them who to love and fear and long have they waited for the Trikloptikon to give them answers and done its bidding always, long have they snorted souldust to share the dreams of their dead. Now the souldust shows them something that they do not wish to see.

The things that are now but fish have learned to walk, speak and think. Eventually they gain the power to understand sigils. They carve them to share desires, fears and pleasures. Sometimes they use them to remind each other to do simple tasks that might otherwise have been forgotten. Their skies are gray with smoke and there are no cities there. They build their cities on the ground and set fire to their skies. Damn the fish! There is nothing that can be done. The earth and sky alike are covered in gray poison. Even the seas the ungrateful bastards crawled from are filled with garbage.

The seers scream as one "the fish, the fish, the fish will destroy the earth!"

Fair Xerath fills with laughter at the thought of something so strange and stupid as fish destroying the earth. The fish always fell for the hooks they dangled down from the sky to tempt them and never did anything to indicate they might one day be an intelligence of some kind, so why would anyone think they were a threat? Stupid seers, high on souldust. The children throw little cakes at them and mock them for their implausible stories of conqueror fish.

The seers are freed from the haze of vision and the sting of derisive mockery by the cry of the Lightbird in the temple of the Trikloptikon. They rush to look upon the Trikloptikon and rejoice, forgetting their visions of fish gone mad and incendiary skies. The green eye of the Trikloptikon has opened and has ordered the harvest to go ahead. The seers climb up to the tower of sounding, playing upon chimes made of preserved ice crystals.

"Harvest time!"

"Harvest time!" the city cries in unison and the preparations are made. The dancing maids begin to weave their mistgarb, the feastmasters meticulously select the best dishes, criminals are pardoned for their offenses. The sculptors of the memorial Trikloptikon replica get to work meticulously chiseling from comet dust. The children mount their skyrabbits and bounce high to pick the fruits now glowing in the clouds. The Green eye had opened again and the Auspicians would prosper another year, though the seers knew the time of the fish would come someday.

III.
Slashcat Saturday Night

"Ronnie Ray, I was thinkin'," Little Teddy began, "I was thinkin' that maybe we should settle in, you know to a different life."

As usual, Ronnie Ray was combing his greasy black hair. Ronnie Ray was usually combing his hair or drinking a Steel Reserve. Sometimes he also ate a chocolate rabbit.

"Watcha mean? Go soft? Be like all the squares who wear

ties and vote for the fella who doesn't hate niggers? That ain't my scene. It's Squaresville and I don't waste my time ridin' through Squaresville. Ain't no good lookin' dames and the cops pull you over for nothin' there, man. Little Teddy, you don't know what it's like out there."

Dirty Ralph spat at Little Teddy and took a bite out of his pretzel for effect.

"You're startin' to act like you might already be a square. I think you're a square!"

Guns were drawn.

"Shit! He's a square!"

"Thou shalt not suffer a square to live, man."

"What are we gonna do about him?"

"If he's a square ain't we square for ridin' with him?"

"I buttfucked him last Saturday! I might catch it!"

"It's okay, there's an ointment for your dick."

"Thank Lucifer!"

"Hey, you think Little Teddy stopped worshipin' Satan?"

"He might! He's a square!"

Little Teddy hanged his head in shame.

"Look guys, it ain't like that. I love Satan just as much as I used."

"Well, Satan doesn't love you anymore, square!"

Ronnie Ray raised his hand for silence and when Ronnie Ray raised his hand for silence, silence was given.

"Let Little Teddy talk. Then we'll decide if he's a square and deal with him accordingly."

The gang applauded Ronnie Ray's decision and went to the cooler to get him another Steel Reserve and then to the candy cache in Ronnie Ray's trunk for another chocolate rabbit.

Little Teddy cleared his throat.

"I was thinkin' we oughta become bounty hunters. We'd get paid for fightin' and huntin' down guys what we don't like."

"See, that's why I'm in charge and you ain't. Catchin' criminals is for faggots, Teddy, faggots and squares."

Ronnie Ray's switchblade was so fast it was barely visible as it cut Teddy's throat. Bounty hunters! Worse than bein' squares, it was almost bein' cops and cops were worse than squares and faggots combined. Killin' Little Teddy should have been enough to make a Saturday night, but it wasn't. Saturday night wasn't just for killin' squares; Saturday night was the time for Hit and Fun.

Rebecca and Leah were on their way back home from Saturday afternoon bible school. They stayed late to pray just a little bit longer for the souls of their twin sisters who had been killed one Saturday night by hot rodding miscreants. Rebecca and Leah were both kind of slow, since they had initially been quadruplets and the other twins had a small portion of their sisters' brains ingrained, so took a fair amount of the family intellect with them to the grave.

They tended not to accept rides from strangers, but they were weary from their day of piety, bible study and baking cupcakes for the blind. So, when the hotrod idled and the young man with meticulously combed hair yelled out the window "need a ride?" they approached the car, ready to hop in. Then, like their sisters, who had also fallen for this ruse, they were run down by Ronnie Ray's friends, who seemingly came out of nowhere, then took turns running them down several times in an orgy of automotive malice. By the time the Slashcats were done, their heads were splattered all over the place. Then the boys cut them open, took out their flattened organs as a sacrifice to Satan, drew a pentagram on the ground, had a righteous orgy that wasn't gay at all and Ronnie Ray ate another chocolate rabbit.

IV.
The Fish are on Their Way

In the library of Xerath, the Auspician seers dream of fish with mouths opened wide in laughter and know there is nothing they can do to change their fate. The Auspicians had recently discovered the notion of pride and reasoned that it would only serve to increase their productivity. Would pride in one's accomplishments not make one wish to accomplish more? Of course it would. But, they had been ignorant of the price of their newfound emotion, not unlike the lightningbeast from the fishfables who created pride only to find it led to upheaval. The Auspicians knew that they were the greatest civilization of all time, especially in comparison to fish so decided that they had nothing to fear. The seers know better than this. The seers have seen fish walking upon land becoming multitudes of animals and eventually grotesque brutes that travel to slave labor camps inside smelly metal boxes powered by burning rocks. They almost do not believe what the souldust has told them. The time of the fish is getting too close to ignore. They decide to try again.

The seers come before the public again with the stories of the boxbrutes and firerocks and war that shakes the Earth and smoke that fills the sky and lies that fill the ears of every bruteman, brutewoman, brutechild, warlies smokelies box lies. They tell the public it all began with the fish and they must be careful not to offend the Trikloptikon, lest they grow extinct and the fishworld begin.

The Auspicians laugh at the doddering old mystics once again. It is obvious that they want more souldust and jewels and silks and they want everyone to rely on them and only them. They want everyone to remember that they are still relevant and still superior and still the only ones that know what the future will bring. How dare they think that way! The Auspicians had discovered pride and each and every one of them felt too much pride to be swayed by any seer's lies. It was the seers who were spiritually inferior, trusting dreams granted them by souldust that they kept to themselves and bowing to the will of a blinking light.

The Auspicians set free their criminals and in the place

of their criminals, incarcerated the seers. They decided that the seers themselves had changed the Trikloptikon, for it was not all that complicated to make a light blink on and off occasionally and to make it seem like it brought on the harvest. The seers insisted this was not the case, which made the other Auspicians mad enough to execute them. The seers did not beg for their lives, only for their kinsmen to watch the Trikloptikon and listen to the cries of the Lightbird, since ignoring these warnings would mean the end of the Auspician race.

The light turned yellow, the skyfruits grew less often, the criminals grew more bold, the skyrabbits grew apathetic and would bear no riders. The Auspicians thought nothing of this and soon became as licentious as they once were wise. Woe! Woe unto the Auspician! The Trikloptikon was growing angry and the fish, the mindless ocean dwelling primitive beasts that they once ate up by the thousands were on their way and would soon have dominion of the land and the sea alike! Weep for sacred Xerath, weep for lost Ruko, weep for bygone Kjishkantha! Weep weep weep! The fish were on their way!

V.
When the Sheriff Up and Hanged Himself

The sheriff up and hanged himself because he didn't have any better ideas. He'd be damned if Ronnie Ray and his boy weren't winning. Little bastards, damn antisocial monsters. And if they were winning, he was a loser and his father, who had once been the lube king of central Kentucky, had not raised him to be a loser. Damned hot rodders, racin' too fast, hangin' around the soda fountain to laugh at him, skippin' school, diggin' up the skeletons of longdead mayors to have macabre shows then displayin' them in lewd positions in the pre-school classrooms. These were the kids that got away with everything, the children of a generation that got away with everything, who were in turn the children of a generation that had got away with nothing.

There was a gypsy lady the sheriff used to make time with when he was younger and she was younger. He still saw her now and again to get playing card readings and engage in some light bondage. She had recently switched to tarot but had a lot of difficulties giving good readings since she did not really get that the cards were metaphorical. When the sheriff asked what he should do about Ronnie Ray and the Slashcats, she drew the Hanged Man, which represented the virtues of patience and fortitude. It was telling him to wear Ronnie Ray down slowly and there would come a day when he'd defeat the hooligans once and for all. He would need to martyr his time and energy in favor of consistent surgical strikes against the Slashcats but at the end of this he would be a hero and none of the terrible events that would come to pass following the sheriff's suicide would have happened.

"This card here says that you should hang yourself."

"Upshidowg?" he asked, his voice muffled by his ball gag.

"No, you must commit suicide properly. Hang yourself for good."

"Canatigavoud?"

"Yes, it's a big decision, of course you should think about it."

So, the sheriff left the gypsy so that he could think about it. After thinking about it, he went to the second person he always sought advice from; his priest.

"So, how is Irina?" asked the priest before the sheriff could so much as greet him. He was not the most caring priest in the world by any means.

:"She's doing well."

The priest let out a yawn.

"A Hundred Hail Marys and a tray of brownies. Homemade this time. The last ones were from the grocery store and that's a sin."

"I need to talk you 'bout somethin' else."

The priest sighed.

"Can it wait? I'm a very busy man, sheriff."

"No, I'm afraid it can't."

"Really?"

"Yes."

The sheriff could hear the priest pouring a drink.

"Alright then, but try to be quick, would ya? These things get awfully boring awfully fast, you know."

The sheriff swallowed a big lump of trepidation.

"Well, Father, I'm contemplating suicide. I heard from Irina that it's the only way I could put an end to them no good Slashcats for good."

The priest flipped through his bible and weighed the pros and cons of the situation. It was difficult for a man of the priest's limited spiritual understanding to wrap his head around. Suicide was a really terrible thing. There was no denying that. But the Slashcats were also a really terrible thing. There was no denying that. But suicide was also a really terrible thing. There was no denying that. He did not recommend suicide too frequently but on the nine occasions in which he had recommended suicide, he did not equivocate, waffle or quaver.

"Suicide," said the priest, "is a terrible thing. There's no denying that. But the Slashcats are also a really terrible thing. There's no denying that."

"Sure are. Worshipin' Satan and rapin' everybody all the time just ain't right for a bunch of young men to do. I went to school with Ronnie Ray's pa and I know he would never have wanted to see his boy turn out that way."

"It is a difficult decision, but," the priest continued, "I've been reading a lot of old Tales from the Crypt comics lately and as an invulnerable zombie you would likely have a much better chance of settling the score with Ronnie Ray. Looking at it from that perspective, it's the only sensible option. Yes, sheriff, hanging yourself ought to do the trick."

"Thank you, father. What's the penance for committin' suicide?"

"Don't you worry about that, sheriff. We're square. I can't absolve you, anyway, if I do, you might not rise from the grave to take revenge."

"Guess we wouldn't that."

"Good luck, sheriff. God will be proud of you."

The sheriff went home and had a good long talk with his basset hound. The basset hound mostly just stared at him (not because he couldn't talk but because he was a good listener). When the conversation was over, he called the old gypsy and she came right over. They danced tenderly, they shared a bottle of wine and for the first time in years, the two made love. These might not have been the actions of a man seeking to be a restless soul or a fella about to commit suicide. They might have been entirely wrong for the occasion. They still took the edge off the whole thing and he was ready as he'd ever been for anything when he tied the noose and prepared to wreak supernatural vengeance. As he died for the town he loved, the old gypsy caught his last breath in a jar as a keepsake.

The gypsy and the priest had made a mistake. The gypsy should have read the book that came with the tarot deck. The priest should have read pretty much anything but Tales from the Crypt comics. Instead of transforming into an unstoppable zombie cop with a vendetta, the sheriff instead ascended to Heaven's Hall of Mighty Heroes where he would eternally be pleasured by The Supernal Chorus of Carnal Perfection. It did not take the sheriff very much angelic pleasure to forget that Ronnie Ray and the Slashcats even existed.

Although the sheriff forgot about Ronnie Ray, it did not go both ways. Ronnie Ray went to the funeral and cried louder and worse than any grieving widow the county had ever seen. He had no authority figure to piss off and terrorize, no enemy to justify his campaign against mankind. He stabbed his way past the sheriff's family to reach the coffin, opened it, jumped in and gave the sheriff a long, passionate open-mouthed kiss, the kind of kiss that made people uncomfortable to witness a living girl receiving, let alone the corpse of a sheriff. He left that funeral feeling empty inside, unable to find any joy in his thuggish heart. It might not have been a Saturday but Ronnie needed a Slashcat Saturday night to cheer himself up since all Ronnie Ray really got any joy from was fucking things up and raping nubile teen girls. If the sheriff hadn't up and hanged himself, this Slashcat Sunday night wouldn't have happened and a great deal of dead people wouldn't have ended up dead.

VI.
The Local Discusses the Greatest Night of His Life

Shakespeare? You like Shakespeare? Shakesqueer is more like it! You Shakesqueer! I oughta kick the teeth outta your face and fuck your pretty little mouth until you fuckin' choke and gag! I should put you in a wedding dress and call you Charlotte and braid your hair til it's all pretty like you was some kinda princess! You'd like that, wouldn't you, Shakesqueer? Well, I don't! I don't like it and you ain't gonna make me do it, cityfag! I oughta kick the teeth outta your face! I promised my mama I wouldn't fight no more and I ain't supposed to swear. I ain't supposed to break that promise, you filthy bastard! Not for you, not for nobody! How dare you try to make me break a promise to my mama! My mama's a saint! My momma's an angel from Heaven! You don't know what it's like to be from here. It ain't like where you're from.

Shakespeare! Ha! That ain't what fun looks like, no sir! You sure got a stupid idea of fun. Let me tell you what fun's like! One time at the County Fair, Ronnie Ray fucked my sister and charged me three dollars to watch. That was three dollars well spent. He sure did her good! He fucked her like there was no tomorrow. Then, he pointed his knife at my ribs and forced me to fuck her. Best pussy I ever had. My sister is one hot piece of ass! But don't you think about touchin' her! She doesn't like out-of-towners, Shakesqueer! You keep your damn hands off my sister.

That was a good time. Would have been the best night of my life if it wasn't for the night of the sheriff's funeral. The sheriff up and hanged himself 'cause nobody fucks with Ronnie Ray! Nobody! Don't you think about it! I know what you out-of-towners are like! Bombin' the World Trade Center, lettin' horses marry dogs, puttin' negroids in the White House. You think you're so much better than me just cause you ain't ever had a pig jizz in your face? You're not from around here, cityfag! You don't know what it's like and I ain't gonna let you judge me!

On the night of the sheriff's funeral, the Slashcats decided that they was gonna have some real Hit and Fun. Not like your Willy Shakesqueer fun! Real fun, motherfucker! Real fun! They gathered up every virgin in town of fuckin' age (which starts at 'bout thirteen) til they had 666 virgins of fuckin' age. You know why 666? Cause it's the devil's number, shithead! Ain't you ever seen the Omen, jizz-for-brains? Can you imagine 666 virgins of fuckin' age? It was fuckin' sweet! I got to watch it from my truck with my binoculars, the ones I use for huntin'. But you wouldn't know anything about that, now would you , cityfag? We're supposed to fuckin' marry the grizzly bears while they're eatin' our children, huh?

So, the virgins formed a great big line. That was one sexy line. 666 virgins meant about 1,300 pairs of tits, some of little nubs what was just growin' in, some of em big fat juicyass melons that you could suck on all night long, and I mean all night. Ronnie got out of his car, and he held up a starter pistol like the kind they use at a race. But you probably don't like races. You like little Willy Shakesqueer stories. It was way more entertaining than those. Ronnie Ray, for one thing started off with a joke.

"Ladies, and I use the term loosely…" he began and took a minute to pause for laughter, cause that was fuckin' funny, right? Jesus Christ, man! And I use the term loosely! Shit, man, that's a joke. Sorry, hang on, let me catch my breath. Don't you get impatient with me, cityfag! You got a pedicure to go to? Huh? Gotta get your little tootsies nice and soft for some little Korean boy to suck 'em? You're gross, cityfag. If that's the sort of thing that people that like Willy Shakesqueer stories are into, I'm awfully glad I didn't finish my literature degree. Fuck Shakespeare! Don't you know nothin' 'bout Geoffrey Chaucer? Fuck Shakesqueer! Chaucer's my man! And I don't mean that like you do when you're talkin' bout the fancypants Jew who's co-owner of your antique hairbrush store! Now quit distractin' me, I'm tryin' to tell you about the greatest night of my life.

"Ladies, and I use the term loosely," said Ronnie Ray, "I have gathered you hear so that we can play a game that you should be honored to participate in."

"We love you, Ronnie Ray!" the virgins cried out, "let us pleasure each other to amuse you!"

Most men would give their right and left nuts and their daddy's left nut to see 666 virgins eatin' each other's tight little pussies, but Ronnie Ray ain't most men and he don't get tempted by the shit most men are tempted by. Even you'd want a piece of that, wouldn't you, cityfag?

"You bitches shut up!" Ronnie Ray screamed at them, "this ain't about somethin' so base and insignificant as fuckin' girls. This is about honoring the sheriff's memory and it's about how Satan is king of the earth and we all gotta show some fuckin' respect to the devil cause he's the only devil we got. This is about the Son of the Morning and it's about Hit and Fun!"

"Please, Ronnie Ray, please, let us suck your dick!" they begged him.

"I said it ain't about that, and it ain't," said Ronnie Ray, "Now are you girls gonna listen to the rules of the game or am I gonna have to kill all your families and all your pets? Don't tell me I gotta do that cause I haven't shot a dog since I was four years old and I don't wanna go down that road again."

"We're sorry, Ronnie Ray, we're sooooo sorry," said all the virgins and you better believe them little bitches meant it. They might have been dumb little bitches but they were smart enough to know that Ronnie Ray meant business.

"That's alright girls. It's easy to get carried away. Any MORE distractions?" Ronnie Ray tapped his feet all impatient-like after that and they knew Ronnie Ray meant double business. You don't fuck with a guy who means double business. If you take nothin' away from our conversations, take that.

"Okay, good. Now, when I fire this pistol, the Slashcats and I are gonna start our cars and you girls are gonna run as far away and as fast as you can because we're gonna try and run you all down. Any virgin that gets run down will get their heads cut off and we're gonna fuck your mouth and eyeballs to honor not just Satan, prince of the Earth, but also our dear, departed sheriff. Any questions, girls?"

You better believe there weren't no questions. Ronnie Ray had explained that motherfucker like nobody's business! You'd have to be pretty dense not to understand that, huh, cityfag? You don't gotta be no William Shakesqueer to explain Hit and Fun.

Ronnie Ray fired the pistol, but he didn't start his car right away, even though he could have and maybe he should have. I would have, but I'm not a classy gentleman like Ronnie Ray. He was givin' the virgins and the Slashcats a head start since he knew he'd be able to just run 'em down like it was nothin' and the whole thing would be done in about five fuckin' minutes. Ronnie Ray could be president if he wanted to but he's too cool for that. The Slashcats are about badass rebellion and you don't need to be president to be a badass. Wasn't more than a minute later that Ronnie Ray was runnin' down virgins and cuttin' off their dumb bitch heads!

The virgins tried everything that they could to escape. They climbed trees, they got on buses leavin' town, they disguised themselves as dragons, they hid in the backs of turnip trucks, they joined the Navy, but that wasn't enough to stop the Slashcats. Shit, you can't stop the Slashcats that easy! No way! You can't escape 'em, cityfag! No matter how hard you try, they're gonna get ya. How long do you think it would take most gangs to kill 666 virgins? A month? Two months? A year? It wasn't like that for Ronnie Ray and the Slashcats! It took them just an hour to get all of them virgins headless. And you know what? The Slashcats just took the heads! Them boys were kind enough to leave 666 dead virgins lyin' on the ground unclaimed for the local boys to play with. And did we ever! Every man in town got himself a little bit of headless tail! Bitches were covered head to toe in spunk, they way they oughta be. Best night of my life!

VII.
It's (Not) The Thought That Counts

Ronnie Ray and the boys hadn't squashed a single virgin head during their game of Hit and Fun. Satan would be pleased. He would have been if he wasn't disgusted and confused. He did not recall every telling Ronnie Ray to do anything like that, or anything at all. Ronnie Ray creeped Satan out. Corrupting a soul like Ronnie Ray's would be like attaching a bayonet to an H-bomb. Watching this, Satan cringed knowing that the chance of Ronnie Ray getting into Heaven via last minute deathbed repentance was slim to nil. He'd have to find some punishment that would keep Ronnie Ray from having any mobility or chance to interact with him. It didn't even matter that there wasn't anything in his diabolical imagination that Ronnie Ray would even look upon as a punishment.

They counted the heads thoroughly several times and were relieved that it had come out to six hundred sixty six heads. Anything less and Satan would not have been satisfied. At least they thought. Satan drew the line at around three, four at the most. Satan considered petitioning God to ask if they could create another Hell for souls too repugnant for the original. He was sure God wouldn't go for it otherwise running Hell wouldn't have been a punishment for him. He really didn't want to know what the Slashcats had planned to do with the six hundred sixty three too many heads but was once again screwed over since the sacrifice had been made in his name so he was obligated to watch.

"Okay, boys, let's fuck them heads for Satan!" Ronnie Ray ordered his troops. And they began to fuck those heads good. Ronnie Ray preferred his men fuck their nice, squishy eyeballs, though being the understanding gang leader that he was understood that some of his more squeamish boys would opt instead for the more conventional mouth. What was important was that they were fucking six hundred sixty six severed virgin heads for Satan and were doing it underneath the old haunted traffic light that was always yellow. Ronnie liked that light because he never told him to stop. He hated it when people told him to stop, with the exception of the sheriff whose pleas for Ronnie Ray to stop had gravity behind them and therefore a certain amount of risk. Ronnie Ray fucked ten of his heads for the sheriff. The sheriff would have been as confused and repulsed by this as Satan was.

The Slashcats fucked as fast as they could, yet still it took them a good three hours to get all of the severed virgin heads properly fucked. It was longer than it took them to kill the virgins to begin with, longer than it took the townsfolk to ravage the decapitated corpses and fill them with semen. To say that the Slashcats were exhausted by the ordeal would be an understatement. Dirty Ralph looked like he was going to have a heart attack, Thesaurus Himmler had a hernia, Jester Benedict's penis was hemorrhaging, Backbacon Jones' seizures were acting up and Rudy Fortinbras was dead. Even Ronnie Ray had started to break a sweat. To Ronnie Ray, breaking a sweat was the sign of a successful and epic party. His parties generally tended to in his mind range from "disappointing", to "pretty cool", well below the point of exertion, no matter how many steel reserves he'd had to drink and how much raping and killing had gone on.

Ronnie Ray folded his hands in prayer and a tear rolled down his cheek.

"Dear Sheriff, I know you gone on to a better place now, even though by defying me, you have defied the will of Lucifer, the Prince of the Earth. I want to thank you, Sheriff for inspiring me to greater heights and for allowing me to come up with this epic game of Hit and Fun to honor you. As you can see, we have filled six hundred sixty six virgin heads with jizz and I'd like to think you're proud of me for that. My daddy was never alive to see my best rapin' and killin', but I'd like to think he saw it and I'd like to think you saw this and you're as proud of me as daddy is. I love you, Sheriff and I always will."

The Slashcats that were not too exhausted to hug embraced Ronnie Ray.

"That sure was a mighty touchin' speech, Ronnie Ray," said Thesaurus, who did nothing to indicate that his newly acquired hernia was killing him.

"Yeah, Ronnie Ray, it sure was," said Jester, ignoring the blood gushing from his cock to praise the leader who he cared for more than even his genitals.

"Very touching," Dirty Ralph contributed, wondering if that pain in his right arm was what he thought it was. It was.

The Slashcats were silent for a moment and not just because of their debilitating injuries. The Haunted Traffic Light was flashing. It did not normally flash. Nobody in town had seen it flash. It was a flashing yellow. Made everybody in town wonder what they were doing with their lives. Made people feel like a waste, made them consider quitting jobs and abandoning families or quitting life, made the men of the town feel guilty for covering all of those virgins in cum. Made people miss the Sheriff, grandparents, stillborn children and celebrities they hadn't even met. Made people feel desperately like yielding to life's indignities and tragedies.

It made the townsfolk feel like shit, but they would have killed to feel like shit if they knew what was going to happen when the light turned red. As it flashed red, every baby in town woke up and cried in unison at the top of their lungs, every alarm clock and car alarm went off in a cacophony of hateful noise. Every dog barked, every cat yowled, every rat squeaked, every bird screeched and every microwave beeped . Even those who should have been spared by deafness developed the ability to hear just so they could experience the sonic agony that everyone else felt. It took only moments of this for people to start bleeding out of their ears.

A few years ago, Ronnie Ray dreamed once that his balls kept growing and growing, until they reached such an incredible size that they smothered the Earth. It was invariably a wet dream. He'd wake up, his sheets soaking because he knew that everybody on the planet had technically died sucking his balls. Now, there was a part of him, a tiny part of him that thought that maybe that dream had actually been a nightmare, not a promise of success in his antisocial endeavors, but a threat.

VIII.
The Red Eye Opens

Weep! Weep! The Auspician, once the envy of all creatures was becoming base and degraded! Murder and rape, once inconceivable were now commonplace. Now, each Auspician's name was Lust Receptacle followed by a random number determined by a complicated system of rooting around in the entrails of their ancestors. Auspician scientists, once known for the humanitarian nature of their experiments had devoted several years of work to figuring out a way to breed with their furniture. Woe unto a people once wise now giving birth to sofas and ottomans many of whom rose to great prominence in their society.

Woe! Woe unto the Auspicians who decided that the highest art was not to create great literature but to burn it! Woe unto the Auspicians, whose every king was sainted and whose every saint was indulged with blood sacrifices! Woe unto the Auspicians who once used the dust of prophecy for introspection but now burnt in public squares and spread it through the air with giant fans! Woe unto the Auspician, whose wisdom and human merit was now judged by the number of tables and chairs in his harem!

Woe unto the Auspicians who ignored the cries of starving skyrabbits who at last in desperation began to hunt the children they once had deep and sacred bonds with! Woe unto the Auspicians as they sat back and watched as this misfortune unfolded, half-mad with the dust of the seers, lust slaked with every person and object they could find!

Woe unto the Auspicians who severed the heads of virgins and teased the omnipotent Trikloptikon by filling the heads with their seed right before its all-knowing and judgmental eye! Weep for the Auspicians who plucked the Lightbird raw and ate its flesh! Weep for the tainted! Weep for the misguided! Weep for the progenitors of horrors and purveyors of the world's finest lies! Weep for the Auspicians, for the red eye of the Trikloptikon was opening, burning with righteous hate for the oppressive wretches that had once been the greatest civilization the Earth had ever known!

As it opened, the ears of the Auspicians bled from the cries of their every infant and the blood that came forth took on a life of its own, transforming into a flesheating blob that crushed their city with flailing spiked flagella. As this happened, the furniture that the Auspicians had taken on as lovers hurled itself at them and there was not a weapon in their vast and wicked arsenal that could defend them from the onslaught. Weep weep for the Auspicians as their lovers and their steeds and their bodily fluids betrayed them and avenged themselves for years of being so ill-used! Weep weep weep for the Auspicians whose world turned red from Trikloptikon floating overhead chanting songs of suicide and words of panic! Weep for the Auspicians as they fought in the streets for the right to cannibalize and molest their dead! Weep for the Auspicians as they chopped off their own limbs and tossed them into the sky in the hopes of killing immortal Trikloptikon and reclaiming their civilization, horrible as it might have become! Weep for the Auspicians who survived only five days of Trikloptikon's fury, though they had ruled the Earth and the clouds for millions of years!

Weep now for a people that had names for every star and a place in their hearts to love them equally, weep for a people that had once no concept of war, that had cured all diseases by calmly discussing their position with the viruses and bacteria so they could live in peace with them. Weep for fair Xerath and the knowledge of eons and a compassion the world would never see again.

For centuries and generations afterwards, Trikloptikon haunted the dreams of wicked fish and wicked apes and eventually wicked men. And one of these wicked men searched the Earth and the sky, flying on eldritch wings seeking Trikloptikon and laughing a wicked laugh as he thought of how he could make the world pay for shunning and despising him. When he found it at last, the lunatic was overjoyed and made many devices bearing the dread god's face, scattering them through every city on the planet, forcing society to bend to its will. Woe unto the fish called man for dancing to the rhythms of apocalypse, woe unto man for bringing the three-eyed god into their communities, woe unto man for having in its hearts an arrogance almost surpassing that of the Auspicians while not choosing to surpass their greatness, for bearing Auspician lust without Auspician compassion, for feeling Auspician impertinence and Auspician hate! Weep for man, for his prayers to Trikloptikon have been answered! The red eye hath opened and the sacrifice been made! Weep for man as he faces three-eyed judgment! Weep! Weep for him!

IX.
The Local Discusses
the Scariest Night of his Life

Blair Witch 2:Book of Shadows? More like Scared Bitch 2! Ain't nothin' scary 'bout those movies. Just a bunch of bitches runnin' round scared! That shit ain't scary! Let me tell you 'bout he scariest sight of my life. It'll make you shit yourself, cityfag, then you'll probably cream yourself too cause you love the smell of your own shit! Ain't that right, cityfag? Well, ain't it? Blair Witch 2: Book of Shadows, my ass!

Scariest night of my life started out good enough. Ronnie Ray and the Slashcats had run down six hundred sixty six virgins in a row and…what the fuck do you mean, you've heard that story before, huh? Wasn't in one of them Shakesqueer plays, wasn't in Blair Witch 2: Book of Shadows, so where the fuck was it you woulda heard it? You better believe you were mistaken. You ain't from here! You don't know what it's like! Only people from around here know this story and you don't come from around here, now do you? I thought not. So let me tell this story.

Ronnie Ray and The Slashcats had just run down all them little bitches and cut their heads off, leavin' us their tight little bodies to play with and cum inside of. I know a cityfag like you probably couldn't appreciate goodass lovin' like that, but if you think of the best lovin' your special friend from the antique store ever gave your tender little asshole and you multiply it by five…what do you mean fuckin' dead girls is gross? Boy, you know less about fuckin' then you know about movies. Next thing you're gonna tell me that the Slashcats ain't fuckin' boss. You'd better not tell me that cause that would be a fuckin' lie like when you fuckers that Barack Osama and his towelhead assbuddies didn't blow up the World Trade Center so that nobody would find out that it was a secret abortion clinic for the Jews.

Greatest night of my life, and then for no reason at all, starts to go sour. There's a buncha awful noises and I feel sad and guilty and my ears start bleedin' and the sky glows bright red. Not just like when the sky usually turns red, it was so red it looked like the whole damn town was nothin' but a great big whore house. And I looked up to see where the red light came from and there in the sky was the ugliest motherfuckin' thing I ever saw in my life. First thing I saw was its head, a giant traffic light about the size of a bus, that was glowin' red. And it had this long neck that was made up of doll heads and a body like a great big manta ray and the two hind legs of a cat and a tail with a giant scorpion stinger. Bastard was the size of a train and that red light meant business.

And all of a fuckin' sudden, the cars are tryin' to run us down and we gotta start dodgin' cars. You ever try to outrun a Camaro? Makes me glad I wasn't a fucking virgin for all that time, that's for sure! It sucks to outrun a Camaro! Usually can't do it. Only thing that'll stop 'em is if you got some poor SOB in front you for them to run down. Like they say about not havin' to be faster than the shark. I feel awful bad about what happened to my brothers, but it had to be done. I was lucky to get inside of a house and climb up to the attic and watch everything with a telescope.

Next thing you know, everything starts gettin' even worse, if that's possible and let me assure you, it is! Deafening babies, killer cars…that shit seems like it's scary as it can get…fuck your Blair Witch 2! Fuck in the ass like your special antique friend does! Next thing you know all the little sperms are flyin' through the air, makin' a big cloud of jizz flies that keeps eatin' people's skin! They try to swat 'em away or clean 'em off, but how are you gonna do that if your skin's gettin' eaten, huh, smartass?

And as if that's not bad enough (AND IT IS!), the headless virgins start wanderin' the streets, breaking into people's homes and tearin' their heads off and puttin' their hands inside em like puppets and makin' people's jaws clamp up and down so they can bite everybody! And it works! Those virgins with their head puppets were killin' people like nothin' else! Way scarier than Blair Witch 2, that's for sure.

But to this day, I'm moved by what occurred next. You wouldn't 't have seen it comin' from a mile away…Ronnie Ray was drivin' around, squeegee in hand cleanin' up the jizz and runnin' down the virgins. Doin' a damn fine job of it. Too bad he missed the one that climbed up into that attic and tore my head off and killed me. Yeah, that's right, cityfag! Killed me dead and I came back to life again and you know what? Bein' dead makes me awful fuckin' hungry!

X:
The Revelation

Thesaurus Himmler was run down by his own rod. Dirty Ralph was eaten by a cloud of flies made of semen. Jester Benedict's penis bled to death. Backbacon Jones was devoured by virgins as he lay on the ground having the worst seizure of his life. Woe! Woe! Woe to the Slashcats! Woe to the citizens of Highfive, Pennsylvania! The red eye had opened and as it had done to the Auspicians before and the Cuddly Starponies before them, it brought inconceivable and sickening punishments. It was not just Highfive, Pennsylvania that Trikloptikon wished to mete out justice to. A mind of primal judgmental light would not be so narrow in scope. It had turned Highfive, Pennsylvania into a wasteland and every single one of the fish, the apes called men would follow. Weep! Weep! Weep for the fish called man!

And yet…could it be? Someone had survived. Though Thesaurus Himmler's hot rod had turned on him, though virgins and semenflies had eaten every man, woman and child, Ronnie Ray yet lived, still in the comfort of his hotrod, which had miraculously remained loyal to him. The extension of the man, of the instrument of evil Ronnie Ray could not be spirited away from its master, even by the deadly sacred light of the harbinger Trikloptikon! The devilcar ran down virgins, spattered jizzflies on its windshield and it almost goes without saying that Ronnie Ray's rod had meant death to any car that came near! The minions of the three-eyed god could do nothing against the sociopathic badass that even Satan feared. If a thing like Trikloptikon could be impressed, it would have been. Since Ronnie Ray, the last man in town was not yet dead, it honored him by not advancing its wave of devastation until it could find some way to destroy him. Though his will to fight had given the three-eyed punisher pause, Ronnie Ray could take no solace in this. He was moved to prayer.

"Satan? If you can hear me, what you're doin' now sure is cool but all my buddies who loved you every bit as much as I did are dead now and I don't like that. So, if you could use your dark powers to bring them back to life so we can build a rocket launcher and shoot that traffic light monster you sent down in your infinite wisdom out of the sky, I'd really like that."

For the first time in Ronnie Ray's lifetime of diabolical petitioning, Satan actually replied. Ronnie Ray was surprised.

:"Hi, Ronnie Ray," said a voice in his head, "you've been praying to me for a long time now…"

Ronnie Ray's eyes lit up.

"Wow! Is that you, Satan?"

"Yes, Ronnie Ray, it's me and I think this is a perfect time for me to tell you that you're weird and a creep and I hate you. I've never answered your or more or less anybody else's prayers and I don't plan on starting now. Leave me alone, you motherfucking freak."

Ronnie Ray was infuriated.

"When I get to Hell, I'm going to cut you so bad, you fucking faggot!" Ronnie Ray screamed. Satan made no further reply because he was scared. Satan regretted saying now. He was sure that Ronnie Ray would have no problem cutting and now everybody felt bad. Words hurt. Ronnie Ray was crying.

"Shucks, now I'm all alone," Ronnie Ray sobbed, "ain't got nobody in all the world and now this traffic light monster's gonna kill everybody on the planet. Life used to be about Hit and Fun and now it's no fun. Why can't it be fun again? I miss you, sheriff and I wish you could help me out. "

When Ronnie Ray was six, the sheriff got Ronnie Ray's kitten out of a tree. And although Ronnie Ray rewarded this act of kindness by punching the sheriff in the nutsack, secretly he had developed a great deal of admiration for the man. He even for a split second considered devoting his life to law enforcement, until he discarded the idea when he remembered that enforcing laws for squares and breaking them was for handsome rebels. Now trapped, he looked back on the day of his decision to become a psychotic hotrod hooligan and wished that the sheriff could get him out of the metaphorical tree he was in as he once had done for the kitten.

"Sheriff, I'm sorry!" Ronnie Ray cried, "I love you, sheriff!"

The sheriff had been having a peerless good time basking in the glory of the Hall of Mighty Heroes and sampling the myriad pleasures of The Choir of Carnal Perfection. If he were not obligated as an angel to answer Ronnie Ray's call for help, he would not have, because Ronnie Ray's call for help really pissed him off. But he had to, so he did, appearing beside Ronnie Ray in order to comfort the hooligan he had killed himself to defeat.

"Well, Ronnie Ray," said the sheriff, "I sort of missed you too."

Ronnie Ray dried his tears.

"Really sheriff?"

"No. If angels were capable of hate, I'd still hate you."

Ronnie Ray moped.

"I sure made a mess of this, sheriff. All I wanted to do was to honor your memory."

The sheriff put a hand on Ronnie Ray's shoulder.

"I know you meant well. What I don't know is why you thought killin' and rapin' six hundred sixty six virgins including my daughter would have made me happy. I'm sure you had your reasons, though."

Ronnie Ray shrugged.

"I don't know. But, do you think you can help me with this? I sure made a big mess out of things here."

"No such luck," the sheriff replied, "all I can do is provide you with a revelation. I don't know if it will help though."

"Guess it couldn't hurt," said Ronnie Ray, disappointed.

The sheriff reached into his pocket and pulled out a ball of light, which he handed to Ronnie Ray. The small ball exploded into a supernova of brightness, engulfing both Ronnie Ray and the car and changing them both. The light seared off Ronnie Ray's flesh until was nothing but a skeleton, a bug-eyed thing with a long, dripping tongue, a hotrod drawing by Ed "Big Daddy" Roth. The car grew and transformed as well, turning into a cartoon jalopy with a prominently displayed atomic bomb for an engine. If angels were capable of fear, the sheriff would have been very afraid.

Especially when the atomic bomb went off, turning the town into a smoking wreckage. That might have been the end of Ronnie Ray and the car and the sheriff, but Ronnie Ray was something not altogether human and the sheriff was an angel. Ronnie Ray and the car reassembled themselves and headed west, to blow the next town to smithereens. The sheriff, being an angel could not be destroyed by miracle radiation. But he could be irradiated. As anybody who has read Marvel comics or seen giant monster movies knows, becoming irradiated makes something bigger and awesomer. This was true of the sheriff who grew to a height of fifty feet tall and developed green wings of radiation on his back. He flew into the sky and began to vigorously wrestle Trikloptikon. They fought for hours, the sheriff being stung by Trikloptikon's stinger once for every time he smacked it in its fat, traffic light face. Unable to resolve their stalemate, Trikloptikon finally gave up, floating off into space to never again be seen by human eyes. It had witnessed the actions of a species that did not need a harbinger of doom. It had cars, satanic rituals, atom bombs and bad attitudes, and these things had come together to forge the malevolent god called Ronnie Ray, more than Trikloptikon's equal and it was headed to the next town and the next town and even if it drove into the ocean, would not be the last such monster to exist. Weep, weep, weep for mankind!

Beast With Two Backs

Mia and him, they'd been doing nothing but arguing. Maybe not literally, but close enough. He'd wanted to go to the opera. He loved the opera and when they were first dating, she had said that she too loved the opera. He should have known when she didn't name any specific operas that she was trying to impress him. She actually hated the opera and wouldn't be caught dead there. What she loved were carnivals. She loved watching him compete at games that were skewed against him, she loved eating funnel cake. She loved the muddy musky dirty smell of ponies. She loved smiling at tattooed creeps suggestively as she got on rides that took her to the brink. She loved sleaze and grime and the magic of lies. Things that always made him uncomfortable.

And she loved the sideshow. They were usually nothing like her conceits and dreams of sideshows. When you thought of sideshows, you thought of human oddities that bent and broke the laws of nature, displaying superpowers or shamelessly parading ugliness. The days of the true sideshow were mostly gone. These were, after all, the days of tolerance and political correctness. Calling mentally-challenged children pinheads or gawking in wide-eyed shock and terror at the morbidly obese were products of a simpler, sicker time. At a modern-day sideshow, you'd get to see a fake Fiji Mermaid (the only kind of Fiji Mermaid) in a glass case, a monitor lizard billed a living dinosaur, a lady with her body in a box with a spider painted on it and some framed photos. A scam posing as a museum.

It was at the third carnival they'd been to that month, this one an hour and a half outside of town. He objected to throwing away six dollars to get into the sideshow, just as he'd objected to the smell of piss over red velvet seat cushions, woodchip fries over a sit down meal and a tilt-o-whirl over beautiful, masterful music painstakingly perfected by people that wanted nothing more than to do what they do perfectly, inspiringly. He had longed for inspiration and had never gotten it from this world of over-inked ex-cons and oil-slick cuisine that had marred their time together. He was starting to feel like he wanted to get out. But the sideshow surprised him.

He had developed low expectations, and was perfectly justified in them. He had reached a point at which he wanted just a night at the opera and a glimpse of mastery, the sort of thing that would make him want to sit back down at the piano and start playing something that wasn't Billy Joel or a Sinatra song to belt out adequately as a de facto wingman for some blue suited hack who'd never met half the people whose names he dropped. A trip to the opera would have done that, at least in his mind. She knew better and he knew she knew better and he resented the hell out of it.

He had developed low expectations and was certain the sideshow as always would fail to meet them. Even if he tried to meet the bullshit with an ironic smirk, he'd still be out three dollars. Three dollars spent for the dubious privilege of walking around a shrine to chicanery and petty theft. But this sideshow was slightly different. In the middle of this tent was a corral, and the corral housed something unlike anything he'd seen at any other sideshow. So they passed the Fiji Mermaid and the woman in the spidery box. A mutated pig fetus in a jar. Went through the motions, halfheartedly wondering what was in the corral. Couldn't be anything that great.

Except that it was. A naked man twisted like a backwards bridge. Toned chest. Cast iron arms holding him up. Overdeveloped wide open legs bent. Head looking to the right. A woman, firm breasted, toned arms, powerful legs pressed against his, was bent into the same position, head facing the opposite way. They were making love. Or else...no. They were joined at the crotch by a bridge of skin. Two beautiful people, stuck together in mock intimacy. Brother, sister. He pulled Mia close. Kissed her. Clamped down on her tongue until he could taste blood. Reached under her skirt and squeezed her ass. Even though they must have been in plain view of the naked conjoined twins and even though they could hear another couple walking into the tent, the making out only got more intense. Soon they were fervently dry humping.

The other couple, lightly pierced but preppily dressed college kids whispered to each other. Quietly debated whether the freaks were real. Cleared their throats to make their presence known. Forced them to find some modicum of common decency. Forced them to break their embrace, cut off their kiss, leaving them to taste their bloody mouths and public shame. They took another long look at the brother and sister bridge before shuffling out, barely glancing at the third monitor lizard of the month. Was it just him or did this one look small and sickly?

They didn't ride any rides. He didn't try and win her another tiny plush pig by popping balloons with darts. They didn't eat any greasy food. They went to the car. They made out like teenagers. He began to notice the gray in her eyes again and the way the pixie cut about which he'd felt apathetic before framed her sweet freckled face perfectly. They pulled over and she gave him a blowjob. He enjoyed locking eyes with her and watching her as much as he enjoyed the act itself, which was plenty. It took a tremendous force of will to last as long as he did.

They waited, not knowing what they'd do next. Were they daring each other to go further? Were they trying to stop something that they knew was coming? He chickened out. He started the car.

"I think we should get some dinner. Like, a real dinner."

It took a second for Mia to crack a smile.

"Yeah. That would be nice."

They were underdressed for the restaurant, which was tiny, dark and intimate. Little Italian place. The food probably not worth the price. Under the table, they moved their legs forward, bodies stretching, unconsciously reaching for each other, his foot rubbing her leg, her foot rubbing his. They talked. Really talked. Ate ten-dollar bruschetta as they waited for their meal. Kissed vigorously in spite of onion garlic blood mouth. Incurred judgmental Connecticut glances of curdled patrician spite. They savored their meals, the restaurant, the moments, each other.

They pulled over again on the way home. Frenetic scratching of two teenage werewolves. Bitter disdain of t-shirts and seats that would not pull back far enough. They fucked. Clumsy, dirty awkward car sex. We've got shit to prove sex. By the end of it, they were sweaty, stinking, content, tired and just the slightest bit afraid. The previous day they had been pulling apart. It was only begrudgingly that he had accepted her suggestion that they should go to the carnival. She had been speaking less often, curtly, muttering things under her breath. And here they were, entwined, bitterly, achingly in love. Neither of them needed to speculate for long. They knew where their passion had come from. When they got back to the apartment, they fell asleep slower than they let on. Eyes half-closed, ears perked-up to wait until the other one had drifted off.

The next day, she went to work and he was stuck at home. Not amused by daytime television. Didn't feel like reading. Or watching a movie. Or going for a walk somewhere. He sat down at the piano and played. It yowled like a cat. It screeched protest. It growled hatred and spat lopsided notes that would not string together. The piano was usually unresponsive, but he had made some headway. It had moved from utter noncompliance to babbled curses. That was something at least. Not enough. He soon found that he did not know what to do with himself. He soon found that he did know what to do with himself.

He called a friend. Asked to borrow his car. Yes, of course he'd fill up the tank. He left a note on the coffee table. Said he was catching up with some old friends. He had no intention of catching up with old friends. There was only one thing he was thinking of doing. Only one person he wanted to see. Two people. He went to the carnival.

***

For once he could ignore the grease urine crime stench. For once he could ignore the sleaze. There was something beautiful to see there in the freak show tent. Ignoring the grimeworld and the gaffed freaks and everything else, he approached the corral and the bent bridge twins. Inseparable. Stuck. Together. He cried. He didn't know why he would cry in the presence of such a perfect, loving monster. But he did. He wondered if the freaks could hear him, if they felt for him, if they could feel anything but their oneness and if they could care for the feelings of a being that was not part of the fleshbridge.

For reasons that also escaped him, suddenly, he no longer felt like crying. He felt content and safe and like life made sense again. He left, drove back home. Found Mia in the living room reading. Locked eyes with her. Used her at length on the couch. Sweating aching, uncertain of what brought them so close, exactly what was unifying their bodies when their minds and hearts had been growing so far apart. Scared by feelings of what was simultaneously consent and rape. When they finished, they sat up on the couch, trying to scoot away from each other, but ending up cuddled together, quiet and unsure. Each thought of making a move for the remote to turn the tv on, neither dared to.

They went to bed, didn't exchange so much as a "good night" before going to sleep. She woke up in the middle of the night, stroked into the land of the living. They fucked languidly at first, still half asleep, sloppy, not sure of what they wanted from it, but it rolled along, gathering passion, gathering strength until there was none left in their bodies and they fell asleep again, knowing that they were having the same dream. Should have been some comfort in that, being protected and unified, safe from it turning into a nightmare. It wasn't.

As they held hands, each knew they were not holding the hands of some dreamself, but the dreamhands of a real person standing behind them, digging into their mind, clinging to their soul. Resentful and nervous. To be the one to let go would mean they were the one that didn't care, that they were the one to face their lover's judgmental gaze upon waking. They were holding hands in the dark, surrounded by nothing but possibilities. Dreams could happen if someone let go and ran into the void to discover. But nobody was going to. They breathed heavy, held hands and hoped the other one would let go and make a move, create some possibilities.

They held hands in the dark and waited. They held hands in the dark wishing they could stop. They held hands in the dark hating each other a bit. They held hands in the dark wondering if it would be like this when they woke up. Was there some balance they could strike up between silence and drooling lust, between worlds away and too close for comfort? Was that the question every couple asked or just the ones that weren't sure they worked. Would you let go? Would you fucking let go? They held hands in the dark and waited. Until the light came on.

The darkness faded and they knew where they were. Either they were tiny or the corral was gigantic. Gigantic like the copulating twins overhead. Holding hands in the dark, they had been beneath a bridge of inescapable affection the whole time. Corralled inside porn promise and sideshow sleaze, legs turned into columns, miles of back giving way into cavernous buttocks. Each one of them wishing the other would let go. Would you fucking let go? We are not this. We are not stuck. We can let go any time. Would you fucking let go?

***

They wake up at the same time, making sure to turn away, as they cannot bear to look each other in the face following the dream. Mia goes to brush her teeth. He goes to get a cup of coffee. She hops in the shower. He toasts a bagel. Wolfs it down. She emerges from the shower. Dresses. Goes to the kitchen. He takes her place in the bathroom. Brushes his teeth. Showers. When he emerges, both of them know that one of them will have to leave the apartment if they are both to be alone. They hesitate and wait. Would you fucking let go?

They both end up on the couch. Saying nothing. Somebody must say something. Just as somebody should have gone off into the dark and explored instead of leaving them standing there beneath the human bridge. If they'd gone off and explored the darkness, while it was darkness, they wouldn't have known it was the corral and that they were trapped. Being a dream, not knowing that they were trapped, they had to be free. Then they realize, at the same time, what must be done. There is only thing they want to do, only one thing they can do. They know they're thinking as one, but they try to resist thinking that they're thinking as one, that there are no mysteries between them. Time feels too thick to pass. It does not drip away. Petrified.

Mia gets the courage to speak. She knows that it must end. Not the relationship. Not the awkwardness. But the stillness. They have somewhere to go.

"I want to go…"

"Yes. We should."

"The carnival."

"Yes."

"You went there yesterday."

He does not admit to this. He gets their coats. They drive past an hour and a half of oblivion and cornfield. They ignore rigged games that barely try to get their attention and food that barely smells like food. There is only one thing they have come for. As it was in their dream, there is nothing in the world but the tent and the corral and the two of them. The few patrons of the carnival back away, threatened by the intensity of their closeness and the singularity of their purpose. Nobody wants to get in their way. Nobody can. Nobody thinks they even exist in the eyes of the inseparable couple.

They enter the tent and the two freakseekers already inside instinctually make their way to the exit. They know this tent is no longer their space. They go to the corral, eyes clinging to the archbacked man and the archbacked woman, the manhood stuck to womanhood, brothersister lovers. They feel the static spark of arousal. The tiny spine shock that declares "I'm afraid, I'm aroused, I need you, go away." They kiss, lips entwined, locked. Truly locked.

Have our faces come together? Are mouths one mouth? Will we taste with one tongue just as we think with one mind? Will our whole head be stuck together? He grabs her breast, surprised that he could let go of her hand. She shakes slightly when he does, puts her hand on his side, thinking that perhaps his letting go means they can't come back together, even as their mouths threaten to merge, melt together. She wraps her leg around his. If the freaks could turn their head, they would be watching them, perhaps seeing that they were alike. They swear the freaks are letting out sighs of pleasure. He has seen them twice, knows they don't speak, couldn't if they tried, but they are moaning softly.

Would they ever want to be cut apart? Can they even see? Are these sounds in their heads? In both their heads, they wonder. They are both wondering and they know it. They break their embrace, but clasp their hands again. Walk out of the tent, to the car. They don't drive for long before pulling over somewhere secluded, to touch, bite, unite. Love. Make love. Hold each other slightly too long for comfort when they are done.

Petrified again. They try to listen for each other's thoughts and to know if their thoughts are being heard. The results are inconclusive. They decide to get moving. That they should get lunch. They go to the Italian place that is slightly too nice for them. They stare at each other. Rub each other's feet under the table. Hold hands, only letting go when the food comes. It is the same thing that they ordered before. It tastes the same. It's pretty good, but they barely notice, although each one gets a slight taste of the other's meal in their mouth. A weird olfactory trick. A slight hallucination.

After lunch, they get back on the road. Resisting temptation, pushing yes, pushing no into each other's brains. They want to pull over. They want desperately not to. If they did, neither one thinks it would be their decision. They can decide when they want each other and when they don't. They can't. Pushing yes, pushing no, forty more minutes of almost kissing, almost sex, almost irresistible loving. It's good to be back at the apartment. Maybe.

Couch calls them over and they obey. Television becomes totem, each one afraid of the consequences of turning it on. Whoever turns it on is unloving. Whoever turns it on wants to ignore the problems that have grown. The remote destroys their world. The remote is an argument machine that should not under any circumstances be activated. They do not argue anymore. They are past that. They are past the television times. They might also be past the talking times. There are things to say, but they might not need to say them anymore.

Bedroom. They know bedroom. They undress. They stare at one another, knowing as they've known everything today, what is next. There can only be one conclusion. He assumes the bridge position. She approaches, sucking him ready. It takes awhile, because of his nerves and the awkwardness of the position. His yoga is out of practice. She assumes her position, wide open, waiting.

He enters her, neither of them knowing if he will ever pull out again.

The Man in the Film Noir Hat

His face is like a calavera, mocking all evils with a serpentine smirk. His eyes are beautiful, yellowy cats eye green and somehow reflect like a makeup mirror. His suit is white with red stripes like a carnival barker's, but his hat doesn't match, that's the thing. His hat is a wide-brimmed gray fedora like a gangster from an old movie with Edward G. Robinson or James Cagney. It's just wrong wearing a hat like that with his suit. Where does he get off pretending to be a gangster?

He's dashingly devastatingly distractingly handsome and when he walks into Beaumont's Café, Lucille the pretty young waitress almost forgets her new husband, a wild-looking musician that she's been married to for three months. She has no clue who the man in the Film Noir hat is, but it doesn't matter. She wants him to hold her, to breathe his breath (peppermint like his suit) in her hair, to kiss her until she can't breathe at all. She sways her hips like Mae West and looks at him with thirst in her dark brown eyes. "Hmm" she says with her lips, but in her mind the sound amounts to a voracious "mmm".

"What can I do for you?" She says half-suggestively catching a drop of saliva with her tongue before it becomes too conspicuous.

He smiles, but doesn't open his mouth at first, until he talks, his voice jingling jangling, tintinnabulations of a tambourine.

"Do you run this place?"

Lucille smiles. She knows it's nothing like the calavera grin, nowhere near as horrifyingly comfortingly lovingly brutally softly warmly coldly seductive. She's ashamed that she might be trying to seduce him back. What would her husband say? What husband? All there is right now is a man in a candycane carnival barker suit and a hat that doesn't belong at all. He is what is there, so he is what is real.

"No. My aunt Jess does."

The smile slides across his face like a blues man's harmonica. It reveals glimmering gleaming teeth, sharp, but not like an animal's, no. Like a vampire's. Teeth to tear and torment.

"Really, that's a surprise. I took one look at you and I said to myself "this pretty little lady runs the restaurant." There seems to be an air of authority about you. Your carriage is very…" The word does not come, or else he delays it to make the forthcoming word seem more felicitous. His brow furrows as if he's deep in thought. "Majestic."

She blushes and her face turns reddish pinkish frostbitten scarlet. "Do you want me to go get her?"

"If it's no trouble." He says it like John Wayne or Clint Eastwood with a hypermasculine inflection. The smile comes back.

She sways her hips again, like Mae West or Peggie Lee or some similarly sultry figure.

Lucille walks into the kitchen where slightly haggard Aunt Jess Beaumont is scrubbing a pan caked with blueberry pie. The smell of Dawn permeates the room yet doesn't get rid of the noxious meatloaf stench around it. "There's a man to see you Aunt Jess," Lucille tells the middle-aged cook and proprietor of the café, "He's cute, but he sounds like a salesman."

"Tell him to go away." Lucille doesn't want him to go away. She clings to her aunt's thighs like a child and begins to sob. After the tantrum, Jess does come out of the kitchen, but she's awfully suspicious. Lucille is usually somewhat calm and down-to-earth, though she does go on and she's certainly not the sharpest knife in the drawer. There's some bad juju around this place and she just can't put her finger on it.

Then she sees the man in the Film Noir hat and she smells the musk of beauty and corruption, of carcasses and violets and dead things and peppermints and…money. She too smiles at him. She too sways her hips, hips supporting her somewhat ample girth. She too hears "mmm" in her mind. Money, violets…she likes him and she can't tell why. She'd have a worse tantrum than Lucille if he had to leave.

"What do you want?" she asks him. She's trying to be the consummate businesswoman. She's trying to sound like one sounds when dealing with a salesman. It doesn't work on him, he knows she smells the violets and the money and the corpses. He knows she is "mmm"ing at the center of her gold-and-gray-flecked hair. Lucille is looking at him in silent worship, eyes as wide as an English girl's at a Tom Jones concert.

"I'm an idea man," he says, "I sell ideas."

Jess' hand ventures ponderously pensively to her chin. "How much are these ideas?" She asks. She's only curious. Yes, that's it. She couldn't be taken in by some smooth-talking stranger selling something she didn't want. Violets and money and…mmm.

"A dollar." He says.

Jess takes out the dollar like one possessed and gives it to him. She mouths the words "I love you" but would never say them out loud. His calavera smile and his yellowy cats eye green eyes say "I know you do."

He stuffs the dollar in the jacket pocket of his candy-cane carnival barker suit. "Your coffee should be a quarter cheaper." He tips his hat revealing a bald head decorated with pretty patterns like those of a Faberge egg. Each bizarre line and swirl forms the letters of an unwritten novel or the scenes of a film that won't ever be screened. Lucille and Jess see in those patterns the blinding light of ingenuity and have a headache just from looking at the bare, bald head of the man in the film noir hat. Then he walks out, bathed in a light of pure and unrefined thought and leaving an olfactory trail of money and violets and corpses and peppermints. As stupid as what he suggested might be, it is positively epiphanous to Jess.

Four days pass and he has gone from Maryland to New York on his flying carpet of dreamstuff. He gets a hot dog with Jess' dollar and walks on to the UN building. He's about to go in, when he is stopped by security. They stop him, but they don't. They just don't dare to make him state his business, because it must be too big to understand. They're right.

Inside, the world is meeting. Population 200 and something. The man who is China is arguing with the man who is France regarding something neither one cares about. The man who is France took the man who is China's parking space.

Everything stops when they see the man in the Film Noir hat. They smell the violets and peppermints and money and corpses. They all like the man in the Film Noir hat.

"What do you want?" says the man who is our great nation feigning frustration to obscure his interest in the man in the Film Noir hat.

"I'm here to sell you an idea," the man in the Film Noir hat says.

"How much?" says the man who is Switzerland.

"A dollar."

The man in the Film Noir hat takes Switzerland's dollar and makes his suggestion: "This world is over. I say nuke the damn thing."

Each one of them stops and thinks about it. And each one of them has to laugh at the absurdities they've lived with.

And everyone smiles. The world joins hands, wraps their arms around friend and foe alike....

And there is fire and screaming and crying children and melting cities and a mushroom cloud...

And the man in the Film Noir hat takes a leisurely stroll through the dust, his work done in this corner of reality. He stops and enjoys the voice of his sister Calliope, singing dirges for the slain woven with threads of great operatic sopranos. He basks in the music for a little while, then looks down at his watch. He's sad to go, but there is promise yet. Other places and other times are calling, other dirges, lament of a thousand bluesmen, hearts that ache to stop to stop the ache. "Goodbye, blue ball," he says to this earth, "a muse's work is never done."

All About the Sheriff

There is nothing to be known in this donut shop. But every day he comes in with his questions and his pliers and his high beaver count ten gallon hat. And he comes around and keeps on asking questions and twisting the fingers of local low-lives until everything they know comes pouring out. It's inconsequential that it's never what he needs. What's he supposed to do? He's the sheriff.

There was a time when this city was just a bare whitewashed wall that walked around with him, interposing itself between him and those he loved, in particular this one woman whose name he has forgotten, but if you ask the wall, it will tell you. You just have to know which wall to ask. And that information doesn't come cheap.

In the beginning, she could sneak behind the wall, trick it into looking away, pole vault over it or approach him from the sides. It was just one wall and she was brave and beautiful and optimistic and used to men and their sad, secret places. Every man has them, after all. They could carry on their life and love almost as if it wasn't there. But it was.

The first wall attracted a second wall, as walls often do. While it is hard to get around a wall that doesn't want you getting past it, it's twice as difficult getting around two of them. Physical contact becomes exhausting, lovemaking virtually impossible. That's what the walls tell me at least. And I have no reason to believe they didn't perform their tasks admirably.

Though the man who would be sheriff wasn't getting any, the walls found time to breed and gave birth to twins. Walls grow up quickly. It was only a matter of days before the man who would be sheriff found himself in a box. The box had almost no cellphone reception, just enough to hear her pick up the phone, say his name, a name he has since forgotten and ask "is that you?" and God help the poor bastard, by the end of the week, he wasn't sure. A week in a box that you know you're responsible for does that to a man. Had he not known from the cellphone calls that there was a girl out there somewhere, there would have been nothing left of him.

At last, a door appeared in one wall. Was it the will of the man who would be sheriff? It's difficult to say. What the man who would be sheriff knew was that he was grateful for it. He opened the door and walked out into a snowbound city, born during his seclusion. There was a cowboy standing in the street, face wet with tears red as a stoplight from misery.

The cowboy hugged the man who would be sheriff. He placed his cowboy hat on the man who would be sheriff's head and a tin star on the man who would be sheriff's chest. The cowboy turned, took a few steps, put his six-gun up to his head and blew his brains out. I meet a lot of people here in this donut shop and I haven't met a single one that knew who this cowboy was or where he came from. There are some folks who are adamant that the cowboy doesn't exist and others who will scream out "by the cowboy!" as an oath.

The man who would be sheriff found himself wearing a tin star and a high beaver count hat and wandering the streets of the city that grew around him during his time in the box. Petty crimes stopped at the sight of the desperate tin starred gentleman whose loneliness was poison and whose fear turned quickly into a rain of lead that would cleanse the criminal souls of their impurities. And it wasn't long before his loneliness and fear spread across this whole damn city.

There is nothing to be learned at this donut shop, although he comes here often enough. The criminal types that congregate here only know about crime. It's what they do. They're criminals after all. There is nothing that can be learned in this donut shop. I make sure of that and he could twist my fingers off and not hear a word he doesn't already know.

I've seen her a couple times. Late at night when the criminals have left and the sheriff has already made his rounds. Yeah. The one he built the wall to protect himself from, the one he built the city to avoid, the one he's still trying to find. She gets a low-fat muffin and a coffee and she tells me "don't tell him that I came." And I never do.

Octopus

He strains. He grunts. His face twists. He throws his back into it. The jar has no desire to give in. It will not be opened. Not by him. Not right now. He runs the faucet over the lid, hoping that it will loosen up a little. He strains, he grunts, he throws his back into it. He takes a fork and tries to use it as a lever. An artifact from six hundred years in the future in the hands of a neanderthal, sealed like a pyramid, stiff, rigid and unforgiving as his seventh grade math teacher. He sets it down on the counter and he stares, as dogs stare at refrigerator doors. "There is food in there," the dog stare says, "but how do I get at it?" Then, the intimacy between him, the jar and existential defeat is broken when she walks through the door, just home from work. She kisses him on the cheek, thanks him for starting dinner and picks up the jar, not knowing that this is between him and it, not knowing the anger and frustration. With a deft little twist, it opens for her. He seethes, he mumbles to himself.

"You loosened it for me," she says, seeing the annoyance on his face. He loosened it. He squeezed, fought, wrestled and agonized over the damn thing and all that became of his little struggle was that he loosened it. He says nothing. He seethes, he mumbles to himself. They make dinner. He picks at it and leaves a lot of leftovers. The conversation lies dead on the dinner table, and neither of them wishes to comment on it. Neither of them will call an ambulance, neither will make an attempt to resuscitate the moment. He can't even reach for the words. They would be tiny squeaks from distant church mice.

They go to bed. She reads as he just sits up and thinks. He moves to kiss her and she rolls over. He places his hand on her thigh and she places hers on his to sort of acknowledge it.

It is merely acknowledged. It is not desired, reciprocated or encouraged. He thinks about sneaking it between her legs, but he doesn't bother. He's pretty sure it won't go anywhere. His body gets a little twitch, a little throb, but it doesn't really matter. He's pretty sure she just wants to sit and read and suddenly, for no good at reason at all, he wonders if it would even work. Is there too much stress? Is it just writhing in its sleep? The twitch and the erection doesn't know. He's thankful he could avoid the embarrassment, but he has to stop and wonder if it will work next time. The sound of the neighbor with the guitar who he can't get to stop playing interrupts his sleep, but he tunes it out. He's starting to get used to it.

He dreams of floating around in the ocean. He is himself, but spineless, his arms, long and limp, each finger a tentacle. His body is stretched almost beyond recognition, and he can barely swim. He sees objects lying on the ocean floor, pencils, pens, things from his desk, mail and he reaches for them, but his weak, soft arms with their long, tentacled fingers don't work right. Nothing is tangible, nothing is accessible here, he can only float around. Suddenly, he swims into his bedroom, the same but beneath the sea. She is lying in bed on the ocean floor, asleep, nude and content. He tries to swim to her, but his boneless body doesn't work. The tides drag him along, into the opening of a great black cave. He doesn't know what lurks in there, but knows it is powerful, it has weight behind it and it could open any jar of pasta sauce it wanted to.

He wakes up at four in the morning, and goes for a long walk to quiet his head. He passes the Speedway, the McDonald's, the church and all the familiar things that make his town just like every other town and then he does it again and then once more. By the time he gets home, she's gone to work and it's time for him to go. He laments the lack of a kiss goodbye, but not so much as the jar and the frailty of long, cartilaginous limbs. As he types, staples and files, he thinks about how small his arms must be. How could he do anything with such small arms?

Little tasks feel twice as hard. The pressure needed to work the stapler must be tenfold. His boss watches him straining and jokes off handedly "you should go to the gym."

So, he goes. He works out for a couple hours, straining to lift the weights, but feeling so much more alive as the pain shoots through him. No more floppy, useless tendrils of flesh and sinew. He will have muscles and would not tolerate any more weakness in himself. He stares at the octopus in the mirror and begs it to disappear and never come back. He will sweat it out of existence, making salt that it couldn't swim through. The octopus had to die and in its place, there would be a man, a strong, passionate, capable man who could open jars and fix shelves and do all of the other things he could do if he was a man. He makes his way on his journey with courage, abandon and obsessive zeal, like some twisted vagabond among the Oz fellowship. At the end of the yellow brick road the wizard would give him some muscles and balls.

He comes home, thick with sweat and pheromone, thick with sasquatch musk, thick with intent and intensity and she pounces. Her kisses are rough and desperate, her tongue pillaging his mouth for all the excitement within. They duel with kisses all through the house, until they reach the bedroom. The musk, the scent of man emerging, the Mithras Osiris Orpheus Christ pulls her to the mattress and rips her clothes off. Their lovemaking is beyond brutal, beyond bestial. Dirt monsoon fire. The urge to create, the urge to die...but the octopus is in him. It won't last, it says, I will take the hard-on that god's given you, it says, and I will make it like me. He fights it, he concentrates on her body and his love for her. When he goes flaccid and he pulls out, he doesn't notice that half an hour has passed and she is on her back, wheezing and panting. All he can think of is the fact that the hard-on is gone. Like his body, like his muscles, it has atrophied. It is all rubber and tentacle.

The next night is the same. Gym, sweat, sex, octopus. This

time he doesn't hear her saying "stop, I'm getting sore." He doesn't see that when he's pulled out, she looks at him as one looks at a neighbor's angry Doberman on a chain. Too soon. Work harder, stay hard. He goes out for a jog for an hour, then comes home, goes into the living room and falls to the floor for push-ups. He goes to bed an hour after that, not at all tired. He watches the octopus under his eyelids for what must be hours, caught up in the current, wobbling weak, boneless. The other fish have human faces and they laugh at it, swimming just out of reach of the useless fleshy tendrils it calls arms. Eight arms and not a one can catch them. When he finally gets to sleep he is a gladiator skillfully decapitating lions, tigers and berserk slaves. He lays down on the arena floor, wallowing in the blood and guts of the battle and feels whole again.

He skips work that day. Family emergency. The gym is calling, the Roman hulk he longs to be is calling. He will not be an octopus any longer. Stay hard, stay strong. Bathe in the blood of the foe. He lifts free weights forever before he begins to break a sweat. He moves up the weights as far as he can, but they don't provide a challenge. He runs on the treadmill far enough to reach the next major city. It is getting dark, and he still isn't sweating. The personal trainers are awestruck and quiet. When the gym closes, he runs home, wondering why the people on the street are avoiding him. They resent him. They know how small and weak he is. They know he can't open jars and when he yells at the neighbor with the guitar, the kid doesn't stop playing. They know he goes soft and he can't satisfy his girl as well as they could. Laughing fish with human faces, an ocean of disapproval. If he were bigger, he'd show them what was what. The octopus must die.

He comes home to the sound of the kid next door with the guitar. He walks into the kitchen and grabs the broom, takes it outside where the kid with the guitar is butchering "Champagne Supernova" by Oasis. As if it needed butchering. The kid doesn't know what hits him as he is anally impaled by the broom and planted in the ground as a flag. You're still small, says the octopus, even though he is growing. When he went in to grab the broom, the doorway wasn't so narrow, but this time it is, this time his muscled frame can barely squeeze through. She rushes to the sound of splintering wood and crumbling plaster, wondering where it came from, and she finds him, ten feet tall, a tiny head sitting upon a great wall of muscle. His clothes had split off and he was naked. His thighs and pelvis are so big, she can't even see his genitals. He grabs her and throws her down. He's not taking any of her shit. He gets on top of her and she tries to squirm out from beneath him, but she can't. He's massive and only growing. The man disappears beneath the muscle. She begs him to get up, but he can't. His arms and his legs no longer move, weighed down by their hugeness. Trapped beneath him as he expands, a sea of pulsing muscle mass, she suffocates. Soon, there is nothing in the room but him, everything absorbed and shattered by hard, angry tissue. First the room, and then the house. It breaks to pieces as he outgrows it and encompasses the lawn and then the neighbors.

The SWAT team arrives, peppering him with bullets, flamethrowers and rockets, but their weapons do nothing. Overhead, fighter jets launch tomahawk missiles as his body absorbs the block, houses drowning in his pectorals. Somewhere in the rippling, cancerous muscle-eaten town, an erection twitches.

Having Set Out to be Vanquished

"The toad," said the elder, "has eaten."

"Then he can eat again," said the young man, defiant, "I will be sacrificed. You will not stop me."

The elder shook his head.

"If we feed him again, then he will expect two next month. I cannot allow you to do that. Die fighting the Voormis if you want a noble death."

A woman had taken her leave of the young man, and she had taken his senses with her, as women often do when they take their leave. He had come to the elder to tell him that he wished to give himself to Tsathoggua, the toad that was death. He could see no semblance of a future, no purpose for him as a craftsman, as a soldier, as a priest or as a man. And there were few in the village that would dispute this.

"I would die before I killed a single Voormis and men would die protecting me from harm. I want to be of help and I could be of help by sating the hunger of the gods."

The elder sighed. The youth before him was obstinate, indeed unskilled with a sword and showed no knack for any trade. And there was no persuading him otherwise, so all he could do was send the dead boy on a fool's errand during which he would, of course, be killed.

"Atlach-Nachta," the elder mumbled.

"Hmm?" the young man's ears perked up.

"Atlach-Nachta. You can give yourself to the spider."

The young man's sunken heart bobbed to the surface again.

"Is the spider a terrible, ferocious god?"

"Yes," said the elder, "one of the worst. Its hunger is nearly insatiable."

"Then I shall go forth and I shall feed it."

The elder embraced the poor suicidal youth.

"May your journey be safe as it can be."

He set out with the elder's blessing, dubious though it was, weaving, ducking and hiding, struggling to stay warm in the wide white wastes. Though he shivered, though he suffered, he was intent. He had surrendered the prospect of living well, so was unshakeable, imperturbable in his desperate drive to die well. In town, they would remember his name forever and they would speak of him forever as a noble, upstanding man who had chosen to die as best he could. The thought kept him warm and kept his eyes sharp for foraging and hunting.

Indeed, foolishness, death wish and lack of skill could not contend with his determination. He came at last to the cavern where he would find the spider. It shimmered with promise and its wide open maw brought to mind the hunger of the gods, a hunger he would sate to become a redeemer of men and a hero in the eyes of the villagers. He was afraid, in part, to die, but more ecstatic by far. He had meditated and dreamt of nothing but, his journey blessed by promise of spiderteeth and eternal digestion and promise that the time would come where he would no longer have to live with the burden of being the man that he was becoming.

He entered the cavern frightened of what was inside it, but with a heart that was joyful, perversely joyful to know that this had to be the place. Walking through, he found lizards of a million colors, birds of brightness, birds of strangeness, plants hanging upside down from the roof above him quietly humming songs, saw-toothed gnomic fiends, who leapt from the dark to frighten him, then returned to the shadows, the unfathomable shadows they came from. He wandered a great while and in his wanderings, he felt he could find most anything here except the spider, except the promise of dying well.

He spent what felt like days in the cavern, days during which his zeal even for dying began to wane. There was no end of wonder and confusion to be had among the shapes and concepts around him, among the dreams and the phantasms, but there was not the thing he wanted. He realized that he had come to the wrong cavern. He had heard stories of this place and they brought little consolation. The cavern was connected to the spider's lair, but the caves did not meet for a great long way and he was sure to perish in here among the archetypes before he could reach the spider.

The girl frightened him at first. He was sure that she would peel away her face and reveal something foul beneath it . She was not a day over thirteen, dusky skinned, hair thick darkness, opaque shadows. Her dress was white as she was dark, her feet bare. She held a candle and the fiends that would frighten backed away from her.

"You are tired and hungry," she said.

"Are you him?" he asked her, not quite lucid.

"You are tired and hungry," she said, cutting through the night with her little candle, "rest and eat."

"I will not rest until I find him. I need the spider."

"Rest and eat," she replied.

And he felt the urge to rest and eat. He hated her for the urge to rest and eat. She made him feel less than a man, tinier and slighter than her, and though her candle was substantial, she was tiny and slight indeed. He followed her for not very long. Her home was close, or it wasn't and she moved quickly. It couldn't matter less which was which. The cabin was full of light and the smells of better food than he deserved. This wasn't the way to death but he did not turn away.

"You're welcome here," she said, "my mother and sister are always expecting. Rest and eat."

He came in and there was food upon the table. A girl was seated there, his age, not young as the dusky girl. Her hair was blood. Her face flushed. Her eyes green as green could be, greener than a man who dwelt on the tundras had seen, greener than the Earth had given up yet. Her dress was white and plain as the dusky girl's. Her smile was sad but inviting. It seemed likely to taste bloody as her hair, sweet as the hut smelled. He hated her because she distracted from the task at hand. The hut and the food and the rest distracted from the task at hand, the task of dying well.

"Will you sit?" she asked. And he would sit. He took a seat at the table beside her and the dusky girl sat down beside him. A white haired woman, old as any he had seen was at a hearth nearby. She was stirring a cauldron as it cooked.

"Company. We've been expecting company," said the white haired woman.

She ladled the contents of the cauldron into three bowls.

"Don't look into the bowl," she said, "just eat. Can you do that?"

"Yes," he said. She served him a bowl. She did the same for the other women and sat down with a bowl of her own.

He tasted the soup. The broth was filled with chunks of meat that he did not recognize, but the taste danced upon his tongue, alternating between a great many flavors, but never did they clash. His stomach filled with joy. His body filled with joy and he thought of the only joy he'd known on his journey.

"I am looking for the spider Atlach-Nachta," he said between bites.

"Odd thing to search for," said the young woman with red hair.

"If he wants it," said the white haired woman, "he will find it."

"I want nothing more," he said boldly, "I have come to die in its jaws."

"Then you'll find it," said the dusky girl, placing a hand on his shoulder, "you seem like the type."

When he was done eating, the white haired woman led him to a comfortable bed. He lay down on it with no reservations, no protest that his journey was slowed down. He dreamed of the spider's jaws again, accomplishing his quest, growing so big in the spider's stomach that it never needed to eat again. He sighed and moaned in his sleep until he was roused, suddenly, violently.

A young woman, naked and golden-haired was lying on top of him. Her skin was wet and joyful, the weight against him felt nice. He tried to remember the woman who had once lain on top of him and see what color her hair was, but it faded from his memory. The spider in his dreams and in his heart had eaten the girl that drove him to find it. Had she had golden hair like this woman? Were her nipples and lips rose pink like this?

She brushed his lips gently with hers. It was not a kiss but an inquiry. His breathing grew heavy in reply to it, his manhood, numbed from cold and numbed from self hate rose in reply. He did not know this woman but he knew her. And as she answered his body by sliding him inside her, he knew her better. She was smooth and life was easy and they moved together forceful but calm, whims uncontested, wants the same. Life grew quiet as he respired excess thoughts.

And as the scent of a man pleased and a woman pleased perfumed the night, he drifted to sleep again. He did not dream of jaws. So calm and clear and still was he that he dreamed of nothing at all. There was nothing he could have dreamed of.

When he awakened, a girl of around 12, pale, covered in freckles, hair blazing orange was seated on his chest, a mischievous smile on her face. He felt as if he had met her someplace before, but it could not be. He looked to his side, confused.

"My sister," the orange haired girl declared, "has gone out to gather flowers."

"I don't know what…"

"Come to breakfast," said the orange haired girl.

She crawled off of his chest and went to the kitchen so that he could dress. He did so hastily, remembering that he needed to resume his search for the spider. The village was depending upon his being devoured. There was no telling what consequences invoking the god's wrath would visit upon them. At least this is what he told himself. He was calm and satisfied and refreshed and thus he had to return in his mind to his quest and the import of his life, which could be measured only in the gnashing of primordial teeth. He went to the kitchen, to find a dark skinned woman, face ancient and craggy, hair wispy and gray at the cauldron.

"My daughter has gone to gather flowers," said the old woman, "we will eat when she returns."

"I thank you for your hospitality," he said, "but I will have to take my leave. I am seeking the spider Atlach-Nachta. I am to be sacrificed, so I will need to move fast, lest the spider but displeased and visit pain upon my village."

The orange-haired girl giggled.

"Sacrificed. You must be very proud."

"You may leave," said the old woman, "if you wish."

"Thank you," he said, "for understanding. It is most important that I find the spider."

Though he said this, he took a seat instead of heading out the door. It would be unwise of him to embark on this journey with anything but a sharp mind and a full stomach. Even though he was seeking death, he was moving with purpose and to move with purpose takes strength, insight and energy. There was also a part of him that had a sneaking suspicion that these three women knew something of Atlach-Nachta and if he stayed here to eat, he would be able to find something out, perhaps even the location of the monster's lair.

The blonde girl, the one he had made love to, soon returned, in her arms a bundle of flowers of all imaginable colors, which she solemnly handed to the old woman. The old woman kissed the blonde girl on her forehead and tossed the bundle of flowers into the cauldron, filling the kitchen with a sweetness that made the young man's stomach growl, but made his heart feel very light indeed.

The blonde girl embraced him, kissing his lips.

"I am grateful that you decided to stay and eat," she told him, "the spider is fierce."

"What do you know of him?"

"He sits," she said, "between here and the world of dreams. Do you ever dream?"

"Only of the spider," he said.

Her eyes moistened with tears.

"That's terrible."

"We should talk of other things," said the old woman and the young man was quick to comply. They conversed, laughed, ate and drank through the day. They got up and danced, all four of them, to a music of no discernible origin. The name of the spider was not spoken. The jaws of the spider were not contemplated. The young man felt as if the world was oddly fresh and beautiful and though he was still in a cavern, vast. They were together until nightfall, full and content.

"It is late again," said the old woman, "you should stay in this place."

He did not protest or bring up his quest or the jeopardy his village would be in if he were to accept their hospitality another night. He stayed up with them until the time came where he was weary to tuck himself into the comfortable guest bed and turn in. And when he did, he was at ease, not anguished not tossing, fright far away from him. He dreamt of nothing and was not jarred by the hand on his face that awakened.

The young woman's skin was a healthy brown, her hair black as black could be, her waist slender, her legs long and powerful, her buttocks round and firm, her breasts heavy with dark nipples, her mouth small and thin. Her brown eyes were calm, but passionate and expectant. She was lying beside him, quiet, naked and ready for his touch. He traced her body with his hand, letting out a sigh that grew tall and vast in the quiet of the hut at night. He let his lips follow where his hands had traced, then continued downward feeling the bristles of dark pubic hair against his face, smelling her excitement and at last planting his lips on her, thrusting his tongue into her and drinking deep of her until the quiet vanished, replaced by pleas for pleasure. Pleas that he answered joyfully until once again sleep claimed victory over him.

No noise til morning when he was roused by a willowy whiteness, young, platinum, around the same age as the dark haired girl he first met and the red-haired girl who had roused him the previous day. The women of the house seemed to grow young and old as he slept, one a child, one a crone and one a woman his age. Such things made sense in the cavern. The blonde was a joyful and quiet child, rousing him with only a soft touch on the cheek and a whisper of "breakfast is ready." And from the smell of roasted meat, he could tell it was.

Though the old woman cooking was ancient, her red hair had only faded slightly into a pinkish color. She spooned him some soup quietly, a sharp, vulpine smile upon her face.

"I trust you had a pleasant sleep," she said.

The dark haired girl, already up and seated at the table looked nonplussed.

"Mother!"

The blonde tried politely to hold back laughter.

"We're all women in this house. We all know what goes on in it."

The young man could not help but blush.

"It…it was a nice night."

The old red-haired woman laughed heartily.

"I'm certain it was. Eat up. Tell us about love."

"Love?"

"Yes," said the blonde, "I would like to hear you speak about love."

The young man had not thought to speak about love before. It had only brought him pain, it had led him in fact to his quest to be eaten and to this cavern. He spoke of his love and of the man she had chosen instead and of the betrayal and the disappointment and of the loss and the unworthiness. He did

111

not speak of the spider but of what had brought him to the spider. The spider was far from his mind. He spoke then of the night he had with the blonde and then with the dark-haired girl and of the satisfaction he had felt staying in this place.

The red-haired old woman planted a kiss upon his forehead.

"And you are welcome here as long as you would stay."

"I do not know," he said, "how long I will stay."

"As long as you will, you will find what you desire."

And there was no more talk of staying or going from there. He enjoyed the company of the women, they were full of stories and songs, as one could truly only expect from residents of the cavern. They had chores to do about the cottage that made him feel useful and the dark haired girl made him feel quite comfortable as he sat and rested his head in her lap. He spoke and laughed and sighed with contentment and the sighing became yawning and night came round again. Though he had only stayed there three days, he treasured the days and nights in this place equally and felt a certain amount of both excitement and regret as he turned in.

Kissed out of slumber, the red-haired woman he saw on his first day at the cottage lay beside him. She clutched his hand tightly and smiled at him, warm as the phoenix plume of her hair, cool and soft as her snowy skin. The kisses they shared were long but gentle then grew in ferocity sharing blood drawn from bitten tongues. The fervor between them grew, taking from the place where they lay into itself, timeless, above and beneath judgment. They loved and played fought at once until nothing was left in them and they needed to rest.

He stayed there through cycles of lovers, sisters and mothers, nights without judgment, days without consequence. He stayed there and forgot sacrifice and the name and the face of the one that had driven him to this place and the end of his life. He stayed and he became joyful, eager for the evening and eager for the morrow. He grew to love the three equally, for their words and their cooking, and their company and their sharp insights and their loving touch. If forced to choose, his heart would shatter but he would never be forced to choose by them. This place was not for that.

But as a man who set out to be vanquished, there came a day when he dreamt once more of the spider and its jaws and the salvation of his village and the purgation of all that he had brought with him, things he had thought were purged among the women. He awakened and there was no bed and there was no house and he was alone once more among the gibberings of the archetypes and the objects without meaning and the objects too full of meaning to comprehend them.

He tried to call out the names of the women and beg for them to come back to him and beg for him to take him back to the place that he had left, a place he knew in his heart was out there somewhere. Heart heavy, he set out, not knowing if he would find the spider or if he would once again see joy and hope and potential. He wandered intent but aimless, full of fear, knowing that he would find whatever he desired.

Dieselpig

Dieselpig Wins the Medal of Honor!

Though life changes, goes from unbearable to bearable from mad to sane, from joyous to sad, there is always one thing one can count on: THE NEWS! Yes, whether it be Christmas Eve or Beltane or Take Your Lion to Work Day, you can always count on news. News is there to document the birth of your child, news is there to tell your relatives that you are starving in the gutter because your child's bail is far too expensive. News is there when hope is gone and you are wondering what is left in your miserable existence! News marches on, an army of dedicated journalists are here to make sure you do not linger too long in the black vestibules of ignorance.

When I was a child, there was no news. You needed to discover all things one at a time or to learn gossip from local harlots by cleaning their cum and shit stained floors. You would stand on street corners shouting, offering blood in exchange for the details of people's days. And when they took up the offer, you usually didn't get very much from them. Clothes were dirty so I washed them. Dinner was cold so I heated it. Wife was a whore so I shot her. The gathering of information was slow and inefficient before the Newsman came.

When the Newsman arrived, he brought with him certain techniques from his home planet, a place where information flowed freely and could be accessed by any man, woman or child simply by eating the proper lizards. Or if they preferred by writing it down or presenting it over the radio. We had never thought to report news on the radio. Radios back then were mostly for presenting radio dramas that were forbidden to teach listeners anything. Didn't get to watch newsreels like this one before the Newsman came.

Certain news hating elements tied him to a burning crucifix in the town square and forbade anyone from watching him die. They waved their pistols and nightsticks around and told us that there would be no spreading the news of the Newsman's death. They didn't count on the people's desire to hear more news. Hundreds of us were on the streets, notepads in hand taking down the events and though many of us were sliced open and turned into propaganda spouting hand puppets, there were enough of us that weren't for hope to keep shining brightly, a news-colored flash of hope that scorched the skies and filled the air with talk of dissent and details about the weather and the scores of baseball games.

News marches on! In Canada, scientists have developed a mind control technique using only subversive literature, provocative images and the power of suggestion.

"It doesn't work," a middle aged buzz cut scientist assures us, "there are other elements that are needed to make it work and none of those are present. Reports of shifting consciousness are deeply exaggerated. There is only one consciousness and it is unperturbable, unflappable in its perceptions and cannot be transformed with awkward attempts at manipulation."

Another middle aged buzz cut scientist thinks differently.

"Science is a delicate process and scientists are not to be trusted. Many of them are opposed to news, an inalienable right that people fought and killed and died for during the Newsman rebellion. It is possible to shift, shatter and slaughter consciousness. This can be done via ideals and images, runes that affect our backbrain and make us do things that we could not conceive of doing. This can be done via news, but scientists do not wish you to know this. They would live in a world with no news again. Can you imagine, a world without news? It would be hell."

Can words and images be used to change the minds of man?

Only time will tell. One thing is for certain, news marches on.

News marches on in the darkness of the human heart, though the Lord of Lies opposes it. But that doesn't deter our boys in black and white! The war against Satan has been rough going in recent years, but Cardinal Flanagan remains optimistic about tomorrow night's mass exorcism at Yankee Stadium.

"Yes, it is true that over 70 percent of Americans are currently possessed by Satan and it is true that twenty of the remaining thirty percent are being threatened by one form or another of Obsession or supernatural temptation. And it is true that corporeal demons pose a danger to women, children and house pets even greater than that of rogue lions, but we've got faith!"

Our boys gather outside of Yankee stadium, praying for success in tonight's mass exorcism, all looking fine in their vestments. Does a soul good to see them. Drawing their swords and their bibles, they're rushing the parking lot. Devout Catholics all, they won't back down from the tasks the almighty has set before them. Which is lucky, because Old Scratch isn't going down without a fight! The devil, that old trickster has a grim ambush prepared! Tentacled frogfaced monstrosities, lobsterclawed apes, nagas, dragons, minotaurs, weresharks… the parking lot is a mess! Looks as if our boys might not even make it inside to the exorcism!

It's a wonderful day for an exorcism here at Yankee Stadium! But it doesn't look like easy going for the Catholics! Cardinal Flanagan, who should be inside right now reading the Roman rite and giving the Big Apple some relief from infernal forces is going toe to toe with a dragon. Dragons are interesting because they simultaneously embody avarice and wrath, which makes them hard for demonlogists to classify. The Vatican's official stance is that dragons serve Mammon, the King of Greed, but some scholars including ironically, Flanagan himself contest this. And with the way that fire breathing serpent claws, bites and roars out obscenities from before the age of man, it looks like Flanagan might have a point. But don't tell the pope that!

Father Benedict Jones looks as if he has a promising military career ahead of him. With the effortless way he clears through gibbering imps, ignoring their promises of whores skilled in pleasures that fragile human minds could not comprehend, he certainly seems like a young man to watch. But will he fare as well against tentacle demons? Tentacle demons, unlike dragons, have a very definite point of origin and place in hell's hierarchy. Tentacle demons are of the third circle, the Circle of Lust. Their soul prerogative is to invade, penetrate and impregnate the soul with multitudes of demons. If Father Jones isn't careful, he could end up being a mommy to a dragon very similar to the pesky fiend that's giving Cardinal Flanagan a run for the money in his collection plate!

"It is possible," says a buzz cut scientist, "to transform the news into a rune of madness, a mark on the psyche that tells it to collapse, to surrender and to acquiesce to the worst in life. This strategy was utilized during the news wars to bring down the Newsman. But could be used in any war, in any propaganda campaign, in any novel, in any film. It is possible to break down or build up the defenses of the viewer with this sort of psychic attack."

What is this buzz cut scientist doing with a gun? Is his buzz cut and scholarly manner an act? Is he actually some sort of madman? Why does he press the gun against his temple? Oh.

Father Benedict Jones has sent many a gibbering imp back to Hell today. In his first month of service to the church, he performed six exorcisms, liberating six souls from the torments of minor demons. Now, faced with the tentacle demon, his faith seems to be wavering. At the age of 12, Benedict Jones was orphaned by Cthulhu cultists. He lived on the streets with his little brother until he was taken in by the church and raised to do battle with the forces of the supernatural. Benedict Jones is not just a warrior, but a mentor to children, and a tireless advocate for the poor. A soldier, a humanitarian, a hero and just

117

an overall nice guy. Men like Father Benedict Jones are few and far between.

The flailing tentacles, the words that shake his soul and the whipping of its spike-barbed frogtongue beating at Father Jones seem to indicate that there might be one fewer and a greater distance between men like Jones. A tentacle is tearing through his vestments and the strength in his sword-arm is failing him. Father Benedict Jones had better rally his faith and strike back or else he's about to get a nasty reminder of his days as an altar boy. With a swift, precise cut, he has severed the tentacle demon's whipping tongue.

Well, it looks as if there's some good news to report! You might remember Smiley the Pig, the brave little fella that fought three great white sharks to save an orphaned dolphin? Modern science has finally found a way to give him back the hooves and head he lost in this struggle. What do you think of that folks? He looks as good as new! Yes, there you have it! Modern science has created a Dieselpig! Is there anything Diesel can't do? Dieselpig trots at a hundred miles per hour, firing hundreds of shots from the Thompson machine gun his head was replaced by at America's enemies! And Dieselpig won't stop until Old Scratch goes back to where he belongs! God bless you, Smiley…or should I say, "Dieselpig"?

Dieselpig sure would come in handy in the Yankee Stadium parking lot! The Catholics are taking an awful drubbing! Fifty seven priests went in, and it looks like only seven could possibly make it into Yankee Stadium itself! Right now the dragon is hungrily lapping up all that remains of Cardinal Flanagan. Though prayers are being hurled at it like nobody's business, it shows no sign of relenting until it has careful lapped up every drop of the priestly puddle! Dieselpig, where are you? If only the Catholics knew that Dieselpig is ready to fight the infernal menace! Looks like they should be watching the news, eh folks? If Benedict Jones knew he had Dieselpig to pray for, he'd be in a much better position then he's in now, that's for sure!

Benedict Jones is on his knees, too breathless to pray, but swinging that sword and severing tentacles, clinging to the hope that he might live to perform the much needed exorcism on all the possessed citizens inside Yankee Stadium. There will be no Dieselpig to save him, only his sword, his willpower and the love of God. He cranes his neck up and down to avoid the frogface's bite he castrates tentacles, he saves himself from violation. And suddenly, it happens. The sword slides into the monster's squishy body. Father Jones yanks on it, wiggles it around. The tentacles aren't flailing. The head isn't snapping! Do you believe in miracles? Benedict Jones has saved himself from the lusts of the infernal host!

Sword and Bible still in hand, Jones is running for the entrance! Three hail and hearty young priests are giving their all to keep the dragon down. Though fire and claws and hopelessness threaten to put an end to them, the Catholics still give their all to protect Jones. And Jones, running like the wind into the inner sanctum of the possessed will not let their surely inevitable deaths be in vain! Jones ascends the stairs, reciting his Hail Marys and knowing in his heart of hearts that he too might end up at God's right hand when all of this is over. Benedict Jones is the face of hope and the face of sacrifice.

Some levitating, some with heads spinning, some pockmarked, some covered in scales and feathers, the crowd is all possessed and they do not take kindly to incursion from the priesthood. The possessed hordes fall on him. Two thousand rabid Yankee's fans under the influence of the underworld. Oh, the humanity! Yanking his pubic hairs out one at a time with their teeth, ripping skin off his face, vomiting, pissing, cutting themselves and bleeding on him.

Benedict Jones is having trouble starting the exorcism rite. The possessed are holding his mouth open and vomiting into it. War is Hell and war with Hell is doubly hell and Benedict is finding this out the hard way. His eyes wide open in pain and disgust, Father Benedict Jones wants to pray and he cannot. He cannot pray for the claws and the terror and the vomit to stop. They will not. Benedict Jones, soldier for God has now become Benedict Jones martyr for God.

This is an ugly day for news. Or is it? What's that up in the sky? Is it an angel? Has God brought an angel to free the possessed from their agony? No! God and America have done better! It's a helicopter! And descending from that helicopter with a parachute on his back is none other than true salvation! DIESELPIG HAS COME TO YANKEE STADIUM! DIESELPIG HAS COME TO YANKEE STADIUM!

Bounding forward on piston hooves, opening fire with his Thompson gun head, no man, woman or child is safe from America's righteous anger! Mouths foam no longer, twisted heads no longer make unnatural faces mocking the glory of creation, the body of Benedict Jones is no longer being defaced! Looks like our favorite hero pig has the situation well in hand! Looks like God had a plan for Yankee Stadium tonight! Hope is a pig with a Thompson machine gun for a head.

But is Dieselpig the answer? Of course he is. We have spoken to this neat buzz cut scientist to inquire of this.

"Dieselpig is a lie. Hope is not a pig with a Thompson machine gun for a head. It is too late for hope. It's coming for us. It cannot be contained. Some things are worse than devils. Worse than death awaits us. Worse than hell awaits us after that. Your pig cannot save you."

Everyone loves Dieselpig!

As the president has proven by presenting Dieselpig with the Medal of Honor! Part pig, part diesel, Dieselpig is the soldier of the future...no, Dieselpig is the American of the future!

"Fellow Americans," says the president, "some of you wonder what valor looks like. Some of you wonder what compassion looks like. Some of you wonder what the new man looks like. You need wonder no longer. Valor is Dieselpig.

Compassion is Dieselpig. The future is Dieselpig."

Meanwhile, in Tinseltown: Hollywood's elite gather to celebrate the premiere of The Wake at the House of Dead Hogs! Director Heinrich Pseudonym has made what will no doubt be the triumph of the cinema season. The Wake at the House of Dead Hogs is a mystery drama in three acts. The Wake at the House of Dead Hogs will leave you changed.

"We cannot rely on priests or Dieselpig," says Pseudonym, "you must tear off your faces and find what's underneath. You must drink your teeth. Can't you see that I love you?"

Even Hollywood loves Dieselpig. Isn't that right, Heinrich Pseudonym?

"Dieselpig is folly. He will not save you. The enemy is in your blood. He is under your face. You must tear off your faces to see what's underneath."

It's a lovely day and jellybeans rain down from the sky on the red carpet, a trail of sugary delight leading into the majestic Chinese Theater. Smiling violins play a jaunty jig that says "this is premiere day, a movie premieres today, a movie premieres today!" Hey hey!

Heinrich Pseudonym whaddya know, how do you feel about the movie show?

"The carpet is covered in candy and the whether is warm and gay, my movie premieres today!"

All the finest lions in Hollywood applaud Heinrich Pseudonym, the man of tomorrow, the director of tomorrow, who bears tomorrow's message with tomorrow's blessing. The carpet is covered in candy and the weather is warm and gay! His movie premieres today!

The time has come. Heinrich Pseudonym addresses the audience.

"Wake at the House of Dead Hogs is a film for families, finally, a film for the public to learn to live and learn from. It features one of the finest leonine actors I've ever worked with and one of the smartest, most distinguished of elephants, the loveliest of dwarves."

Smashing a smiling violin, he takes a bow and starts the projector. His eyes widen as he looks to the screen and sees...

nothing.

Heinrich Pseudonym is crying tears of blood. News marches on as directors stare in bug-eyed horror, black and white tears smeared on their cheeks and they wonder how it was that their film ran away. News marches on as faith is lost and sanity doubted. News marches on as Heinrich places his fingers in his mouth, one by one, biting off the tips.

"It has escaped. The film has run away. Tear off your faces. It's all that you can do. All hail the marvelous thing beneath! Hail the true face and death to the false!"

As Heinrich Pseudonym swallows his fingers afraid of what he's wrought, afraid that the thing he's made is coming for him and for you (which it is)and a doubtful president fears that even Dieselpig will not be enough to liberate the souls of America from what they've done (which he won't) as you sit in your seat waiting for the film and the book and the pain and the loss to start you will hear whispers that will come together to form a mighty shout of furious impact so great and so thunderous that you will never be able to flee the truth again and the truth that more and more and more it is inevitable that we'll be left alone with only bad news.

The Wake at the House of Dead Hogs

There is a man in your house playing the calliope. He will not stop until the job is done. Try as you might, you cannot find him, as it probably impossible. Following the music, you will find it comes from inside of closets, down the shower drain, under carpets, under stairs or the space between the cushions of the couch. You are lucky that you cannot see him; he has the head of a nutcracker, painted on eyes, big wooden teeth in a perpetually open mouth, he wears no clothes save a tie with musical notes on it and his body is covered in coarse, bristly hairs that stand up on end and are sharp as the quills of a porcupine. He never speaks, but if he did, his voice would sound like fingernails against canvas, so you should be grateful he does not. A silent movie intertitle appears out of nowhere, projected in mid-air. A film is starting.

The Wake at the House of Dead Hogs: A Mystery Drama in Two Acts

On a rocky, craggy overpass above the village of West Crogdonshire stands the ancient and elegant House of Dead Hogs.

A marvel of engineering, the house awaits guests for the social event of the season, the wake of Sir Edgar Throckmorton the Second.

Made up of thousands of cadavers beneath a dead hog roof, The House of Dead Hogs keeps sinister watch over the village far below. The great front door is not made up of dead hogs, but rather it is a large, round wooden clown face that continuously shifts expressions; one moment, it smiles, the next it frowns. Then suddenly the mouth opens wide in shock and dismay. The man at the calliope holds his note for far longer than he there is need to. Your ears hurt, but you've forgotten where you put your headphones. Did you leave them on the bus? Did you leave them at the elephant show? Is the man at the calliope wearing them so he can drown out the hideous sound of his music? Would you blame him if he was?

Inside...

A tall, buxom young woman is brushing her hair in front of a mirror. The mirror is framed by piglet skulls and hanging on a wall, that is of course made of Dead Hogs. She is dressed in a maid's uniform. Her skirt is short enough that her bare bottom sticks out of it as she leans in to get a closer look at herself. It is a pale gray with freckles that are a darker gray, the color of her hair. She kisses her reflection.

Bridget, a sassy young Irish domestic...

A striking, yet somewhat ugly man in a black suit pressed so neatly it looks like it might be his skin sneaks up behind her. In one hand, he holds a cat of nine tails behind his back, with his other, he holds a finger up to his lip.

Shhhh!!!!
Branwell, a randy and contemptible butler

He whips her and she turns around, alarmed.

"Faith and Begorrah!"

Branwell grabs her by the waist. She kicks, she struggles,

she bites his arm, but it is all for naught. The look of rowdy, eager sadism on his face says that there is no way he will give in. He throws her to the floor and begins whipping her with the wild abandon of a dog splashing around in the bathtub. Black blood streaks down her ass.

"On your knees spread those legs, you tart!"

She complies, getting down on her hands and knees. He continues to whip her, though he is less frantic. He is savoring the act, almost implying a kind of intimacy.

"Now moo like the cow you are!"
"Moo! Moo! Moo!"

A portly, serious man enters. He is wearing a powdered wig, short breeches, buckled shoes and a look of patrician hauteur.

Sorghum, a very successful barrister...

Bridget crawls to Sorghum on her hands and knees. She sits up in an overblown pantomime of somebody begging for mercy. Sorghum looks down on her severely, his puffed up, fat, serious face resembling nothing so much as a constipated bulldog.

"Bridget, this is highly unorthodox! Shame on you for this display! Branwell, scrub her filthy peasant arse off. The guests are arriving soon!"

Branwell stands up straight and salutes. Sorghum exits. Branwell opens his mouth and lets out a long, inaudible villainous laugh. Bridget places her hands on her hips with annoyance. She moves one hand from her hip to literally thumb her nose at him. The Man At The Calliope plays a sickly, dumb imitation of a merry little tune.

"Hrumph!"
Meanwhile, along the mountain pass…

A young man and a young woman sit on plain wooden chairs. The young man who has a look of blithe, ignorant animal contentment on his face is working an invisible steering wheel with his hands. The young woman's skin is an awkward peach color. She looks like a flamingo in the middle of a flock of penguins. It's kind of disgusting. Her hair is as yellow as straw. They are engaged in a deep conversation. At least as deep a conversation as one can engage in with someone who lives a life of blithe, ignorant animal contentment.

"And that, my dear is why we should feed the squirrels to each other."
Reginald and Miriam: Two Young Lovers

Reginald's eyes widen and he smiles a gigantic smile devoid of subtlety or guile.

"I love you!"

He kisses her. She slaps him and giggles tiny silent giggles.

"Keep your eyes on the road, you silly, silly boy!"

The chairs belch black smoke. Miriam holds her hand in front of her face. Reginald holds his hand in front of his face.

"AAAAAAHHHHHHHHH!!!!!!!!!! Look out!"

The two step out of a ruined Model T. They are on a barren country road. There is a dead cow lying in front of them, recently run over. As Reginald kneels down to see if the dead cow is alright and not in fact dead, a filthy old woman walks up the road. She seems like someone you might have seen before, though you're not certain how this could be possible. After all, it's not like you're prone to keeping the company of raggedy old women. She jumps up and down, shaking her fists at him.

"Damn tourists! My cow! My precious, precious cow!"

Reginald places his hand on her shoulder.

"I am terribly sorry. We have the money to reimburse you for your cow."

The old woman cackles noiselessly. She spits on him.

"Your filthy Jew money is no good here! I bet you've stolen it!"

He shrugs, then does a happy jig. It's very humiliating. The old woman bounces in place like an eager toddler, applauding. Miriam awakens. She stretches as if it were a nap she had just indulged in instead of a faint.

"Goodness, Reginald! What have we done?"

He embraces her.

"It's alright, my love. She has been more than compensated."

Reginald turns to the old woman, his posture manly and dignified.

"So tell me, where might we find somebody who can repair this here jalopy?"

The old lady picks up a heavy stick that has appeared on the ground and smacks the dead cow on the head, which pops right open. She rifles through the animal's brains. She looks at you, all big eyes and prophetic madness.

"It's all here. You must go to the House of Dead Hogs. There you will find everything she needs."

Reginald puffs a pipe. The Man At The Calliope repeatedly changes back and forth between the same two chords. In his hands, the instrument is quite disturbing. It is clear that he plays badly because he wants you to feel badly. A sudden hunch leads you to check under the rug for him. Reginald stands completely still for over two minutes, doing nothing but puffing that pipe. When he is finished spacing out, he smiles his idiot grin. You feel like punching it off his face. This is an odd impulse, because you are not usually a violent person.

"Dead hogs, you say? Sounds fantastic!"

He kisses the old lady full on the lips and fondles a sagging breast. Miriam rolls her eyes and shrugs.

And up the pass!

Three burly men dressed in potato sacks wearing coffee cans for hats push a giant Jack-O-Lantern up the mountain pass. Sitting upon it are Reginald and Miriam. She rests her head on his shoulder, her face sleepy and glowing with a childlike innocence.

What a jolly time!

A man and a woman approach the House of Dead Hogs. The woman is tall and slender with vulpine, patrician features. Her lips are thick and black and contrast nicely with her skin, which is almost perfectly white. She wears the skin of a little girl around her neck and a unicorn fur coat. The unicorn coat still has the horn on it, or else people would mistake it for a regular horse, and a fine lady like this could certainly not bear that. The man with her is stout, well mustached and completely naked…with the exception of a pair of black combat boots.

Major Fank Grosvenor and Dame Astrid Grosvenor: respectable socialites

The door opens and Bridget steps out, reaching for Dame Astrid's coat and wrap. The angry socialite slaps her hands away.

"How dare you lay your filthy Irish hands on me! Get away! Get away!"

Bridget turns around and touches her toes, presenting herself to Dame Astrid. Dame Astrid kicks her soundly in the rear.

"Thank you, ma'am!"

Branwell emerges from the house and leads Dame Astrid and the Major inside. A short, mousy looking man in glasses holding hands with a short mousy looking woman in glasses comes to the door. The woman might be the man's identical twin brother in a wig.

"Norton and Josephine Throckmorton: Edgar Throckmorton's nephew and his wife, a gorgeous movie star."

Bridget puts her hands on her hips and winks at Norton salaciously. He winks back and squeezes his wife's breasts. She puts her hand on his crotch. A frustrated Bridget folds her arms indignantly.

"Well, nerts!"

Norton shoves Bridget to the ground. The two trample over her as they walk in.

On the mountain pass...

Reginald and Miriam are still being pushed on the pumpkin. Reginald strums a silent ukulele. Miriam points straight ahead, brimming with excitement.

"Look Reginald, there it is!"

The House of Dead Hogs is only a few feet away. It dwarfs the Jack-O-Lantern. The clownhead door is frowning. Reginald and Miriam get off the pumpkin. Reginald hops up and down spastically. Miriam smacks him with his ukulele. He hits the ground. Tiny children in devil costumes float around his head. He sits up, rubbing a huge bump and shrugs. He smiles his gigantic, "I'm-barely-sentient" smile. Miriam raises the ukulele over head and...

Ten minutes earlier...

An elderly woman approaches the house accompanied by a lion standing on his hind legs. The lion wears a monocle and a pith helmet. He is puffing on a pipe.

Dame Smegma Healfdene and Panthera Leo: Important aristocrats with a mysterious past

Bridget escorts these two in without incident. Right behind them stands a gaunt, serious gentleman. His mouth is small and stingy with almost no lips, as if it were drawn on as an afterthought by a careless cartoonist. He has a sharp Roman nose, cold eyes and only wisps of hair grow on his bald, liver spotted head. He gives the maid a long bow. He then gives her a longbow. But she does not know what to do with this and discards it. Your neighbor's house is burning down and somehow it is your fault. Your sister is calling to tell you that your father has died but you won't hear it. Somebody has hidden your cellphone. It might have been The Man At The Calliope or it might be this suspicious gentleman. The Man is probably innocent. He would want you to take in the misery. But, then again, alienating you from family during a time of crisis is the sort of thing he might be into. It is difficult to say.

Raymond Dubarge, an expert on the occult. He does not know where your phone is.

He kisses Bridget's hand.

"Enchantez, madame."

She swoons. Dubarge steps right up to you. He shakes his head gravely.

"It is too late. Too late for your father. He has

died. It is too late for your neighbor's children. They have burned to death. It is too late to leave, for soon the wake will begin."

Just as you're beginning to get used to the Man At The Calliope's sloppy playing, it emits a single, long unpleasant noise that has abandoned any pretense of being music. You suspect that he is sitting on the keys.

Reginald and Miriam come to call...

Pipe in mouth, Reginald is doing a happy jig right outside the door. Miriam breaks into an ecstatic Charleston. Reginald pets the dead hog walls. He kisses them. He bites into them, then spits out a ball of lard. He turns to Miriam, grinning his dopiest grin.

"Baby, this place is the bee's knees!"

Miriam stops dancing. She sulks, deeply distraught.

"I don't know about that Reginald. There is something different about this house, something unsavory, which worries me."

The door opens and a monster with an elk's head pops out, raising his arms to indicate that he is big and scary. Miriam swoons. The Elk's head pops off and reveals that of Branwell underneath.

"Ah, it's only you two. You're on the list."

Reginald shakes Miriam awake. She stands up, spots Branwell and then swoons again. Reginald shakes her awake.

When she stands up, he jumps for joy.

"We're on the list, darling! We're on the list!"

Miriam resumes her ecstatic Charleston and Reginald joins. Branwell pulls out a derringer and shoots himself in the stomach. He reaches into the wound and pulls out a teddy bear which he holds like an infant. He kisses it tenderly.

At the reading of the will...

The drawing room of the House of Dead Hogs is enormous. It is lit by phosphorescent fish in fish bowls that hang from the ceiling by pig intestines. There is no furniture in the room. The guests are instead seated on the backs of several Irish maids. There arc more guests now, some that you haven't seen before. There are seven shapely and vampish flapper septuplets and a dwarf with a goose on his head. Sorghum the barrister is looking nervously at his watch. A few dozen opossums carry in a coffin on their back. They scatter, letting the coffin fall to the floor. It opens up, revealing either a dead gorilla or a dead man in a gorilla suit. Sorghum inaudibly clears his throat.

Greetings, we are here to deal with a grave matter...

Everyone pantomimes riotous laughter. Reginald laughs so hard that he falls off the maid on which he was sitting and rolls on the floor uncontrollably. He coughs up some blood. Sorghum chuckles himself...of course inaudibly.

Oh, my! How very clever of the lot of you! As I was saying, Sir Edgar was a man of some peculiar tastes. Such as the gorilla suit he wore

every day of his life. Instead of more conventional clauses in his will, such as a duel to the death or a semen swallowing contest, Sir Edgar shall leave the house and the majority of his money to…"

All over the room, everyone is filing their nails, with the exception of Reginald who is doing a humiliating jig in his customary fashion.

"The first one to find the telephone, which has been deviously hidden in one of the house's seven hundred fifty nine rooms."

Dame Astrid shakes her dainty white fist.

"This is an outrage! We all know who Edgar would have left his money to."

Dame Smegma shakes her fists as well.

"Outrage! Outrage!"

Miriam swoons. Reginald shakes her awake as he has before. As she gets up, his mouth hangs open in disbelief.

"You're alive, darling!"

Reginald celebrates with another of his humiliating jigs. Miriam does an ecstatic Charleston, which everyone joins. A jolly time is had by all. And then things go black.

DARKNESS!

The Man at the Calliope stretches one chord as far as it goes, then extends it farther still. Having had enough of this, you get the shotgun you keep under the couch and you fire it in every possible direction, hoping to hit him. It does not, and it looks as if there is no possible way for you to stop him from causing the calliope to wail in agony. That's it. You decide it's time to walk out. You've had enough of this torment. That's odd…didn't you used to have a front door? Didn't you used to have windows? Yes, you certainly must have had windows. What else would have possessed you to buy curtains? And everybody you know has a front door. It comes standard on the majority of dwellings. When the lights come back on in The House of Dead Hogs, it is a relief to you. At least for the moment it is, for as soon as the blackness fades you can see that Panthera Leo, the noble, affluent gentleman is dead. Miriam swoons. Bridget, shocked by Miriam's swoon Mousy Norton holds his nearly identical wife to comfort her. Dame Astrid wags a judgmental finger in your direction.

"Somebody do something!"

Sorghum kneels over Panthera's body to examine it. He sniffs it, shoves his fingers into its mouth, sniffs them, then listens for a heartbeat.

"It appears that Panthera Leo has been murdered, and we have a mystery on our hands."

Dame Astrid sits down and folds her arms.

"Hmmph! I hate mysteries! They're for poor people! I refuse to participate!"

She makes a good point. You don't have to get involved. You could find some means of smashing through the wall and have done with all of this. Who needs this nonsense? Who needs mysteries? Well? Are you a coward? Are you some kind of piss pants little coward? Is that why everyone hates you? Dame Astrid might be onto something. And yet, you can't, can you? Everyone in the room is quite shocked at what Astrid has said. As well they should be. Dubarge slaps her in the face then faces you.

"There is nothing to do but to figure this out. The mystery shall be solved."
End of first reel. The reels are changing themselves. You won't have to wait too long, I assure you.

As the reels change, you hope there is some kind of trouble with the machine. If there is trouble with the machine, you might not have to suffer through this film anymore. Not suffering through this film would be a refreshing break from suffering through this film. Though you hope this will happen, you do not expect it to. The reels are changing themselves. This projector is a capable and healthy one.

The reels have changed. Thank you for your patience. Enjoy the picture!

The movie returns with a close-up on Dubarge's rather unsettling face. He looks rather shocked.

"It appears we have not one but two mysteries!"

Dubarge points at the coffin. Everyone's attention moves over to it. The coffin is open and empty. Branwell looks inside.

"The coffin is empty."

Dubarge raises a finger in an "aha" gesture.

"Empty because the body is gone!"

The women swoon halfway, then stand up again midswoon. Reginald moves to embrace Miriam, but fails to notice a scratch in the negative. As he walks through it, his body is split in half. He is full of grasshoppers, which the guests get on their knees to catch and eat. When they are done feasting on Reginald's tasty insectoid innards, they return to their seats on top of the help. Dubarge both places his hand on his chin AND shakes his head gravely. There is something to be concerned about. The Man at the Calliope plays his "something is terribly wrong" motif.

"It seems we might be faced by the presence of..."

Miriam places her hand over her mouth.

"No! Don't say it! It couldn't be!"

Dubarge raises his finger in the air to further dramatize the point.

"Yes! The occult!"

Miriam swoons. Josephine places her hand on her mouth in shock, silently gasping. The Man at the Calliope plays those same tired notes of dissonance. Major Grosvenor gets up off of Bridget, on whom he was previously sitting. He places his hand thoughtfully on his chin.

"Could you show me to my quarters, miss?"

Bridget curtsies.

"Certainly, major?"

The two vanish. Dubarge puts his hand on Josephine's shoulder to comfort her.

"Do not fret, pretty miss, for I, Raymond Dubarge, am an expert on the occult."

Miriam stands up, wiping off her brow.

"Thank goodness!"

Sorghum shakes his cane emphatically.

"Hmmph! Are you opining that black magic killed such a hail and hearty gentleman?"

Dubarge laughs loudly, but inaudibly. He places his hands at his sides like an arrogant Errol Flynn.

"Ha! Black magic? Hardly! The occult is a most vast and relevant subject!"

Norton finishes the martini that has manifested in his hand.

"Come now! The days when the Throckmortons feared black magic have been over and done with for years, Monsieur Dubarge!"

The goose atop the dwarf's head unhinges its jaw like a serpent and swallows him whole. Branwell shoots the goose with his derringer. It stumbles, whirls around, falls down and dies. Branwell looks into your eyes intensely.

"It's over."

The calliope plays a strong, hopeful, effervescent song. He plays a song of the sun rising, conquering the darkness. He plays a song of light and joy and triumph.

THE END

Napoleon Bonaparte…himself
Music by Napoleon Bonaparte
Written and directed by Napoleon Bonaparte
Release comes slowly
Pain lives on and on
Every blade of grass is suffering
Every raindrop on the window waits to evaporate
If you hold onto hope
You have already lost…
The reels are changing. A goose is dead. A dwarf is dead. It will not be so simple. Just one more reel. Just three more reels. The reels are changing themselves. The film will be back.

The film returns. One of the flapper sextuplets, this one wearing glasses to indicate she is the more bookish of the seven is shaking her head defiantly. It looks like she has been doing it for awhile.

"Dear cousin Norton, while it easy to dismiss the occult, it is not always practical!"

Dame Astrid applauds politely and noiselessly.

"Well put, Cynthia! I myself have found the occult pragmatic from time to time."

Miriam places her fingers over her mouth as she emits a silent girlish giggle.

"You, Dame Astrid? You've made use of the occult?"

Dame Astrid punches Miriam in the face, causing her to spit out a frog. Dubarge tramples the poor creature to death. He then steps up to you, getting right in your face.

"There are occult goings on in The House of Dead Hogs, you'll see!"

As he says this, the gorilla-suited corpse (or just someone in a gorilla suit very much like that of the corpse) creeps up on him, wrapping hairy hands around his throat and then…

"Darkness!"

As the intertitle implies, the drawing room is overcome completely by darkness. Is it a real or metaphorical darkness? How can one put out a fish? Is it their darkness? Is it yours? Is it The Man at the Calliope's? There is a wise and ancient squirrel outside your window that could explain this to you, but your windows are gone and he does not have a telephone. Suddenly, the light returns. Its return is definitely a literal one as you certainly don't feel illuminated. Dubarge's corpse lies on the floor. Beside it is your cellphone. Didn't you used to have stairs? Bridget has reappeared with two black eyes, crawling on her hands and knees and dripping semen down her chin. She is bleeding profusely from her anus. The major reappears, dressed as a sultan, wearing a turban and an open silk kimono that reveals his large, blood-caked erection. The only thing missing from his sultan costume is a pair of curly-toed slippers, which of course are absent since he is a military man and would never take his boots off. Sorghum shakes his cane angrily at Bridget.

"Bridget, this is highly unorthodox! You must have razors in your cunny! Clean off the major posthaste!"

Bridget produces a feather duster and kneels down before the Major, dusting him off. Dame Astrid gets behind Bridget, eagerly slurping up the blood from Bridget's ass. Sorghum silently applauds this spectacle, then stiffens up more than ever, clutching his cane tightly to his chest.

"Ladies and gentlemen, strange occurrences have been occurring, but we must not be hasty and rush to judgments. But one thing is certain, if you wish to find a suitable beneficiary, the telephone must be found."

Everyone goes down on the floor and begins to search the drawing room for the telephone. Finding no telephone on the floor, they check up each other's skirts and down each other's pants.

Half an hour later...

Everyone is once more sitting atop the Irish maids. Their hands are on their chins to indicate that they are extremely

141

deep in thought. The bookish flapper excitedly rises to her feet, waving her arms.

"Perhaps we should check the ballroom!"

One by one, the guests rise to their feet. They line up to shake the bookish flapper's hand. Sorghum hands her a cake, which she shoves her face into like a dog, devouring it in moments. Bridget and three other Irish maids dutifully lap icing off. The maids look sweaty and sick, they squat down, each of them excreting an entire cake. The guests take up the cakes, feeding them to one another. When the cakes are finished, Sorghum thumps his cane on the floor.

"Alright, everyone! To the ballroom!"

Bridget places her right hand on her waist and sticks out her right leg. She winks seductively.

"Well, nobody likes a good ball like I do!"

Even within an engineering marvel like The House of Dead Hogs, the ballroom is an architectural masterstroke. For one hundred years, the ballroom has remained in its present state. That is to say, changing the ballroom was unnecessary for all this time for it was easily one hundred years ahead of its time. The ballroom's sophisticated automatons remain a testament to the ingenuity of the Throckmorton family, even when compared to the wonders of this modern age.

The ballroom is gigantic, but lit only by a single colossal

fishbowl containing a shark-sized phosphorescent fish. While this is impressive, it is not in itself deserving of the accolades on the intertitle. The marvel of ingenuity is the ballroom's permanent occupants: a dozen or so dancing clockwork couples clad in the fine dead hog waist coats and dead hog pantaloons. If they were to dance a simple box step or go around in circles they would be quite impressive but their dancing brings them into the realm of the technologically sublime. They indulge in slick foxtrots, gorgeous tangos, brilliant flamencos. The faceless dancers are every bit as familiar with the language of dance as any human couple could be, perhaps moreso. They are impressive enough to move the man at the calliope into creating actual music. Listening thus far, it might not have seemed possible, but then again, it makes sense that somebody capable of playing so miraculously bad, with such deep malice, they would have to have the ability to evoke real emotion with their art. It is not appropriate to the scene, however. It is a strangely poetic variation on the music used to introduce clowns at the circus. Not right to document the perfection of the dancers, but you must take what you can get. At least he is not ruining it with his own inimitable brand of sonic ugliness. The guests watch the dancers, mesmerized by their movements. A solitary tear falls from Miriam's eyes. She places her hands upon her heart.

"This is so beautiful here and I feel so safe... for the first time since I came to this wicked village, since I came to this wickedest of houses..."

Sorghum pats her on the back. His face shines with nostalgia.

"There is a deep complexity in this house that is beautiful. It makes this house beautiful and wondrous as few places can be. This house is as nature is, free from man's ideas of justice or injustice. As a man who has studied the law his whole life, it is a relief to be in this house, watching clockwork men and women dance."

Miriam leans against the barrister, eyes wide and bright as the sun.

"They are fantastic."

First, the music changes. This is new. Usually the Man at the Calliope waits and reacts, but this time the music makes a preemptive strike against sanity, changing from music to noise to something worse than noise. The calliope makes a sound like hundreds of dogs howling for food, The calliope makes a sound like brakes screeching a second too late to stop a child from getting run over. The calliope makes a haunting, drawn out sound akin to a cry for help, but altogether different. The cry is stretched to its very limit, as if the sound waves could snap if they were strained any further. You get the impression that it is your dead father, coming before you like Hamlet the elder telling you that only you can free him from damnation. This isn't so. It is the sound of a calliope. It vomits out another noise, a vengeful wheezing emphysemic laughter. In this moment of taxed sanity, you are tempted to shoot yourself. You cock your shotgun. You put it in your mouth and fire it. Sour milk comes out. Beyond sour. More like expired cottage cheese than sour milk, which would be bad enough. You run to your bathroom to throw up, only to discover that you no longer have a bathroom. Did you ever have a bathroom?

Miriam is startled. She points.

There is a puff of smoke the color of strawberry soda. It

144

expands into an ethereal figure, a red-tinted magician with a big red top hat, wisps of clownish hair on the side of his head, a big bulbous glans of a nose and wicked, glowing white eyes. He floats about, waving a magic wand. The Man at the Calliope plays the laughter wheeze once more, though it is unclear whether it has been invoked by the spell or whether The Man at the Calliope is making this noise because the thinks this is what black magic sounds like. Luckily, you find your headphones and will not have to suffer this noise if he plays it again. It's too bad your headphones are crawling with centipedes. The countless tiny stings are somehow refreshing. You could run a marathon if you could walk out your front door, if you had a front door to walk out. You would need a much larger living room to run a marathon. The Magician floats close to you.

"This is not the dance. These are not the steps. Life is not the dance, you silly fools. Exalting in your pretty things. Love is not the dance. You think yourself above the pretty puppets? That's a laugh!"

Miriam covers her eyes.

"Please stop!"

She opens her eyes to find the Magician right in front of her.

"It is you who must stop, delighting in the beauty of the world and fainting at its ugliness! Watching puppets dance and thinking that you are any freer!"

He disappears with a puff of white smoke. Sorghum holds Miriam close.

"It is alright, dear child! This fiend has taken his leave."

The clockwork dancers stop dancing. This change is so off-putting for you that you take off your headphones. The Man at the Calliope takes advantage of this by musically sodomizing Lady of Spain. The centipedes scamper about on the floor, trying frantically to flee. You take this hint and put the headphones back on. That was a close one. Another figure is materializing and you have no doubt The Man at the Calliope accompanies its coming with sounds man was not meant to hear. The figure goes from blurry to clear, from incorporeal to shockingly present. It is a medieval jester with a skeletal face. His coxcomb and suit are jet black. There is a tiny head atop its marotte. Its eyes are open. It has a full head of hair and a full set of teeth.

The jester is not alone. Something else appears beside him, a wizened old man, naked, save, a cloak, a crown and a chastity belt. His face is a sad looking golden death mask, mouth nothing but a straight line drooping downward into a permanent frown. As the other guests cringe, Norton finishes a martini. He looks on the arcane happenings with an arrogant smirk.

"Ha! It's all done with mirrors! Keep your heads, people!"

With a wide, dense grin that would have done Reginald proud, Sorghum steps forward.

"I quite agree! There is, after all, no such

thing as the occult! There must be a mundane explanation for all of this."

Bridget runs around back and forth in circles. She tries the ballroom door and it will not budge. She pounds it, kicks it, runs into it head first, falls down and gets up only to repeat the process. The door still does not budge. She runs to Branwell, clinging to him.

"Woe is me! We're going to die! This house is full of haints! It's hainted!"

An unfamiliar hobo in blackface dies of fright. You've seen him some place before, but it was long ago and has nothing to do with The House of Dead Hogs. He peddled a swan boat for awhile. You have always been fond of swan boats. Miriam, Josephine and the septuplets join Bridget in her running around in circles. Each of them takes turns swooning as the others wake them up. The king stares at you for several minutes. You don't know if he has eyes so it is difficult to tell what he's trying to convey. But you know what he intends to say when he puts his hands on the side of his face, a Macaulay Culkin, Edward Munch scream. Abundantly clear.

The jester dances an awkward jig. The sort of jig Reginald used to dance. As he dances, the clockwork dancers imitate him, indulging in Reginald's humiliating jig for a little. They stop cold and begin to slap each other. The slapping escalates and the dancers rip gears and bits of clockwork out of each other's bodies. Norton sips two martinis, shaking his head in disbelief.

"Ha! It is easy to manipulate simple machines!"

Sorghum places his hand on his chin to think. Just as

Norton cannot be cynical without a martini, the others seem unable to think if they do not place their hands on their chin.

"Yes, perhaps there is a secret switch around here…"

Bridget sassily places her hands on her hips and her nose in the air.

"Hrumph! Ain't no switch that can shut off a house full of haints, that's for sure!"

Sorghum raps her on the head with his cane and wags a judgmental finger at her.

"I'll have none of your sass! You Irish are all alike!"

Bridget runs around in circles, hands in the air.

"Help! Someone help me, please! This house is full of haints and the barrister is trying to kill me!"

The king hangs his head. He paces the floor, back and forth, back and forth. He falls to his knees and clasps his hands to pray. The jester dances around him cruelly, smacking him with the marotte as he tries to concentrate on his prayer. The jester jumps up in the air, kicking up his heels. He does Reginald's idiotic jig as he juggles the heads of the clockwork dancers. The king turns around, kneeling before the jester, no longer praying but begging. A wisp of black smoke appears beside the king, growing bigger and bigger, more and more solid. The smoke forms into a shadowy winged serpent, a hideous dragon glowering at the guests through milky white empty eyes. The dragon flies up to the bookish septuplet, opens its fanged maw and bites her head off. The jester waves his marotte as if composing an orchestra. Miriam pulls at her hair. Sweat pours down her forehead, not drips, pours. It looks as if someone standing in the rafters has dumped out a bucket of sweat.

"What's happening, I feel very..."

One of the surviving septuplets rips off her dress and crawls on the floor like an animal. She rubs Dame Astrid's leg. She licks it. She bites down into it as if it were a chicken. Dame Astrid absentmindedly pets her. Miriam crawls to Sorghum's feet. The Major grabs Josephine, tossing her to the floor. Norton drops his martini out of shock. A new one appears in his hand instantly.

"See here! That's my wife!"

The Major shrugs. Josephine shrugs. The Major enters her, pumping her hard. Dame Smegma takes off her dress. Underneath it, she's wearing a whalebone corset and bloomers. Norton licks his lips and drops his trousers. He masturbates as he smashes his martini glass on her head. She strains her tongue trying to lick the martini off her head. Another septuplet kisses one of her sisters passionately, ripping the dress from her body as she does. They fall to the floor, tickling, groping and probing each other. Another sextuplet joins in biting and licking her sisters all over. For reasons that you do not understand, you feel an urge to remove the headphones and experience the accompaniment to this riotous debauch but you do not. That's what The Man at the Calliope wants, for you to let down your guard and let in the noise and punishment. The jester looks on, laughing silently, or maybe the calliope is laughing for him. It's possible, that damnable calliope has made laughing sounds before, wheezing, inhuman laughter. Branwell falls to the floor to perform enthusiastic cunnilingus on a septuplet. The final unoccupied septuplet watches him devouring her sister's pussy and pleasures herself with his derringer. There is a mild look of disappointment on her face.

"Oh, how I wish you carried a bigger gun!"

For once, Bridget is the one thinking, as indicated by her hand on her chin. She gets a "eureka" look on her face. A tiny fishbowl appears over head with a tiny phosphorescent fish swimming in it. She takes Sorghum's cane, inserting it into the septuplet, who rewards her with a kiss. And then another kiss. And another. And another. And another. They exchange kisses and caresses as she works herself with the cane. The jester gets on the kings back and rides him around the room using the marotte as a crop. Meanwhile,. Miriam rubs her large peach tinted breasts in Sorghum's face. He pulls away, looking somewhat quizzical. Miriam in turn gets a quizzical look.

"Mr. Sorghum, do you get the feeling as if something unusual is going on, perhaps something sinister?"

Sorghum does not reply. The Major pulls out of Josephine and forcefully thrusts his penis into Sorghum's mouth. Miriam continues to tease him with her breasts. Josephine picks Branwell's gun off the floor and uses it as a sex toy as the sextuplet had done. The gun goes off inside her. The sextuplet with Bridget abandons her in favor of Josephine. She plunges her tongue deep into her, drinking up the blood. Josephine rolls her eyes in hazy delight.

"Ooh! That's so much better!"

The septuplet spits out a bullet. Bridget taps the girl on the shoulder to get her attention. She doesn't. Bridget tries spanking her but does not get her attention. She taps Branwell on the shoulder but fails to get his. She folds her arms in discontent.

"Hrumph!"

As Bridget expresses her displeasure, Norton takes pleasure in beating Dame Smegma to death with a brick. He pours martini after martini on her wizened, inexplicably naked body and licks them off. He bores of this quickly, so wanders over to where Miriam is displaying her body to Sorghum. He gets behind Miriam, pries her legs open and fists her anally. The shadowy flies dircctly ovcr Norton. It opens its fanged mouth to reveal a long, black forked tongue which it forces into Norton's mouth. Norton closes his eyes in sheer bliss. Dame Astrid takes a cue from Norton and sodomizes her septuplet lover with the heel of her shoe. The king struggles to wrestle the laughing jester off his back but he cannot. As punishment, the jester dances on the king's back. The septuplets end their Sapphic ecstasy to take turns fingering their decapitated sister. Josephine gets up and joins them, rubbing her oozing vaginal wound against the headless girl, leaving a thick trail of blood. The four septuplets lick their lips and then go to work cleaning their sister's corpse. Josephine collapses from bloodloss. Her soul separates from her body. She looks over it, at first disappointed then aroused. She grinds, pinches, touches and generally molests her own corpse. Norton, very turned on by making out with the dragon ejaculates the word "satisfied" onto Miriam's back. Miriam breaks away from Norton and marches around in a stiff, naked parody of a soldier. The Major throws his head back, letting out a bunch of guffaws at Miriam's performance. He ejaculates a moustache onto Sorghum's face. Whether this has anything to

151

do with the laughter is impossible to tell. Sorghum in turn pulls down his pants and ejaculates a moustache onto Norton's face. The four march together, a small battalion of mock soldiers, then break into the sort of jig both Reginald and the jester have done so often. Bridget, still unpartnered, sways unseductively, performing a series of awkward chorus line kicks. She falls down, gets up again and resumes it. To change things up, she turns around, wiggling her scarred, blood-streaked ass then bends down far enough to present a rear view of her labia. She straightens up, turns, performs more kicks, winks and blows a kiss.

"Yoo hoo!"

The dragon's eyes are on her. It slobbers, exhaling a gout of white flame. The jester appears beside it, whispering in its ear. The dragon bites the jester's head off. A new one grows in its place. It flies away from the jester, to Bridget, who it envelops in its big shadowy wings.

And after many long years of loneliness and despair, it seemed that love, once a stranger to Bridget the maid, had entered the life of the ill-bred potato chomping domestic. With the coming of the dark stranger, Eros was now a compatriot. She would be changed forever.

The maid is on her knees, working its great ebony length with her mouth. She pulls away, then smiles big. The massive dragoncock lets loose a small flame, singing her face. She turns around, presenting herself, this time not to tease. It takes her, slowly, tenderly, lovingly. You have no desire to find out how The Man at the Calliope is accompanying this. Tears flow down Bridget's cheek.

"I have never known such joy as this! 'Tis a pleasure to have you for my handsome knight! Your bonnie lass loves ye, my darling!"

Lady Astrid's septuplet is now riding on her back, there is a bridle in her mouth and an obscenely big dildo has been affixed to her forehead. The four who have been playing soldier see this and conclude their games so that they may pet the "unicorn." The mischievous twinkle in her eye shows that Miriam wants more than to pet it, however. She gets down her hands and knees so that Lady Astrid can insert the horn, which she does, with the animal intensity of a dog in heat. The septuplet spanks Astrid with a crop, spurring her on, making her go faster. There is a look on the septuplet's face that screams "I'm in charge."

"Go, horsey! You mustn't displease your mistress!"

Meanwhile, Norton fondles his wife's soul as it makes love to her body. The septuplets that were just a minute ago so interested in Josephine have lost interest, now preferring to strangle each other and bite one another's faces. Branwell's septuplet, now returning the oral favors he granted her, bites off his penis and swallows it. Branwell reaches down her throat and pulls out a long line of interconnected handkerchiefs. The septuplets cease their violence so that they may applaud. Branwell flagellates himself with his cat o' nine tails as she silently recites magic words.

"Abracadabra, Alakazam, Shazam, Teth Adam, Cthulhu Ftahghin Tim Tom Tot!"

The handkerchiefs transform into crows that peck Branwell's eyes out and eat them. When they are done, one by one, they fly up the septuplet's vagina. The septuplet puts her hand over her mouth in embarrassment. Steam erupts from her head like a geyser. The crows fly out her mouth and rip out her eyes. Branwell reaches into his eye sockets, pulling out two diamonds, which he places in her sockets. She swoons, but gets back up immediately.

"Of course I will marry you!"

For so long that you lose track of time, the film focuses on Branwell beating his fiancée with the cat o' nine tails, hundreds and hundreds times as he gains sadistic momentum. You have to wonder whether her death is more of a relief to you or her. Branwell withdraws the diamonds from her sockets and puts them in his own. Each facet has a tiny pupil, making him look something like an anthropoid fly in this way.

"You've made me so happy, darling!"

Bridget and the dragon have moved into missionary position. The dragon's tenderness has given way to demonic savagery. There is a fanged smile on the dragon's crocodilian face and a toothy one on Bridget's. It pulls out of here, rears up to its full, impressive height. It sprays the king with a blast of flame, setting him aflame. The jester dances around the immolated king, taunting him. The rest of the orgy has devolved into pure chaos, a big ball of sweaty bodies rolling around the room. It is hard to tell where one begins and one ends. Bridget lies back contently and waves to the other guests. The jester makes a hand gesture and the king is no longer, aflame, but has been transported to the top of the sexball. He rides it like a circus bear as it rolls around the ballroom. The clockwork dancers somehow reassemble themselves and waltz around the room. Bridget rises to her feet. Her already large breasts balloon in size, her stomach grows big and wide. Her smile too seems to grow, it is as big as any human being can smile.

"Faith and Begorrah! I'm with child!"

The guests separate from the ball and gather round Bridget. Champagne bottles are opened. All present embrace Bridget, with the exception of Norton, who is masturbating into the stump of the headless septuplet's neck. A six foot long sunflower grows out of it. Although it is almost his size, Norton picks the flower. The clockwork dancers enter explicit poses. The jester sits on the king's shoulders, strangling him with his knees. In your living room, it begins to rain. The rain is cold and chunky, almost frozen. Damn! You left your umbrella at the elephant show! Bridget's stomach continues to expand. Sorghum produces a cake, which he rubs on the maid's pregnant belly. The dragon becomes less tangible, gray and smoky where it had once been black. It wraps the room in its great gray smoky wings. It breathes out tiny etheric jesters, then fades into a tiny black puff of smoke. Music by Wagner echoes through your headphones even though they are not plugged into anything. It is possibly just your imagination. Probably just your imagination.

Puffs of gray smoke come out from between Bridget's legs. Each puff of smoke turns into a small, black worm. The black worms crawl around the floor in circles. There must have been a dozen puffs of smoke, since there are now a dozen or so of these little black worms crawling around the floor. The Major gets down on the floor and chases after one of them. Catching it, he pops it into his mouth. He stands up and rubs his belly.

"Delicious! I have never tasted such a treat!"

Sorghum shakes his cane at Bridget.

"Bridget, this is highly unorthodox!"

Sorghum chases the new mother around the room, brandishing his cane. The crop wielding septuplet saddles up Dame Astrid to pursue Sorghum. The others are too occupied in chasing down Bridget's offspring to join the chase. The clockwork dancers explode. The jester grabs their heads and tosses them one by one at the king. The dragon reappears and with a single unholy gulp, swallows Josephine's soul. Norton stops chasing after the worms, so that he can see if he is able to fit his wife's corpse's head into his mouth. He cannot. He kicks and pounds the floor in a childish tantrum. The others fail to catch the worms, but succeed in a moment of brilliant physical comedy by bumping their heads in unison. Even in the midst of your discomfort, you must laugh at it. The guests (save Sorghum, Dame Astrid, her jockey and Norton of course), laugh at the hilarious accident, each one coughing up a few drops of blood. Norton swings the sunflower in the dragon's general direction. The dragon belches fire at him, which he sidesteps to thrust at the monster with the sunflower.

"Have at thee, knave!"

Dame Astrid's jockey turns her around and she joins Norton's attack on the dragon, charging with her dildohorn. The jester and king ignore the commotion and waltz. The king's body language is even more droopy and defeated than before. He is barely standing. The laughing guests cannot seem to stop coughing blood on themselves. The worms disappear in more puffs of smoke. Dame Astrid successfully runs headfirst into the dragon. Norton slices it with the sunflower, causing it to bleed kernels of popcorn. The dragon stumbles back in pain and Dame Astrid charges it again. The dragon reels from the dildo impalement. Norton tosses the sunflower, hitting the dragon dead center in the chest. It fades away, as do the king and jester. The clockwork dancers reappear, once more completely intact.

"A most unusual calm settles over the ballroom…"

All present survivors of the draconic orgy tragedy are once again dressed and upright. While Bridget's stomach has returned to its normal size, her breasts are still quite swollen and large. Miriam adjusts the collar of her dress.

"Well, it is clear that the telephone is not in the ballroom."

Bridget runs around in circles, fearful of haints. One of the five surviving septuplets dons a pair of glasses. She looks quite bookish.

"Then perhaps we should check elsewhere."

All present engage in a huddle. Sorghum steps forward.

"Yes, a splendid suggestion."

The rain in your living room comes down harder. Fortunately, you find a scuba suit hidden in your couch cushions. You haven't a moment to spare since the ice cold water is rising, turning from a big puddle into a small pool. Without the suit, you would inevitably drown or freeze to death. The guests exit the ballroom, finding themselves in a hallway that branches off in several directions. Miriam swoons, as she does whenever she is faced with conflict.

Fifteen minutes later…

Miriam gets up. Everyone is still in the same position, overwhelmed by the number of options available. A small fishbowl appears over the newly bookish septuplet's head.

"Perhaps if we split up, we can cover more ground."

All present go into another huddle, conferring briefly. They all nod in agreement. Sorghum inaudibly clears his throat.

"Miriam, you shall come with me and the septuplets and we will go down the hallway to the right."

Miriam silently applauds his decision.

"Norton, Dame Astrid, Branwell, Bridget and The Major shall go straight ahead. I believe that hallway leads to Lord Throckmorton's personal zoo."

Miriam silently applauds his decision. Sorghum leads the way down the right hallway. All present fail to notice the gorilla-suited figure behind him. It throttles and strangles him to death then looks directly at you. There is nobody in the suit.

Intermission

During the intermission, the rain stops. The pool of water has thankfully not gotten too large. You splash toward the bathroom before you once more realize that there is no way to get there. You also realize that you have trapped yourself in this scuba suit. This is unfortunate, because you have just soiled yourself and there is no way to avoid sitting in your own filth. The Man at the Calliope has decided to entertain during this intermission by projecting a short film entitled "You've Done All This" on the walls of your living room oubliette. You of course wish he didn't. The film begins with a close-up of your father's withered lung. It cuts to your sister sitting by the phone, crying and crying. And then you are born. A jeep explodes somewhere in the Middle East. You fall off your tricycle. Princess Diana dies in a car crash. At age six, you refuse to eat your broccoli. African tribal elders perform a graphic female circumcision. In the third grade you cheat on a math test. These things cannot be your fault and yet the threads of being connect. Your mother and father are conceiving you. They're really going at it. The Man at the Calliope appears in the bedroom, a pipe wrench in his hand. He sneaks up behind your father and smacks him in the head, knocking him out. Your mother laughs and pushes the limp, unconscious body of your father off of her. The Man at the Calliope enters her. You have a thought. A disconcerting thought. You never had any eyes. They have always been painted on and yet they see so well. They do not have any problem watching the hideous nutcracker musician having violent sex with your mother. Your so-called father looks up at you sadly from the hospital bed in which he lays dying and wheezes out his last word.

"Why?"

The short film ends and you are not entertained. It was all terribly shot. Your eyes no longer feel like they were painted on, though. Or do they? No. They are actual eyes. You have just been tricked. Your teeth are not wooden. Your body is not covered in coarse hairs. There is no way you were being shown the truth. When all this is said and done, he will reveal himself and when he does you will certainly show him what's what. He is not your father. This is not your fault. You are not a bad person. You would have called if you could. You weren't even sure he was sick. He might not actually be sick or dead. These could have just been things you were seeing and feeling. Unreal things. A test. And if you pass it, there might be a reward. What else is life if not a series of small tests? And at the center of it all must surely be the knowledge that everything is going to be alright. What if it wasn't? What if you could tell it wasn't and you kept going anyway? What if all these things that you had seen and felt were the truth? Wouldn't that be quite a thing? It is hard to tell what to do with yourself during intermissions, but the things your brain has been doing could not possibly be the right answer. You couldn't have deserved that. Could you? Calm washes over you as the intermission ends. Is that feeling calm? Is the intermission over? Don't worry. The intermission is certainly over. The rain doesn't start again. There has been enough rain.

The reels are changing. Intermission is over. Are you relaxed?

Act the Second

For a frame, the face of the sad king. If you had blinked, you would have missed it. You haven't been blinking much. Perhaps not at all. As if…no, they're not painted on. That was a trick. People do not have big painted on nutcracker eyes. You don't at least.

Twenty years ago, The Laboratory…

A fat disheveled professor downs the contents of a smoking test-tube. He clasps at his throat, falling backward. When he gets up, his head is a lit jack o' lantern. He bangs his pumpkin head against the wall until it splits open, releasing a wisp of red-tinted smoke. Ten young ladies with black circles under their eyes perform a breathtaking, flawless ballet. The red smoke washes over them, melting the flesh from their bones. In the smoke, a pair of evil white eyes shines brightly.

Meanwhile in the present, the guests make their way toward the manor's fantastic zoo. Throughout his travels in Africa, the Orient,

Hybrasil and West Atlantis, Lord Throckmorton acquired specimens of many a marvelous and ferocious species...

The guests are, as the intertitle said, at Lord Throckmorton's private zoo. Dame Astrid is terrified by the specimen in the nearest cage. She blocks your view of the specimen so you cannot be sure what it is that scares her so.

"It's ghastly!"

The others come closer to look at the cage. Norton drops his martini. Miriam faints. Branwell removes the diamonds from his eye sockets. Bridget holds The Major tight. They do not linger in their positions for long, backing away from the cage so that whatever is in there does not get them. This gives you an opportunity to see the denizen of the cage: a sumptuous and delicious-looking layer cake. The group have eaten many cakes before, but this one is completely objectionable. The guests move away from the caged cake to check out the specimen next to it. They applaud the specimen wildly. Inside the cage is a bucket of something. Miriam weeps for joy at the sight of it.

"My god, it's so beautiful!"

All present join in, each guest trying to outdo the last one's display of weeping. A fly buzzes around the bucket. Branwell shoots it with his derringer. All place their hands on their chin, pondering the mysteries of the peerlessly beautiful bucket. Miriam weeps again, this time appearing saddened rather than elated. All the others join in. Norton hangs his head in shame.

"Look at it! Wasting away in there! Something must be done!"

All present nod in agreement. They shake hands. Branwell opens the door to set free the bucket. It doesn't leave the cage. Should it have left the cage? It is, after all, a bucket. Should it leave? If your door was open, if your living room had not become a tomb and a dungeon, you would walk out. You cannot pity the bucket's captivity when you yourself are so thoroughly trapped. "Walk away, dammit!" you shout at the bucket, "Run! Get help!" The bucket does nothing. Branwell walks into the cage, grabs the bucket and sets it down a foot closer to the door. The group stares at the bucket expectantly. The bucket does not move. All present weep once more. Branwell brings the bucket to the Major, who takes a sip from whatever is in the bucket, then passes it on to Bridget. Bridget takes a sip, then passes it onto Dame Astrid. The bucket makes it around the circle three times before they return it to its cage and lock the doors. The Major heaves an inaudible sigh.

"The poor bastard!"

A priest appears and leads the guests in a silent prayer. When they are done, they give him a round of silent applause. The priest fades into nothingness. Miriam trembles. Norton drops his martini. Branwell tears the diamonds from his sockets. The Major crosses himself. The cage containing the cake is empty. Not a second after the film divulges this information, everyone runs around in circles, pursued by the ravenous, bouncing cake. Courageous eyeless Branwell faces his foe, shooting the cake with his derringer. The bucket's cell door opens and it slides toward the cake. A cardboard winged angel appears in a burst of washed out light.

"Fear not! Even in this place, hope still shines through!"

The cake and bucket float upward on a beam of light.

The Major's head detaches from his body and floats upward alongside the bucket and cake. All present wave goodbye.

That day in the zoo, three worthy souls ascended to Heaven. Hope springs eternal.
Bucket…Sidney Vargas Shimura
Cake…Nostrils the Wonderdog
Major Grosvenor…Nostrils the Wonderdog
The reels are changing. Is there nothing you can do to stop them? Can YOU accept change?
The reels have changed. The time for talk has come and gone.

All present have joined hands. They take an extended bow. They stare blankly at you, expecting something important. You get up from the couch to try your front door. No. It is still just a wall. You never had a front door. You sit down again. They are still waiting for you to do something important. You do not do anything important. You don't know what they want. They shake their heads in disapproval and return to surveying the cages in the zoo. The next cage contains a rotting pig head. The guests pull out cameras and take pictures of it. They point at it and silently laugh. The pig head silently laughs back. Norton drops his martini and enters a comical boxing stance, prancing and preening in what he thinks constitutes the demeanor of a fighter in the ring. Branwell opens the cage and Norton enters it. He punches the pig head several times. The pig head continues to laugh in spite of Norton's best pounding. Norton hits harder and harder until he starts to break a sweat. Branwell pours a martini over his head to cool him off. Norton returns to the fighting, but is not holding up well. The muscles in his arms are clearly straining, his face is clenched tight and covered in sweat. He throws up. He throws up again. He throws up again. And again and again and again. He vomits out a tiny Norton which marches solemnly into the pig head's mouth. A wizened old woman appears. She is probably over one hundred years old. You swear you have seen this old woman's face in an old photograph. Was it in your grandmother's attic? Is she your grandmother? Is she The Man at the Calliope's grandmother? Couldn't be. Her eyes are actual eyes and were not just painted on her. She jumps up and down.

"What have you done? What have you done? You've doomed yourself, Norton Throckmorton. You'll doom everyone! You shouldn't have come here!"

She focuses her gaze on you, which reminds you that movies really aren't supposed to do that. She extends her hand. You could almost take it. But it is not a real hand. This woman is probably not even alive.

"I remember you from when you were small. You'll do okay for yourself in the end. You'll figure out what is what and all shall be well."

You breathe. You breathe well enough to realize that you have not been breathing right. It has not been real breathing. Sighs of resignation, huffing frustration. Now you breathe. Norton's fist slams into her face. She takes up his challenge, prancing and preening in a boxing stance not unlike his. They fight. With a succession of surprisingly hard jabs, she has Norton in a daze. With a powerful uppercut, she knocks him out. She dances around him, kicking his prostrate form until he stands up, punching her again. She mustn't have been ready because the punch breaks her concentration. He presses his advantage, laying into her with punch after punch after punch until she hits the floor. He kicks her in the head until she bleeds to death. He returns to the pig head cage and pounds on the pig head until it stops laughing. All present bow before Norton. There is a puff of smoke. When it clears, Norton has the rotten pig head for a head. The guests pick at it, ripping off pieces of pig flesh until there is nothing left of it. Norton's regular head grows back right away. The group approach the next cage, finding inside it a headless pig body, standing on its hind legs and shaking the bars.

"What a jolly time!"

The guests are now outside at a large, empty courtyard. Everyone has a balloon. Sorghum is there, his face thin and sunken in. There are large, black circles around his eyes. Bridget tries to hug him, but he pushes her away and looks at her as if she is completely unfamiliar to him.

"May I seat you?"

A large table appears, fully set. Everyone sits down. They get up and switch places several times before settling. Sorghum pours everyone a glass of thick beef stew. He uncovers a large platter, revealing…himself. He stands on the table, carving his body up. It is stuffed with tiny Mary Janes, the kind Shirley Temple might wear. He serves each guest a plate of himself. They devour Sorghum and the tiny shoes with gusto and ravenous hunger. Sorghum places the lid back on the platter.

"Alakazam!"

He raises the lid. There are now a dozen or so little monkeys on it. They leap onto Norton and begin tearing off his hair. Norton's mouth opens wide in a silent scream. Miriam faints. Sorghum mopes. He places a conciliatory hand on Norton's shoulder.

"I am sorry, young Norton. The prophecy is fulfilled."

Norton vanishes. Everyone pops their balloon with their fork. It is alarming to see a balloon pop without hearing anything. The priest appears at the table, uttering a silent prayer before once again taking his leave. Miriam takes Sorghum's hand and looks into his eyes.

"It is good to see you again."

Sorghum shakes his head in violent opposition.

"I am of the house. You have not seen me. You have not partaken of me. You do not know the truth. You know the house's truth. There will be more suffering yet. Perhaps. Perhaps not."

Miriam clings to him.

"Please, tell me what you mean."

Sorghum pushes her away.

"I do not know what you speak of! I do not know who you are!"

Sorghum disappears. The table disappears. The courtyard disappears. The guests find themselves once more in the great entrance hall.

Elsewhere in the house, the other group of guests were approaching Lord Throckmorton's sewing room. While some might consider sewing an effeminate pursuit, Lord Throckmorton was a man of many, many talents.

Miriam and the septuplets cautiously enter the sewing room, characterized as such by a multitude of tables and many dress forms, wearing exquisite evening gowns tinted in blue, yellow and green. The girls all disrobe, each trying on and modeling a different evening gown. The dress forms spring to life, at first covering their nakedness then chasing the girls around the room. A dress form, catches two septuplets, taking a thread and needle from one of the sewing tables and sewing the girls together facially, turning them into conjoined twins, bound at the head. Although the dress forms return to their regular inanimate state after this gruesome punishment, the girls still flee from the room as fast as they can. The Siamese septuplets flee slowly as they are still unaccustomed to having another person attached to their face. Once more out in the hallway, the girls must choose another room to investigate. The bookish one places her hand upon her chin.

"When I was a girl, visiting this place, I recall there was an art gallery. That would have been an excellent place at which to hide a telephone."

The conjoined septuplets, nod in agreement. With great difficulty.

The Throckmorton gallery houses paintings from the finest artists in Europe. Throckmorton devoted most of his adult life to collecting them. These paintings show facets of Throckmorton's psyche and personality that he kept secret from his friends and family.

The girls tour the room, examining the paintings. The paintings are all paintings of telephones. They are all the same telephone, save one that looks an awful lot like your cellphone. The bookish one is examining this painting intently.

"It looks like someone is screaming for help."

Miriam nods in agreement, then places her hand upon her chin.

"Yes, somebody has missed a call. A very relevant call. A call for help."

There is a look of rage and consternation on the sewn together faces of the conjoined septuplets.

"Hrumph! This gallery is a terrible place to hide a telephone!"

The bookish septuplet puffs a pipe.

"Yes, I think it is time we returned to the hallway."
The guests, having explored more of the house's horrors and fascinating delights, come together in the hallway.

All surviving guests bump into each other in the hallway. There are two Miriams among them. Both faint. Only one gets up, the other having disappeared.

Together once more, the guests share stories of what has occurred during their separation.

Everyone is silently laughing. The old woman who might be your grandmother or something is among them. She wasn't your grandmother. She was actually the old lady whose cow Reginald and Miriam ran over at the beginning of the film. Imagine, you not knowing your own grandmother! It is still not altogether impossible that she is The Man at the Calliope's grandmother and if The Man at the Calliope is who he claims to be via those films, then…no, you know a trick when you see one. There is no reason for your floor to be covered in razorblades. You never found razorblades to be especially aesthetic and they are a poor replacement for a carpet. There's some reason for them to be there. Has the room gotten even smaller? Why is the room nothing but your sofa and a bunch of razor blades strewn about? Are you sure you haven't seen her photo somewhere? She waves hello to you before addressing the guests. Norton appears beside her, huge black circles under his eyes. He opens his mouth. She slaps him. She raps her stick on the floor inaudibly and all eyes are upon her.

"We have come bearing a message of great import. To ignore it will have consequences most dire. I assure you all that what I say is truth and these things are not to be trifled with. Not ever. Don't go into the library. Misfortune waits for you there. The truth waits too."

Miriam steps forward, posture straight, confident and determined.

"I have come here to find answers and know myself. I do not fear the truth. Whatever knowledge this library might contain, I am ready for it."

169

The black circled Norton looks at the old woman disapprovingly. He shakes his fists in anger.

"What has been done shall be done! What must be shall be! Who are you to stand against the will of The House of Dead Hogs? No man has that power! No man!"

The old woman stares into you, through you.

"He speaks the truth. I am sorry. There is nothing I can do. Soon, all will be revealed. For good or for ill."

Norton and the old woman disappear.

And so the guests made their way to the house's marvelously appointed library. Like Lord Throckmorton's other collections of curiosities and works of art, the library was proudly assembled over many years. Few other places can compare in sheer breadth and depth of occult lore...

There are no bookshelves in the library, only a multitude of dead women in maid's uniforms, their hands nailed to the floor. Books are stacked sideways on their backs in tall piles. Miriam reaches for a book at random, examining the title.

"On the Worship of Dark Powers."

She opens to a page on which there is a crude woodcut of a man trying to fit his wife's head in his mouth.

"Since time began man has used worship in his celebration of dark powers opting to venerate and placate the foulnesses of his life instead of to antagonize or ossify them. This shows both a tendency and a predilection in human nature, a rationalized disorder of the spirit..."

Miriam turns the page. On the next page is a crude woodcut of a dancing jester.

"Often associated with the worship of dark powers, clowns bring delight with their merry capering..."

On the next page is a big black dragon surrounded by a litter of tiny worms.

"Dragyns (or dragons) are associated with the devil and are generally omens of the coming of rainstorms and vampyres..."

The next page depicts a giant Santa Claus. His mouth gapes wide and several babies are trying to crawl out of it. There is a red tinted bloodstain on this page.

"The vampyre is a seller of souls and a purveyor of dark bargains. The vampyre fears nothing but daylight or its mortal enemy..."

The next page depicts a teapot.

"The lion, king of beasts, may frighten the vampyre with its mighty roar. Thus, the vampyre shuns the company of lions, even when the invitation is extended."

The next page features a crude woodcut of a dancing jester. It is the same crude woodcut from four pages back.

"Often associated with the worship of dark powers, clowns bring delight with their merry capering…"

The next page contains a familiar woodcut of a dancing jester.

"Often associated with the worship of dark powers, clowns bring delight with their merry capering…"

The next page features an infuriating woodcut of a dancing jester.

"Often associated with the weapons of damp pigeons, clowns bring defeat with their many caltrops…"

Miriam turns the page incredibly fast. The next page features a heavily detailed drawing of an apple.

"The wehrwulf is a formidable opponent to all but the most dedicated of sorcerers…"

There is a drawing of a pig on the next page.

"The most loathsome of all the powers of

darkness, the pig is a deceiver. It knows you. It knows why your living room was flooded. It can tell you why your living room was flooded. It can tell you if the old woman is actually your grandmother. If you ask it right."

Miriam closes the book. Reginald is standing beside her. There are telltale black circles under his eyes. He is dressed in a maid's uniform and carrying his own head on a platter. He smiles his idiot grin.

"What a delightful book!"

Reginald's face melts off, revealing that of the skeletal jester. Your headphones break. The Man at the Calliope is playing Take Me Out to the Ballgame at a crawl as if he does not know where the next key is. Miriam touches the jester's face. He disappears. Miriam shrugs.

"Reginald never did like libraries."

The Man at the Calliope switches to The Daring Young Man on the Flying Trapeze." The room fills with the red-tinted smoke.

"So the fools come seeking wisdom! Looking for order in what is essentially a series of accidents? I will give you order!"

The red smoke twists and swirls, at last becoming the ominous magician. He points at you, his crazy, bloated face hateful and judgmental.

"You offend me! You're as bad as these brain-dead fops! How can you continue to live as you do?"

He knows something, like the old lady does, or the cats.

"What are you talking about?" You scream at him.

Miriam puts a finger to her lips and groin punches you with her cold, blue eyes.

"Shhh!"

The magician sits beside you on your couch. He slides right up to you and blows in your ear. You hear nothing. You feel nothing. Of course. He is only the image of a magician. He is not an actual magician. When he speaks, you cannot hear him. If he tried to touch you, his hand would go right through you. His purpose its to look like an evil magician and nothing else.

Seven years ago, in Spain...

Several men in bull suits chase The Major and Dame Astrid down narrow streets of featureless, boxy buildings. After a few such streets, the bulls turn around. The city gives way to a forest. Instead of buildings, there are many trees bearing skulls on their branches. Dame Astrid picks one and takes a bite. The Calliope makes a "crunch" noise, which you did not think was something that a calliope could do. They keep walking and come upon an encampment of cardboard tents and poorly built plywood wagons. Gypsies dance frenetically, far too frenetically for the accompaniment, The Man at the Calliope's dreadfully slow The Daring Young Man on the Flying Trapeze. Dame Astrid stares at a cute and striking eight year old gypsy girl's dancing. When the dance concludes, she approaches an old lady, the same old lady whose car Reginald and Miriam ran over, the same old lady that issued the warnings, the same old lady that might be your grandmother. She taps her on the shoulder.

"How much for your daughter?"

The old woman shrugs.

"Oh, not very much, not much at all. I'm not especially fond of her, you see."

Dame Astrid skips merrily along the path, the skin of the gypsy girl wrapped around her neck as a stole.

The Present

Dame Astrid is on her knees, weeping.

"Those were such beautiful times…"

The Man at the Calliope plays Take Me Out to the Ballgame. The guests make a circle around Dame Astrid, joining hands and boisterously but silently singing.

"Oh, he flies through the air with the greatest of ease…"

Dame Astrid rises, joining hands with them.

"The Daring Young Man on the Flying Trapeze…"

Dame Astrid smiles as they sway in unison.

"He'll dine on your dog for the taste of the fleas, my love he has stolen away…"

The magician waves his wand and the worms that Bridget

gave birth to reappear. Miriam and Dame Astrid lick their lips. The mouths of the conjoined septuplets water. The bookish septuplet pops one in her mouth. She spits it out. Her eyes tear up. Her lips quiver.

"Something is wrong. Terribly wrong."

The room fills with red-tinted smoke once again. The worms are gone and in their place are a dozen identical pinup girls dressed in black bras, big black silk stockings and boots with eight inch heels. They all have the same full lips, the same statuesque proportions and the same thoroughly filthy expression on their faces. They form an awkward kick line, dancing very poorly, while the guests, still in a circle, silently sing to them.

"He rides through a hoop on the back of the king, drinks the blood of your children, flees into the night, he cries acid tears and he steals from the mice, in search of his next sacrifice. .."

The bondage girls stumble and fall down in a big pile. They giggle without making a sound. Why doesn't anyone ever make a sound? You should have more to listen to than that damned calliope. The guests in turn form an awkward kickline and fall down on top of each other. The magician bows. All present bow to him. He tips his hat.

"I must take my leave now, but do not fret. Have no fear. I will be back soon."

All present, guest and bondage girl alike embrace. They weep. The Man at the Calliope plays Merrily, We Roll Along. One of the septuplets dies of grief. Four remain, two conjoined at the face, one looking quite bookish and one untouched by this whole ordeal. The bondage girls run around in circles spanking each other. Miriam quietly giggles, then joins the game, spanking the bondage girls. They in turn chase her and spank her. The chase game stops. One of the girls jumps up and down excitedly.

"Let's punish Lucy, she's a bad girl!

Another girl puts her on her forehead in mock despair.

"No, you mustn't!"

Her sisters bounce in unison.

"We must! We must!"

Miriam puts her hands on her hips and her nose in the air.

"Yes, punish wicked Lucy!"

Miriam grabs one of the bondage girls, who she has somehow figured out must be Lucy by the waist. She struggles and kicks until one of her sisters grabs her by the hair with one hand and gags her with the other. Miriam lets go of Lucy's waist to bind her hands. Lucy does not stop kicking. Miriam bites Lucy in the throat, tearing off a large chunk of flesh. Lucy kisses her, taking pleasure at Miriam spitting the flesh into her mouth. The bondage girls laugh, applaud and kiss. The guests laugh, applaud and kiss. The bondage girls reach into their satin undies and pull out switchblades with which they engage in an ill-choreographed knife fight, stumbling on their ridiculous heels with each awkward thrust and clumsy stab. The guests throw coins at the bondage girls to egg them on. Stab by unskilled stab, the ballet goes on until almost as if by accident or actually by accident, one of the girls gets stabbed. Dame Astrid laughs. The bondage girls gasp in unison. Looks of anger cross their uniform, heavily made-up faces.

"MONSTER!"

The bondage girls grab Dame Astrid and vanish in a puff of smoke. The guests place their hands on their chins and walk around in circles searching for her. The bookish septuplet puts her finger up in the air in a "Eureka!" gesture.

"I've got it!"

The guests vanish in a puff of smoke.

Elsewhere...

The guests are in chains in a room filled with all manner of torture equipment, things ranging from racks to spiked cradles to a mechanical shark, mouth agape. A smiling bondage girl leaps into the shark's mouth, clawing her face in ecstasy as the robotic teeth chomp on her. Dame Astrid is suspended naked from the ceiling. Her body is crawling with scorpions. The ghostly figure of Norton manifests itself beside you on the sofa. He offers you a cupcake. You eat it. It tastes like dirt, but you feel a sense of wellbeing and understanding. It was you in the gorilla suit. Its warmth and security envelop you, filling you with warm gorilla feelings. You are safe. The Man at the Calliope plays music with a gorgeous logic to it. The bondage girls approach the chained Bridget, tear off her maid uniform and suckle at her large pregnant breasts like the infants they are. Suddenly, Miriam experiences a surge of strength and breaks free from her chains. An axe appears in her hand. She pushes the bondage girls out of the way and chops off one of Bridget's legs. She inserts it into the pregnant maid and masturbates her with it. Things change. The dead septuplets appear and return to life, Charlstoning with bondage girls. The black-circled Reginald returns, joining the dance. The walls of your living room become smiling dead hog faces and you are satisfied. But something is still undone.

"Come on out!" you shout.

The magician appears and you strangle him like the mighty gorilla you are. He thrashes, he shrieks…and when he shrieks, you hear it. He dies, and in death becomes the naked nutcracker at the calliope. Your true father. Of course! It should have been so obvious. You kick him.

"Hey!" You shout, hoping he'll get up.

He does not wake up. He's dead after all. And everything is so quiet. He used to play such lovely music for you. He showed you that nice home video and projected a silly movie on your wall made just for you. Dammit! Dammit!

"Wake up, father, wake up!" you beg him. He doesn't. He's dead. And then you're someplace else. You're seven on the school bus. Still in the gorilla suit, though. You have a crush on the girl sitting next to you. She is in her twenties, covered in piercings and works as a professional goth fetish model. Her hair is such a nice shade of charcoal and her skin a luxurious light gray.

"Hello," you say.

"Hello," she says.

"How are you doing?"

She pulls a gun out of her backpack, puts in her mouth and paints the seat with her brains. You put your fingers in the blood to make sure it isn't fake, that she isn't pulling some sort of trick. It's not a trick. It's a bloodbath. People love, people die. It's not so bad, is it? And then suddenly, you are floating above the bus, flying up into a gray, celluloid sky. The clouds are tangible. They are part of a movie screen. You plunge your fingers into them and you tear away the sky. Behind the screen is the House of Dead Hogs. You are glad to be there. Miriam and the bondage girls are milking and masturbating Bridget. Miriam stops masturbating Bridget for a second to wave up at you. You stop floating and land. Miriam, eyes full of love, peels away the gorilla suit and you are free. She embraces you, kisses you tenderly. It's not so bad. Your mind gets sharper than it's ever been before. You understand now. You take the axe and split open Miriam's stomach. She smiles at you, her face glows with gratitude. You reach into her wound. Inside it is a telephone. It rings.

"Congratulations," says a staticky voice, "this is all yours now."

And the calliope plays a song of joy.

Coathanger

It is not in the habit of caressing. It will not approach slowly
or softly. It does not knock on doors, seeking permission, but
rather beats down walls, chloroforming you in the shower or
dragging you out of bed like a secret police force from Hell. It
might do all of these things, or it might be none of them, but
it still gets the job done. Today, you're out on a bench not far
from the little lake where you go to retreat from all the clutter.
The dirty clothes might pile up as you sit there, and so might
the bills. Your email box fills up with pleas from men with
the scientific scruples of Mengele, who ask, no beg-beg you
to let them double the size of your manhood so that it may
triumphantly rip through your trousers and like the sword in
the anvil in the churchyard, proclaim you absolute king of all
you survey. All of these things might be happening in your
house, but outside, the water and the air are as clean as man's
progress lets them get. It is you, the bench, a book and a turkey
sandwich the way you like it. You couldn't be more present
in this moment of escape and succor, but then all of a sudden,
you're not there at all.

You're warm and alone in a place where this is no
difference at all between the sea and the sky, between the
mind, the heart and the intuitive whispers of the soul. Pictures
and ideas float past you, facts, concepts, vegetables, fruits and
angels. For once, everything comes to you; wisdom, security,
entertainment and nourishment are all yours without fighting
for them. There is no need to walk at all. You can kick, you
can spin, you can swim and you can fly, but there is no need to
walk since there is no solid ground to place your feet on. It is
an easier world than any you could ever know.

And then suddenly, a vicious tangle of metal rips its way into this sanctuary. It is long, thin and very sharp. You want to get away from it, but there is no chance. It smells you, it wants you, it's made for you. You feel the pain of its prodding and stabbing as it mangles you and drags you out. You suddenly give in to the peace and comfort of death and the silence it brings, not unlike the silence on the bench by the lake.

But it doesn't come. Even when a pair of hands places your bloody little bits in a glass mixing bowl, death doesn't come. And it doesn't come either when the man with the hands turns on the eggbeater and whips you into a nice, fine paté. He passes the bowl around to fancy, bleach blonde ladies in nice Bloomingdale's dresses that look like they were all made to accommodate the tastes of the same pretentious mannequin. They spread you on their crackers and you can feel the grinding of their surgically whitened teeth on each bit of you.

There isn't death after that either. There is another violent realization. It is the realization that the earth is too damn crowded to accommodate you. Too many pairs of feet have been weighing it down and it can barely spin. Like the men who sailed past the boundaries of medieval maps, someone might just fall off the edge into the waiting jaws of some dragon that floats in the void. Then again, maybe the void is worse than the dragons, maybe the notion that there is no more room is worse.

It isn't about pro-life or pro-choice, or any of the things people stand outside clinics with signs for. It isn't even about the thing you just underwent It is not about abortion. It is about war, no shirt, no shoes, no service, soccer practice, playground fights, the Oscars, absolutely no Irish, deportations, homelessness, Munch's the Scream, Birth of a Nation and the Butter Battle Book.

Then lucky you, you're alive again and you're on that bench with that sandwich and that book, sitting by that lake and you wonder what it is you taste like, and when the experience will come again, and whether you are actually on that bench at all or just a piece of gooey protoplasm on a cracker. And when you go home to the world of dirty laundry, bills and penis enlargement, you cannot escape the fear of a Mother Earth who will always have the right to choose.

The Granny Crunchbones Gospels

TheGnome's Warning: mycophage.net

It is possible for two people to have the same dream. It is unlikely, but it is possible. It is possible therefore for two people to have the same trip. I'd like to believe this is an internet meme, but I have known too many people that could swear they saw her and too many of you have written in to me claiming to have made contact with this entity.

I am really leery of spreading this information. I don't want this site to have any Blair Witch/Slenderman style bullshit. This is not 4chan. This site is to educate people on responsible consumption of hallucinogenic mushrooms not to spread fear and create spooky new internet memes. But I have known too many people that could swear they saw her. And I want it to be known that this happens sometimes.

Stay away from the rings. A lot of you have thought it would be cool to sit in the rings and take shrooms. Stay away from the rings. There is a myth that eating shrooms while sitting in the rings, or crop circles will enable you to make contact with the ships or whatever that left the circles. This has happened, but something else is happening. There are reports of seeing something different, something really fucking awful.

Tripping on mushrooms is rarely accompanied by full on visuals. You want visuals, try salvia or really good acid. Shrooms are not about visuals. They are about feeling a strong sense of wellbeing and connected to the Earth. That's right I said EARTH. I'm not going to debate whether or not aliens exist, but if aliens exist, they're not looking for people who just ate a bunch of shrooms to beam transmissions into their head. Don't be retarded.

What do you get when you sit in "crop circles" and so shrooms? Well, I'm going to tell you. You get fucked. That's what you get.

Let me tell you about her.

Llorona

Maria sits alone with the baby, looking at the clock on the microwave. She doesn't like being alone in this building. She doesn't like this neighborhood. The apartment building is full of sounds of arguing and sirens slice through the night. She wants Eric to come home, but it will be another hour. He's working late again. Least that's what he says. He'd better be working late. He'd better not just be at a bar with his buddies trying to pick up some puta.

The baby begins to cry. Is it the noise in the apartment? Is it the absence of his father? Or is it something else? Is it the thing that crawls between the between? She tries to tell herself she's seeing things as she watches the old woman crawl under the door as though she were flat. She tells herself she doesn't see the yellow-fanged, crusty-haired hag coming toward her extending gnarled, clawed hands, open as if expecting something.

It does not take Maria more than a moment to realize what it is the hag wants. She holds the baby tight, grabbing a kitchen knife in her other hand, trembling. The hag keeps holding out her arms expectantly. Maria keeps pointing the knife at her. Green, wispy figures materialize behind the old woman. They start to hum in unison. A sickly sweet tune, a song of wellbeing and safety.

Maria takes it in, sighs, eyes open wide. She places the child in the open hands of the old woman. She immediately knows she's done wrong, giving it to the hag with the abattoir stink and the skin of a toad. Still, she drops the knife, still she waits and watches, wondering what she has done.

The infant skin drains of color, the dusky brown of life giving way to moon-pale, giving way to albinism and emptiness. Makes a tiny rattle, a tiny gasp and no more noise, never, never again. The old woman smiles and hands the dead child back. She is flushed with health, as much as an aberration crinkled as a paper bag can be.

The old woman slides back under the door, accompanied by the green spirits, leaving behind no trace other than a feeling of culpability and shame and a baby that will never cry again. Maria cries. Maria will do a great deal of crying.

Wandering the street below, the old woman lets out a series of loud howls and sobs. She remembers the days when they would bring the children to her and she could rend their flesh with sloppy, satisfied abandon. Those were better days.

Mycophage.net: TheGnome's Warning Continued
User Dunsaniac was the first one to post about the hag.

"I'd heard about the faerie ring from a friend. She told me she liked to go there, smoke up and write poems. Said she could feel the Earth and all of its energies surging up. She felt like there was all this...she called it "feral magic" in the air. Sounded like a cool place to go and trip. What better place to do it than in the middle of a ring of a mushrooms? So I went there. Wasn't that far into the woods. Just half a mile off the trail. No spooky old trees, no winding vines, no wolves howling in the distance, no weirdass markings in the dirt. Just a circle of mushrooms. So I sat down and I ate the shrooms. And I felt the energy surging up and the wild magic. But, a few minutes later, just when I'm starting to really appreciate these energies, this hooded figure appears in the middle of the ring. It extends a bony vein hand, wants me to take it and I get this weird sinking feeling like if I stick around, I will. So I ran like hell. Never went back there again. Don't trip in the rings."

See, kids? Dunsaniac did the right thing. He saw that shit was about to get real and he ran, while he still could run. On the other hand, User CFORT666, was not as smart. Knowing CFORT, this shouldn't surprise any of you. And knowing

CFORT, it would seem unlikely that this happened. But, Dunsaniac is a pretty stable guy (much as any of us regular shroomers can be) and CFORT's into David Icke and shit. This delusion does not fit in with the narrative of his other delusions:

"Holy shit. I can't believe this happened. You're probably not going to believe it either. And no, it doesn't involve reptiles or anything like that. This is fucking different. This doesn't make any sense. I didn't expect to see the mushrooms like fucking bursting out of the ground to prove that they were there under the ground like you always said. And I'm surrounded by a ring of the things and these hideous little men are looking at me and laughing and making faces. And there's weird, green ghostly outlines in the center crop circle. I figure this is important, so I watch and I wait. Maybe these guys are experiments that the Grays made. You know, like they were children before. And then out of nowhere this twisted old woman in a black robe, her face all scaly and warty and covered in tiny hairs extends her hand to me. The green things are singing this weird song and the little men on the mushroom hum along. They tell some part of my brain that I should take the old woman's hand. So I take it. I feel my head filling up with facts and weird images that I don't understand, like maybe this is the stuff I wanted the reptilians to beam into me. She wants me to lead her out of the circle, like she couldn't have gone on her own or if there wasn't somebody that could see her. I lead her out of the circle and the feeling that I'm full of the knowledge I wanted grows and grows. I sit in the circle laughing and she disappears, off to somewhere else. And then the little men put their hands on the side of their heads and they scream together. I forget everything and I'm filled with panic. I know I've done something really terrible and I have no idea what it is."

It's just CFORT. He's crazy, most of you think. Well, I hear that and I think that's the first time I've really believed something he has to say. I think most of you will believe it to you. It doesn't stop there.

Five Years Gone

When the others at the shelter sleep, he swears he sees their mouths still moving and hears them telling him things. He had to stop himself from taping up their mouths, because he knew that it would do nothing. They tell him to come back. He wakes up in the morning with caps in his pocket. He could eat them and she would come and he could go back, back where he belongs. Come live with me and be my love...

And go back to the moon where in chains of moss, gagged with exquisite sweets stuffed into his face by shimmering blue-skinned pixie handmaidens, he would wait for the queen for what felt like days, tortured by the sharp fingernails and unwelcome pawing of Granny Crunchbones, yellow-eyed dirk-clawed fat ugly old beast. She'd breathe in his face, let him smell the stink of crib death and ruin the wonderful sweets. And he'll be happy there because that's where he belongs. Not in the city in the odor choked men's shelter.

He holds the caps in his hand as some men hold heroin needles and others hold the gun they're about to put to their temples. He hears a woman crying in the distance. He knows what she's crying about and the caps look more dangerous than ever. He puts them back in his pocket, remembering her claws on his bare chest and how he longed for the kisses of the Queen as he endured them. She's deprived herself of another chance.

He can hear her sobs, the wails of an aging zoo lion angry that stakes are not being tossed her way. It's one of the worst sounds he ever heard. If these men who'd lost their homes and lives to that kind of greed and privilege could hear it, they'd slash their wrists he imagines. Would they? Is he that much stronger for coming out of something like that a broken man tortured by temptations worse than death?

He proves how strong he is by sobbing uncontrollably along with the monstrous hag hiding somewhere in plain sight. He stops only when he realizes that she could come and slide under the door, flat and hungry and ready to bring him back to the lunar kingdom. Or, in her state of desperation simply rip him and everyone in the room to shreds.

He lies quietly on the bed remembering the mushroom songs from the court and the cosmic caresses of the Queen, all the more rewarding after the humiliations endured at the hands of Granny Crunchbones. He stays awake through the night, listening to the gibberings of his housemates.

"You don't belong here."

"Eat the caps."

"Back where you belong."

In his memory, the Queen slides off her garment of lichens, revealing glowing skin, purple nippled breasts and a thatch of verdant mossy pubic hair that moved about it and twitched. The hair would sing to him, inviting him in and telling him that he'll be loved for always. If he comes back, he will be loved for always. It smells so bad at the shelter. And no matter how many times he throws out the caps or how hard he tries to drown out the voices of the men around him, it doesn't stop.

He takes the caps out of his pocket. He examines them intensely. Another five years that felt like five hundred. Like heroin, like a gun to the temples. It's inevitable. But not tonight.

Mycophage.net TheGnome's Warning Continued
CFORT is not the worst offender. I have heard from some who have gone much further with their stupidity and reckless behavior. User DanDeLion decided CFORT and Dunsaniac were clearly full of shit and that he would prove them wrong. User NatalieSmythe69 suggested she drive up and they would make a day of it. Longtime Mycophage members will remember that Dan and Natalie got pretty hot and heavy with the online flirting to the point at which many of us were positively grossed out. I was secretly relieved that these two would finally take our advice to "get a room" (as Squid_Charlemagne would say).

"All I can say," says Dan, "is shit, man. I'm sorry, CFORT. I hope you're okay. I'm not feeling okay. But I'm here, on the board because I don't want anybody doing the thing we just did. Don't do it. I'll leave it at that."

Dan was greeted by a lot of insults, a lot of jokes about how Natalie must have fled in terror when she saw him naked and links to sites with cheap Viagra and the Amazon page for The Joy of Sex. Some of those users are still around, so I'm not going to editorialize about this behavior...oh, look, I just did... moving on...

"I should just let you assholes be punished like I was. Like Natalie was. But I couldn't live with myself if I did that. So, fine. We'll get into it. You notice how Natalie hasn't been around? It's not because we hooked up and she didn't want to hang on the board and fuck around. Some of you are going to assume that no matter what I say. But if I can stop one of you from shrooming in the circles, it will be worth it. Faerie rings and crop circles are not good places to do drugs. Should be common sense. But that's why we do drugs in those places, right? What happened or didn't between Natalie and me isn't important to the story. I hope. I'm telling myself that. We went out into the woods, sat down in the ring and we did shrooms. We had a god time. Natalie's every bit as sweet and cool and smart and great in person, she really is. We were tripping for awhile before either of us felt anything. Natalie said she felt something funny in her stomach. Shrooms can fuck up your stomach, so I didn't think anything of it. She took my hand and started squeezing it really hard. I've got some serious scratches. She screamed out "It's not human!" And I start to feel like we're not in the woods anymore. And like I can't get out of the circle, but I have to to stay alive. I start to see these green lights darting around and hear music. Someone is singing and pleading me to stay and telling me I can be happy here. I don't even know where I am and I believe it. Natalie doesn't look happy at all. She keeps screaming "Get out! Get out!" She's crying. It looks like blood, but it might just be that I'm tripping. It's hard to tell if that's what it is. And not just because

I'm tripping balls. And out of nowhere, there's a disembodied face, pale skin, purple lips, perfection. And it's not subjective. You couldn't argue about this face. The face wants to kiss me.

And I've never wanted to kiss anyone so much, even if it's just a face, or someone whose face is the only thing I can see. But Natalie's crying and clawing at me. I have to hold her, even if this face wants me to kiss her and these voices want me to stay there. But Natalie's crying and clawing at me. I have to hold Natalie, even if this face wants me to kiss her and these voices want me to stay there. I put my arms around her as she screams. I can see the outline of the hooded thing, but her wide eyes are on it and I can tell she can see all of it and she can't look away.

"Take it! Just take it!" she screams. I can see the hooded thing's hands reaching out toward her, bony, gnarly, scaly monster hands that want something from her. I squeeze her hard as I can and the shapes fade. I'm back in the forest, but from the look on her face and the ranting she's doing, I can tell she isn't. I have to drag her out of the ring and call for an ambulance. I don't think she's left the forest. Her family won't speak to me so I don't know what's happened to her. She can't call. She can't write. Don't go out into the rings. Something might follow you out. "

It's serious. I don't think Dan would make something like that up.

The Heroine
Kelly doesn't feel very good. It's not just the cramps and the embarrassment. The stew mom left to reheat had funny chunks of things in it and didn't go down well. Her brother can't stop crying. He's three years old. He shouldn't be screaming all night like that. She puts in the headphones and listens to her ipod. The ipod plays only one song. It's unfamiliar to her. It stiffens her joints, chills her blood, aggravates the cramps.

191

"Mother's girl's fed at the breast
When mother's girl's life starts
And mother's the one that's loved the best
In baby's tiny heart
Mother's girl's fed at the breast
Til mother's girl is able
To eat the meat that granny brings
To mother's kitchen table
But then the Moon sees mother's girl
A bathin' in the river
When Mistress Moon sees mother's girl
She makes her her's forever
The Moon's your mistress now
And she brings blood to you
And you're no longer Mother's girl
So granny gets her due"

She drops the ipod, looking at it as if it had suddenly transformed into a snake. Craig is crying louder and pounding on his bedroom. She would never have agreed to stay and look after him if she'd thought it would be like this. The worst part of it was that she is starting to think he has a reason for crying so loudly. It isn't just that he was a baby and he missed mommy and daddy. She once again looks to the ipod on the floor, unable to stop thinking of the song it had played. She doesn't want to be in the same room with the device and maybe Craig is crying about something worth crying about. She goes to the three year old's door.

Craig rushes to her, hugging her tight. He tries to choke back his sobs so she can understand him.

"She's at the window."

This is not the sort of thing she likes to hear while babysitting. Not the sort of thing she likes hearing anytime, but when a scared three year old was saying it, it hit her hard. Fist against her resolve, boot on the throat of "I'm a big girl,

I'm not going to cry." Worse yet, it makes her feel inclined to look out the window. She didn't want that. He was a baby. Only three years old and she...she's a grownup, as evidenced by the blood and her responsibility for him. She doesn't have to believe him. She was better off not believing him. But still, she tried not to let her eyes wander to the window, the window, where she, whoever she was, was at.

"There's nobody at the window," she lies. Craig looks at the window. He begins crying again. He has to be looking at something.

"Shh," she lies again, "there's nobody there."

It strikes her that when she was a child, her parents had told her that there was nobody at the window when she had thought she'd seen someone at the window. Her parents may have been lying. Every child's parents may have been lying...

No. Kelly is shocked that she is thinking like this. This is crazy. She isn't a baby like Craig. Grownups don't think that children are right about the stupid things they believe. They assure them they are wrong. Unless they're right. And someone is at the window. Nobody could be at the window. Although, were that so, then why would the boy be looking? This logic feels alien to her. This is not the way she thinks.

She looks out the window. Nothing is there. Her parents were right.

"See? She tells Craig,"nobody's there."

The paranoia pushes its way back to the front of her head. The pain from the cramps and the stomach ache brings her almost to her knees. More devastating than they had been yet. The song plays back in her mind. She puts down the boy.

"It's going to be fine," she tells the both of them. And both know she's lying. Something is terribly wrong. Something is at the front door. She locks the boy's bedroom door. She goes to the kitchen and gets a knife. She sits down in the living room, listening to the sound of scraping at the door and the song playing over and over in her mind. She considers turning on the TV, but is frightened of what might be on there, or what might come through.

There were funny chunks in the stew. Mushrooms. Funny texture. Funny taste. Something was wrong with those mushrooms. Her stomach hurts for a reason. Her brain is funny for a reason. There is scraping at the door for a reason. She's been drugged.

The hag slides under the door flat as a shadow. She doesn't need to be invited in. She is no vampire. She does not approach Kelly, but gives her a moment to take in her presence.

"Put down the knife, little lamb. Bring me your brother. He was promised me."

Kelly stands up, pointing the knife at the monstrous old woman.

"I don't believe you," she says. She doesn't know where this courage comes from, but she's glad to have it.

"You ate the mushrooms. Your mother made the deal. Give me what is mine." The old woman presents yellowed fangs, no doubt honed on centuries of bones.

"She gave me the mushrooms. I didn't choose to eat them. She made no deal."

The old woman laughs. Wispy green figures appear from nowhere and join in the chorus of mockery.

"When your mother was your age, she gave her brother and when her mother was your age, she gave hers. And so on for generations. The deal is made so give me what is mine."

Sounds reasonable enough. It was done often enough. The boy belongs to the old woman and that is that. And you're no longer mother's girl, so Granny gets her due. No. It isn't so.

The old woman grinds her teeth resentfully.

"I haven't got all night. Bring me the child."

Kelly does not stand down. She doesn't drop the knife. She understands the old woman isn't lying and that she was fed what she was fed and left alone when she was left alone for a reason. And maybe that reason wasn't her mother's reason. The old woman takes a step closer, gnashing teeth and brandishing razor sharp claws. The girl charges, knife in hand. She thrusts it at the old woman with all her strength. She plunges the knife into the old woman's head, the warty, scaly skin surprisingly penetrable. The old woman shrieks, stunned by the pain. The girl pulls the knife out. Thrusts it in again and twists it. All she knows of knives, she's learned from carving pumpkins. The old woman lets out another howl of pain.

The old woman backs off, beady eyes full of shock and contempt. Though no blood has come out of the wound, the great gaping hole in her skull is more than enough to let her know that she will not have what is hers this night. She slides back under the door hungry and disappointed.

Kelly unlocks Craig's door and picks him up, bringing him into the living room. They watch tv together for another hour before mother and father get back. Her mother almost faints at the sight of her daughter holding her brother close, breaking with tradition, failing to give in to intimidation. They lock eyes and mother's heart breaks. She has a son but has lost her daughter forever.

Mycophage.net Comments Section
Anonymous
Bullshit Bullshit Bullshit Bullshit

Riboflavin Jonez
Thank you, Gnome for taking time out of your busy schedule to scare kids out of doing drugs. Do you not notice what forum you're running?

Yeah, I agree. I don't get the scare tactics, Gnome. This post made me lose a lot of respect in you.

Shawna766
Didn't think you were that starved for attention.

Anonymous
This is real. This is all real. This is more than real. Stay out of the rings.

IntotheMystik
You've been played. I've heard of this shit on other boards. Granny Crunchbones is just another urban legend. Don't you check Snopes?

MaDDHatta
How do we know?

Riboflavin Jonez
Classic Hatta.

MaDDHatta
Fuck you, flave.

TheGnome
Go fuck yourselves. I tried.

Anonymous
This is real. This is all real. Stay out of the rings.

The Donor

He adjusted his tie. Was this a perfect Windsor knot? It had to be a perfect Windsor knot. Was his collar too stiff? It might have been. It might have been too stiff. He fiddled with it but it distracted him from the knot. And if the knot was not than it would come to nought. Shit. It had to be a perfect Windsor knot. Her breasts were perfect, at least for him, for he was of the "more than a mouthful" school and when the photo came, school was in session. It had to be a perfect Windsor knot. Maybe she would notice.

He looked at his phone again. He knew it would read something different as time did not stand still, though it slowed and it got awfully slow when he was waiting. The moment given time to breathe will creep away and breed and it will breed broods and broods and broods and broods. The moment is the envy of rabbits, of Kipling and Woolf and Darger even, with his codices of the eccentric, his curious, monstrous girls. It puts them all to shame in its generative power. The moment's brood were upon him, tearing his hair and pinching him, imps from a woodcut of a witch's sabbat. Agony starts at the itch. Then the scrape, then the wound. Then death, the itch was death. It was the scrape becoming the wound.

You've waited awful long to get impatient. It's been an awful long time, not right for you to start now but now's the time. It was bursting through his skin now, through his goddamn skin. A stereotype? Perhaps. They'd seen the movies and there were two kinds of guys like him and only one of them was anything akin to sexy. He ordered an Old Fashioned to take the edge off. He liked the drink. He liked bourbon and the little touch of extra sour sweet and the single Maraschino made it a thing. He bounced a little in his seat as if needing to take a piss. The discomfort in his crotch had nothing to do with that. What was he? A child? A man not yet born for sure, so natal, perhaps this was a natal thing, a natal experience, a man about to emerge. He looked at the photo, the blue eyes, button nose, the smile, shy and sharkish as if she was shy but sharkish, which she was. He didn't mind that she was naked as the day she was born and he was at a bar and maybe someone if they craned their neck could see.

Let them look. Let them envy. He was proud. He looked up Windsor knot on YouTube. He'd done it right. Thank fucking Christ. What if what if what if....what if she saw it was wrong and she walked away and if she walked away then he'd be waiting more, another life when he'd wanted to end this one out of shame for what he was. The moment is a killer but shame is genocidal. If Shame was put to trial, it would hang by the neck til Ragnarök. But his tie was right, there was that and he'd been working out. Much as he could. He'd bought that MMA thing at Target. The one with the gloves. The gloves were helping. He could jerk off to that photo til his foreskin was the color of a watermelon.

But she didn't let him suffer that much longer. That wasn't Annie. She was six minutes late and she knew it was an entire axle heavier. She approached him and put her hand directly on his shoulder.

She didn't say "hello", she said "hey, you." like she'd just walked off to use the bathroom since their last conversation online. He turned around, stood up, extended his hand, which wasn't taken since she went in for a hug. Because that was Annie. She was not a mystery, there was never no good reason why, there was not a man she knew who thought of her when they heard Ruby Tuesday.

"It's a pleasure to meet you," he said, capable of only euphemizing. He didn't know shit about pleasure. He had squandered paycheck to paycheck to paycheck bringing exotic delicacies, a culinary Noah's Ark to the pots and pans of his studio apartment in a part of town where a man who wasn't scared of himself couldn't live. That wasn't pleasure, that was something less. He couldn't pick pleasure out if it were standing between his nuts in a police lineup. But he meant it though he didn't know what the fuck it meant.

He held onto her too long, although that wasn't quite possible. She kissed his cheek, moved up to his earlobe. Whispered. Shy but sharkish, naive but damn cagey, like someone who bled chocolate milk but spiked it when the chaperone wasn't looking.

"We don't have to stay here, I know you don't like bars."

"You need a drink," he said, a statement that slithered on its belly beneath understatements.

"We can get a bottle of something."

The waitress arrived with the Old Fashioned. Annie took the cherry, pretending she was preparing the Audrey Horne. She ate cherry and let out an all too exuberant laugh. He wasn't sure that it was that funny, Marx Brothers on Nitrous funny but he laughed with her. He hadn't had a lot of cause to laugh. He sipped the Old Fashioned. She sipped the Old Fashioned. He sipped the Old Fashioned. She sipped it some more. He killed it, the scoundrel. That was the short, sad life of the Old Fashioned.

They left the bar. She was right. He didn't like bars. He liked booze but didn't like bars. She bought a bottle of Cruzan, a four pack of ginger beer. They got on the Orange line to start toward the ugly part of Forest Hills. It would be half an hour but that didn't concern them any. Her head was on his knee like a prom date four sheets to the wind. Looked like a coin toss between throwing up and a blowjob and she only had half a drink in her. Was this sentimental?

He ventured a kiss on her forehead, then silently stared out. There was no talk between them but straight ahead was potential. As Boston passed him by, he traveled time, past the real and into the ideal, sailing into the mystic. She looked up at him and smiled. He smiled back.

"You know how hard it is not to kiss you?"

She sat up and shook her head.

"I've never had to not kiss me before."

He laughed.

"It's rough."

"I have come," she said, "to liberate you from suffering."

He kissed her. Mission accomplished.

"There some reason you're doing this?" he asked.

"I'm going to suck your cock," she whispered. This was not a suitable explanation. This was a superlative explanation.

"I don't get what you say about your breasts," he said. Somehow it was not a non sequitur.

She lightly slapped his face. Giggled.

"You are very fresh."

He couldn't help but laugh. He wondered if she had any idea what she was saying.

"Well, I certainly hope you are."

"Two showers. And I moisturized like nobody's business. Am I smooth?"

She brushed his face with her arm. She knew damn well she was smooth. She had no idea how smooth she was. She defined smooth. Nobody had told her she was smooth in her entire fucking life. He wished he could have her for bathwater. He wanted to cry. He couldn't possibly cry. He swore for a moment on his arm was printed the phrase "Homo Fuge" but that was free association. Free association with an awful stiff price.

"You're very, very smooth."

"I moisturized. A lot."

"You can tell."

She scrunched up some.

"You're not disappointed, are you?"

He looked her over, trying to see what she could be

talking about. He could not. He wanted to know, so he could tell her specifically which objections were complete and utter bullshit, ex-boyfriend propaganda, New England matriarch perfectionism. He could not so much as determine what she thought was wrong with her, except the thing she said about her breasts. He was not sure she believed him.

"No. I wish I knew why you want this though."

"We talked about it."

The darkness, the urine smell of Forest Hills Station. They emerged among a throng of people they could never say three words to, walk out of the station, past the now closed flower and fruit carts and then out into the night air. He holds her hand and she was surprised he held her hand and surprised after that at how tightly he held her hand. She gave a feeble smile, one wounded by oxygen, dying from the germs around it like a martian stepping out from its tripod.

"I was never pretty," she said, though she was pretty, "and my sister got the grades. I never made much of anybody happy."

"I'm happy now," he said.

She shook her head.

"You're anticipating something. That doesn't mean you're happy. I haven't made you happy yet. You're not happy. I wouldn't know, I don't think I've been happy much but you, you're not happy yet. You're expecting something nice."She had a point. He was anticipating something downright grand, something that put a lot of things into context. Maybe he wasn't happy yet. But he liked this.

"I like this," he said, "this thing we're doing now."

"Yeah," she said, "that's good. I like it too. It's nice."

Both of them searched themselves a moment to determine exactly what it was right then that was nice. And neither of them could find it. The future was nice, when the thing they came together for was done, that was nice. And this right now was nice or nice enough or else it was nice. This right now was nice. He pointed out toward Forest Hills, the part of Jamaica Plain where it abruptly stops looking like Sesame Street.

"I live this way," he said, half saying that he wouldn't blame her if she got back on the train and turned around. She didn't get back on the train and she didn't turn around. So, hand in hand they continued on ahead.

"Mostly," she said, "I just paint. I've showed you photos of my paintings, right?"

"They're very good," he said, because they were. He always had trouble saying that to people whose art he didn't like. A lot of the women he'd talked to before made paintings he didn't like much or wrote poems that didn't have much imagery and were made of more adjectives than verbs. He liked her paintings.

"But I wanted to do something bigger," she said, "you know?"

"Yeah."

He didn't. He mostly just wanted to walk down the street without thinking an angry mob should stone him to death. The angry mob never showed. They must have had better things to do. He could not think of doing something bigger. She was right that this was big. It was awfully, awfully big. Especially for him. He had thought of little else but this, all research, all work, all diligence. Hours on the internet, hours on the chatrooms, failed encounters, abortive phone calls. And now, this, this, this was big. So maybe he could think of doing something bigger.

"I'm gonna suck your cock,"she whispered, nuzzling his earlobe with her nose.

She may have had a drink or three before the bar.

"You know," he said, "you don't have to do this."

She backed off, let go of his hand. Her eyes widened into planets at the very end of days, her eyes became Krypton and Alderaan, her eyes said "no survivors."

"Are you having doubts? Do you not want to do this anymore?" She crossed her arms like she was trying to push her heart back into her chest and keep it there.

His heart sought to break out and run off as hers was doing.

"No. I can't say I'm not scared but no, I promise. I don't have any doubts."

He approached, put hands on her shoulders and drew her in. He became awfully assertive awfully fast.

"I want this. Okay?"

She nodded.

"I just wanted to make sure."

"I'm sure. I promise. I'm sure."

So they made their way together to his apartment, cheap enough because the building was something awful. The building looked like it'd been whitewashed in curdled milk, with tiny brown spots peeking out like rabbit shit. He fumbled for the key, hands like teamsters; sweaty, slick,uncooperative and outta shape. As front doors tend to, it eventually acquiesced. This was no fortress but a Forest Hills apartment building, a cheap one, an old one that didn't care much who got in or out.

They climbed up the creeking stairs and made their way to the unadorned door of his apartment, tried the key again, a second too long, with a second too much tension and a second too much annoyance. There had to be something they could have been doing during that second and whatever it was might as well have been the Sistine fucking Chapel, it might as well have been harvesting grapes in Jerez. Whatever they could have been doing as the key struggled with the lock was better than the sum of everything they'd done up until meeting in that bar. For two such people, that did not amount to much but still, it can be said that the time the key had a substantial hitch in the lock during which time its comrades on the keychain went to college, found girlfriends and started lives of their own.

There was thankfully not much of a threshold. The neighborhoods and stoops of Boston are their own thresholds, whether to treasure or winos picking apart a frozen brother for sustenance. There was, in this apartment, a front door and then a couch. This couch was a verdant monstrosity the color of some rotten reverent from an EC Comic. The color could be described with a bastard melange of Lovecraft and AC Moore; "Putrescent Mint." It was not much of a couch and nobody liked it.

"Nice couch," she said.

"Thank you," he said. He hated that couch. She sat down on it and beckoned, making him hate it a whole lot less.

There was no trembling and hesitation, no distance or politics between their bodies. He leaned in without politics and met her lips with no hassle from customs. He lingered there and emboldened, he took a tiny bite before retracting. She smiled and put her hand on his knee.

"I meant what I said," she said, "I want this and I mean it."

She unzipped his pants and freed the wilted thing inside, green thumbing it to bloom big. She rubbed her face against the head, tickled the shaft with her hair. Kissed the tip gently.

"I'm going to suck your cock," she repeated, as if suddenly this were something hard to believe, as if starting to give him a handjob would remove credibility from her ever-more-reasonable claims that she would do so and possibly put it under dispute. He didn't know what came over him. He knew exactly what came over him. And he liked it a great deal.

"Prove it," he said.

Either she was quite fond of him or she was deeply averse to looking like a liar. As promised, she sucked his cock. He could have romanticized it, added deeper shades of meaning or become sentimental or invented poetic superlatives for the quality of the blowjob but none of that was necessary because she was sucking his cock. Having one's cock sucked is, generally speaking, a temporary respite from language, an intermission from interior monologue to grab a snack in the lobby, or in the case of a blowjob like he was receiving, to step into the bathroom and shoot up on something glorious. He got stupid enough to live, to actually live.

She worked him for some time, pulled him from her mouth, made deep, piercing eye contact before returning to the task, up down, tongue, teeth, tenderness and passion. Up, down, tongue, teeth, I cannot say but I'm saying it, up, down, tongue, teeth, please understand that I'm saying, what I'm saying is, what I'm saying is, what I'm saying...up down, down, tongue, teeth, swirls and kisses and gazes that froze him in place like nails in his hands and feet, up down, tongue, teeth, what I'm saying what I'm saying what I'm saying...

"You're having a good time, right?"

She had been going for some time and was referring now to the fact that his cock was all business, its focus intense and laser-like on things that it wanted to do much more than getting sucked, things it would do as long as it could out of fear that there was only so much of the crisp, warm nectar it lived on and that the sea in the lover would run dry and it would have to gasp for air and shrink and die. It was hard as it was because the time was as good as it was and he and it feared that the time was as fleeting as all time had to be.

He took the moment she took to ask to take her face in his hands and kiss her hard again. She didn't seem to know what to make of it, what to make of having such value to him. So she went with it. She let him get to know the taste of her mouth and her neck and her shoulder. And after that, he released her imperfect breast, too conical, too girlish for her taste, smallest in her family. Suckled it and his mouth and then started to bite. She mouthed "don't", she mouthed shame. Then she mouthed "ooh."

"How is that?" she asked.

"Nice."

"The taste."

"It's good."

She smiled coyly, devilishly.

"So, should we start?"

He stood up.

"Are you sure?"

She replied with a kiss. An awfully eloquent one at that. There was a great deal of information he could have gleaned if he hadn't had it in the first place. But largest among all the little details about her nature that he swallowed from her mouth was the great burning affirmative. He momentarily lost himself and descended once more upon her nipple.

"Like it, it's yours," she said, "I didn't come here without thinking about it. I didn't come here without knowing this was important. This is important. We can kiss, we can fuck but that's not what I'm here for. I like you."

He walked into the kitchen, tall and straight, eyes a little watery. But he was quick with purpose. It had been awhile since he'd been quick with purpose. All in all, he moved a little slow, common for a man who hadn't been heading much of anywhere. He got a carving knife, slim but sharp, precise. He was good friends with his whetstone in ways that he hadn't been with anybody else since seventh grade. Except maybe her, even though she'd been a voice and a face on a screen and nothing more. But more.

She smiled. Closed her eyes and breathed deep.

"Okay. go."

He raised the knife.

"No! I'm not ready."

They stopped together. She opened her eyes and giggled.

"Jesus, what is fucking wrong with me?"

"This should make you nervous. It's..."

"Death?"

His hand trembled a little.

"Yeah. I'm going to..."

"Unless the next word coming out of your mouth is "cum", do us a favor and shut the fuck up."

He nodded gravely and caught her eyes again. He searched again and again for omens like a nervous New Ager whose tarot habit was eating his calm and contentment. He was looking for

The Tower but it was nowhere to be seen. How would this fail? He kept inquiring in her and he did not find his answers. He saw no signs of catastrophe and he wanted to flee screaming, to turn his back on her and let her get out of this while she still could. He didn't.

He made the first cut. A tiny sliver of breast that brought up bubbles of blood. She did not scream, she bit her tongue through a smile, made a face that looked like subtle hands just out of view were working between her legs. He sucked on the wound some, took in the warm, savory, coppery sweet of first fluid, first essence. He withdrew when the protein hit him, made another cut, a bigger sliver. She did scream this time, but it was short, sharp and ecstatic.

He poured butter and red wine onto a nonstick frying pan. Waited for it to heat up, and chopped some shallots. He tossed the two white strips of pale, soft sacrifice onto the pan, turned them with a fork as they browned slightly, waited for the meat to take on a thin crunch, like that of a good steak. He didn't let it fry for long, wanted to preserve the taste and texture as best he could so it could best be complemented by the shallots. It was only minutes before he was ready to plate it. It was important to her that she witness this and in turn important to him.

He entered the living room with two plates.

"Me first," she said.

"Of course," he said, serving her the first slice, wine-soaked and surrounded by shallots. She took a bite and the bite took her. The feeling and the situation and the old desire to be part of and inside of something, an old, old feeling captured her. This was what it was to be a piece of art. The dish was simple but the tenderness and dedication shined through every bite as did the desperation.

"There was a woman," he said, as he started to cut up his meat, "she took a picture of her earlobe, frying on a pan. She saw my profile and told me to come right over. Bunch of nudes too. It did everything to me, set my body on edge, reminded that this was too big a thing to hide behind. But you can see sometimes in their eyes..."

He took a bite to try his first bite. Flee flee flee. This wasn't right. Couldn't be. This was not what he deserved. Freaks that eat people did not deserve to taste such things, did not deserve to feel such things. But damned if there wasn't a problem with that line of thinking, damned if the evidence didn't contradict it. Damned if the taste of her wasn't proof that something in him deserved to know it. She was sitting there, chewing on herself, holding only a sweatshirt from her handbag to her bleeding breast. She let him finish after his first swallow.

"Sometimes in their eyes, you can see that they just saw that show. They want you to be a monster and you know, even when you are, you shouldn't hang around anybody that wants you to be one. That's what I figure. This is different."

She stretched her leg out over his lap.

"I'm a work of art now," she said, "I think I think I'm something important."

He didn't bother saying that she always was.

"You don't have to stop. You know why I came here."

He nodded, an invisible anvil atop his head.

"We'll finish but one thing, just the one thing."

"Yeah?"

"Waste nothing."

He wasted nothing.

And You Told Me Again, You Prefer Handsome Men

Four am again and look at you. Dallying downtown drunker than drunker than drunker than…drunker than that. Drunk enough. You can't go home yet. You could take another bus. Two blocks down there's a different one. You could get on the subway. You could get on the subway and there's no chance of it. Calm down. There's no chance of it, okay? There's no fucking chance. But the bar has closed. And you are sitting there about to make a really nice lady call the cops on you. She's a really nice lady. She was good to you all night. She listened. Even when you stopped making sense. And you didn't tip her that well and you were staring down her shirt and you were just you were…

Have some damn self respect. Gotta get up off that barstool. I know it hurts. Your joints are aching, your bones feel fragile. But you gotta get up off that barstool and you gotta prove that it's not going to happen. It won't happen again. Just find another bus or take the subway. The subway station isn't far. Get on the subway. Yeah. You're drunk and you're aching but if you get on the subway, there's no chance it will happen.

Yes, those kids are staring. Of course they're staring. I know it hurts worse cause you're drunk, like they're looking at you louder, like the unspoken laughter is coming out through a phantom megaphone. Stay cool. Just get on the subway and it won't be long. Like the Beatles song. Won't be long now.

See? These people are nice. You got a seat to yourself. Heh. Yeah. Have a fucking sense of humor. Would it kill you to have a sense of humor? You suck sometimes. No, you suck all the time. You…look, I'm sorry. It's just sometimes, you know…I know you do your best.

I don't want you to panic. Let's not panic. But yes, she just got on. On the subway. The shoes and black nylons. And that coat, blue, like a Jehovah's Witness would wear. But the black silk chemise is not the black silk chemise of a Jehovah's Witness. And her hair is platinum like it always is and her eyeshadow is green and somehow it's fucking working. Maybe she won't...of course she's going to notice. Come on, man, let's just be realistic.

"Hey, what's with the burlap sack? You The Elephant Man?"

You could just not...

"Yes, miss. Though I prefer to be called Joseph."

Hard for her to miss The Elephant Man.

"Would you like to get a hotel room with me?"

You don't have to tell her yes. You don't have to do this. Or maybe it will go different this time. You don't have to panic. It could go better. At least she doesn't remember last night or the night before. There's that. Focus on that. It's a new night. Maybe a new hotel. You couldn't possibly end up at the same hotel.

So, it's the same hotel. This doesn't mean it will wind up the same. The clerk looks familiar though. Yes, it's the same Japanese girl with the pink hair.

"Hey! You're the Elephant Man!"

And still you're blushing underneath the sack. Have a fucking sense of humor.

"Yes. Joseph Merrick, at your service, Miss."

Yeah. It is kinda weird that she has a copy of that DVD at the desk of a hotel.

"Autograph?"

Humor her. You want to get upstairs.

The same sparse room. The same disheveled red blankets with black zig zags on them. And the same blonde on the bed taking off the same black chemise to reveal the same cute but pyramidal big nippled b cup tits that you wish you could suck through your sack. And she pulls you into her mouth for what feels like the same blowjob. Her tongue is wet and thorough, her soft moaning vibrating up and down your cock.

Just enjoy this. Just enjoy it. Just enjoy her mouth on you. Just enjoy how she doesn't mind your bumpy rough hand on the back of her head. Her hair is one of the few things it doesn't hurt to touch. So focus on that. The world is warm and wet and it kind of loves you, Joseph Merrick. Maybe it's not so bad being The Elephant Man, huh? You don't need to drink so much or cry so much or bother that poor bartender so much and…aah. Yeah. The blowjob. The world is warm and wet and it kind of loves you, Joseph Merrick.

And even though it hurts and aches your bones when you roll her over, when she pulls down her panties it's all potential. It's all potential, Joseph Merrick. And in spite of your flesh and bone and your fear and your isolation and the booze's conspiracy against your manhood, your cock is hard. And you're ready and the world is warm and wet and it kind of… it loves you. You can wrestle the pain in your joints and your bumpy skin and your awkward, heavy bones and you can enjoy it.

The world is warm and wet and loves you. Her rhythm is slow and considerate. She knows you're in pain and she cares. You know that, right? She's considerate til she's not, and goddammit, don't blame her, enjoy her. She's squeezing you tight inside and out and she's spasm and holding you sacred, her womanhood thirsty as her mouth and eager to get what's in you. Your shudders are coming up and down and in and out of her and you ain't the elephant man.

She loosens again and gives you room to grow back. It always surprises you that you're ready again cause you never you never even thought you'd get there in the first place. But you're in there and this world loves you. The planet Earth loves the Elephant Man and you don't even know this woman's name and if she does but it doesn't fucking matter because life loves you. And you spill again and you spill again and you grow again. She is dripping down her legs and your bones and your body and she's squeezing squeezing hungry happy satisfied squeezing…

"Please," she pants, "I gotta…"

For thirty seconds, you've been a rapist before it sets in and you're out and breathing hard and your bones are wooden and heavy. And your cock withers down and sleeps tight. It's not gonna happen this time. It's not gonna happen this time.

No. The lips of her pussy are quivering and there's that sound. She's got the look on her face. The really ashamed one. It's not gonna happen this time. She's not going to scream about how it was supposed to be perfect. About how it was going to be perfect and you've ruined it. She's going to scream about how it was supposed to be perfect. She's not going to cry. She's going to cry. She's not going to pull the devil mask out of the drawer. It's looking at you with that big, bulbous nose and vacant smile and nothing you say's gonna reach her now. And she's gonna get on her clothes and get on the raincoat and walk out again… maybe tomorrow night. It's not going to happen again. 5 am again and look at you. The fucking Elephant Man.

Along the Crease

Edward

The angel was a burst of flame, a pair of wings, a sword that looked like it could split atoms on its edge and a pair of blue eyes so piercing and metallic they served as a sidearm, two daggers to whirl into war beside it, devastating the foes of Heaven. Edward got a feeling like he had finished a milkshake too fast, then something akin to orgasm and in the distance he heard a reverberating string section. It culminated in a heat, another chill and a smell like the incenses and oils of an enormous New Age store. The angel spoke in a voice that ought to have ripped mountains and caused repentant heathens to walk into the sea as an act of contrition. It may well have been used to such errands, but it had come not smite Edward (who had committed very few sins in his 22 years), but to bare a message. It would come to tell him that the next day, he would meet the love of his life and that he was not to talk to her, consort with her and most certainly, under no circumstances was he to make love to her. Edward had never had a second date in his life, so fear and awe were transcended in favor of a state of abject befuddlement.

"I'm not very good with women. I'm fairly sure that if I met the love of my life, she probably wouldn't return my phone calls." The thought made Edward kind of sullen. The last date he'd been on was a blind date with a friend's sister. The girl had a round head and a long nose, qualities that in combination made her look something like a snowman.

The angel didn't bother reacting, or in fact had done so but quite imperceptibly. Before he could get his bearings again, he had to remember whether he had some Oreos before bed and where the tiny, sharp pain in his right eye must have come from.

"You cannot have her," the angel boomed, "you cannot lay with her. You will unmake existence, you will break down and put an end to the acts of the lord and nothing on Earth or in Heaven shall remain."

"How do I know you're actually an angel?" Edward asked. He had seen and felt enough to know that it probably was the case, but he felt somewhat like being defiant and contrary, being young and at least in a way, standing in the face of a God he had been uncertain of for most of his life. Edward had a small, and frequently insincere defiant streak that occasionally got in the way of his cowardice or existential confusion.

From the flames surrounding the blue eyes, a pair of large, strong hands shot out, surrounded by a glowing purple fire. The fingers traced along the young man's bare chest and with an astounding speed tattooed a half a circle onto his skin. "If the circle is completed, all things in Earth, in Heaven and in all other places will be undone and unmade."

With that, the angel disappeared, leaving Edward alone, horrified and clutching at the burning symbol on the left side of his chest.

Renee

When Renee was premed, she attempted via a defibrillator and a vastly overpriced book of black magic to bring back Kierkegaard, her Siamese kitten. For a moment she swore that his little legs twitched and his poor kitten eyes opened, but that moment , being brief as it was, did not hold enough appeal for Renee to commit to medicine. If she was to be a doctor, she desired to be a Doctor Frankenstein and if that was too much to ask than medicine didn't have enough to offer her. She had grown up intrigued with the idea of creating life, but having had two younger siblings, wasn't especially satisfied with the sort of golem a womb could produce. And maybe a schoolgirl crush on Peter Cushing didn't help matters either.

So, Renee abandoned medicine for Philosophy, Philosophy for Literature and Literature at last for wine coolers and sleeping late. For awhile, she attended parties to find better conversation and maybe somebody with more direction in life to help her along, but that time passed. She was a beautiful girl and it had never gone unnoticed or unexploited. With her tall, curvy figure and eyes the "the color of the sea" (said people who had never seen the sea), she stumbled frequently into romance, which took her nowhere she wanted to go. She never realized that she didn't really need to be wanted, and that she was meant to be a customer and not a commodity. This is why, by the time the angel came, she was already quite tired of love and most things that resembled it.

The angel, like the one who had come to Edward, gave no name. But, unlike Edward's angel, this one had something of a shape, that emerged from a shimmering yellow glow. There were three wings, like the other, but this one had a pair of heads; one that of an alligator with bright, pearly teeth, the other that of an old woman with gleaming silver hair and amber eyes that had no pupils. When it spoke, a warm wave of pure calm filled the room and Renee tasted a chocolate orange, like the ones she got in her Christmas stocking as a child. Each word it said was spelled out in an elaborate pink and purple calligraphy that was more legible than anything typed. Somehow Renee was not surprised and more oddly than that she wasn't surprised that she wasn't surprised.

"I come bearing a message from the Alpha and the Omega." Renee listened and read.

"What does God have to say to me?" she asked. Renee had never been a churchgoer, and while she had read Aquinas and Augustine, she hadn't put a whole lot of stock in it. On the other hand, she could no longer deny God or angels. After all,

215

something that hideous that behaved that strangely and didn't cause trepidation or nausea had to be somehow heavenly. Whatever God was supposed to be, its will was upon her and there'd likely be no escaping it.

"Tomorrow you will meet the love of your life…"

The half circle drawn on her chest burned with need for hours after the angel left.

Kismet

Of course, the two met. They had once been at the same party, although neither knew it. She had cut him off in traffic once, she had twice gotten the soup he had ordered at a restaurant they both dined at and frequently threw out the ATM receipts that he carelessly left near the machine. He had beaten her to the video store's sole copies of Ran, the Blob, Masque of the Red Death and Ilsa, She Wolf of the SS. She had beaten him to Tetsuo: the Iron Man, American Splendor, Metropolis and the Adventures of Milo and Otis. There had been a longstanding record of sleights between them that they knew nothing about, but had occurred startlingly often. Which one of them laughed hysterically and which felt a bit frustrated and hurt would depend only on the circumstances in which the information was revealed.

But, the first time they met that they were aware of, neither Edward or Renee did anything to transgress against the other one. They were both standing in line at the Borders, when searing pains assailed their chests. The pain flared, and burst and glowed like pink floral fireworks until it cooled down and in this coolness came all the relief of a glass of ice water on an August day. The half circle on Renee, exposed by her immodest black tank top, began to smile causing a sensation like the texture of half-melted ice cream as it turned from lumps to puddles. Underneath Edward's shirt, his circle smiled as well, the smile of someone who had found what they wanted.

When Renee looked behind her in line, she expected someone taller or better dressed or someone with higher cheekbones or more chiseled features in general. In short, she expected someone who wasn't Edward. But, she didn't find herself disappointed by him, and stranger yet, she wasn't surprised that he didn't disappoint her. Renee at this point in her life knew she had no clue what she wanted from it, so it would have been something of a tragedy if he had been ideal. She wanted to speak up and make it known how the circle felt in Edward's company, the hot, cold and bright, the leaping and bounding and the colors that could be seen as they touched her, but she stayed silent. The angel's words the previous night were a boot pushed down on her throat stomping and cracking her own like twigs underfoot. Be that as it may, her eyes didn't look like those of a woman who had been told she'd be a catalyst for the Armageddon. She had always been into guys who her parents disapproved of, or her friends said were dangerous, so there was a big appeal to this taboo. What makes a guy more dangerous than if God forbids you from seeing him?

Edward was nervous, as he almost always was. But this was a bigger, alien breed of nervous, with massive fangs and claws, more distinct than his typical twitch and doubly threatening. Edward wasn't ready for either a relationship or the end of the world. He decided at once to forget her, then after that, decided at once to remember her again. And then to keep thinking about her until he could do nothing but speak. "I'm Edward Brown. Have we met?" he asked. His voice was smooth and assertive in ways it had never been before. He said it with the authority other men reserve for pick-up lines, yet with a deep, endearing sincerity.

Renee couldn't remember the last time a guy had asked her that question and meant it. "No," she replied, "but I think we should." She scrawled down her phone number and handed it to him.

He couldn't help but think it was amazing. For once it was as easy to get a girl's number as it was for everyone else.

Cowards

It wasn't long before Edward had committed the number to memory. He committed it faster than he learned his social security number, or as a kid, his home phone number. But even after committing it, he recited it, he tested himself and continued checking back at the little sheet. He added up the digits and they came out to 33. He was surprised to find that the digits of his own phone number added up to the same. He was not a person used to superstition, or faith, or fixations on strange objects, but in a matter of hours, he had become one just because of this sheet of paper and the series of magic numbers he would invoke to summon forth the woman of his dreams. He didn't bother to reprimand or make fun of himself for being so obsessed, as it seemed only natural with a thing of such great power in his hands. It had been so long since anything else had held magic for him.

But, he had yet to pick up the phone or even approach it. In fact, he had neglected to eat because his phone was in his kitchenette. The phone felt to him an even more impressive, marvelous and frightening thing than the sheet of paper, so did not think to move it so it would not intimidate him out of his lunch anymore. If he picked up the phone and dialed the number, then he would have to talk, and once he talked then surely she would hang up and no longer display even the slightest modicum of interest in him. So, calling was right out, in spite of the unbearable excitement that the number generated.

Renee too was facing mixed feelings. With all of the things she could have done, she still found nothing better to do than to reflect on the previous evening. Ever since the angel had arrived, the whole crisis had of course occupied most of her thoughts. First off, she had been preoccupied with the thought of the end of the world. It was the strangest thing that it could be coming soon. After that, it occurred to her, that even more bizarre, she could be the catalyst for such a thing. No matter how many times it came up, the thought never lost its novelty. It made her vacillate between thinking "I'm very important" and "I must end up doing something REALLY wrong", both things that Renee found a little exciting and stressful. She had also met the man who would be the love of her life. One Edward Brown in line behind her at the Borders.

This too was a source of torment. He seemed nice enough, his presence felt wonderful, but he dressed poorly and had no interesting scars. He seemed sort of fidgety and was no more handsome than the next guy, and maybe no more interesting. If she had not been told these things about Edward, it's quite likely that she wouldn't have thought about him again at all, but she had been told these things and they had become immensely important. Edward Brown, aptly named with his dull anglo eyes and flat, unstyled hair was something so special, that Heaven didn't want her to have him. It had become even more intriguing a prospect than it was in the line. So, Renee got a phone book and she began calling people named Edward Brown. Though not a particularly focused girl, Renee was a persistent one and would find this man. She had given him her number, but she knew how attractive she was and how nervous a guy who looked and dressed like Edward must therefore have been, so she would have to make the first move.

Edward thought about the first move for hours and still fixated on the mantra and the prophecy and all sorts of things like that. He went to bed and fixated himself to sleep at around three am, although he was awakened at six by noises coming from his kitchen.

He walked to the kitchen, feeling not fear but a strange excitement, an excitement validated by the sight of Renee seated at his table enjoying a bowl of Fruity Pebbles.

"Thought we could have breakfast," she said.

The First Date

"I'm not really worth ending the world for," said Edward. He hanged his head in quiet despair. Embarrassment and quiet despair were the two feelings Edward knew best when it came to dealings with women. Sometimes in his better moments, he made his way to contrition, although that usually meant that somebody had been drinking. The odd part was, that Renee instead of being bored to tears by the statement decided to keep enjoying the Beaujolais she'd brought over . He reached the same conclusion Renee had, the conclusion that heaven doesn't just go around painting half circles on people for no good reason. She smiled coyly.

"Would you end existence for me?" she asked. She somehow made it sound like the kind of question women ask all the time.

"I don't really know you," Edward began, thinking he would end the statement there, but he saw that Renee was somehow prompting him, and that she knew damn well that was not where he sought to end his sentence.

"I don't really know you," he repeated, "but you're more beautiful to me than most other things out there." He poured another mug of wine and realized that he didn't seek to retreat back into himself or run and hide or correct the statement. Renee found herself just as surprised. She had suspected that Edward had no semblance of a spine at first, but saw that it was something he just kept hidden from day to day .

"What do you think you'd miss?" she asked, hoping to see more boldness in this shy, possibly very dull young man.

"What would I miss about what?" he asked, realizing only a second later what she had clearly been talking about.

"Existence."

"Yes," Edward replied, "I just figured that out. That's a very tough question."

"I know," said Renee. She had fun making him nervous, as

much fun as she had making him brave. She wondered why she had the perverse urge to see what he was made of, especially considering the consequences.

"I'd miss chocolate milk I think." He felt both honest and stupid.

But Renee understood. "Yeah, things like chocolate milk. I always wondered if I died, what I would miss and if it would be the same thing other dead people miss."

"I don't think it would." Edward noticed he really liked her chin. It was round, smooth and not pointy at all.

"I guess it wouldn't be the same for any two people. I would really miss Halloween. I like seeing all the kids marching down the street dressed as Scooby Doo and Freddy Krueger. It feels like everybody has the face they want." When she said that, Edward thought about Halloween as well. He thought about how he had never liked his nose and the masks fit so snugly. He thought about universal generosity, even from the cranky old people who were usually a plague upon the neighborhood. He came to the conclusion that it would be better off if day to day society was just run like Halloween, but he was sure that the idea would certainly not get the support it needed from the government.

"I'd miss animals," Edward said, and was surprised he said it, because he had never had any great rapport with animals, "I think it would be a shame if there were no more animals."

Each of them sucked in a gasp of dread. There was silence until they each poured more wine. Edward wanted to apologize, but it wouldn't have been right. He realized now it would not just be the little things in their life that they appreciated, but the life of all other things. Together, they would shred the world, make the blood of each species flow down the streets. He had never had such important decisions in his hands before and regretted it more than ever as he sampled the awkwardness between them that had been a growing rapport only a few seconds back.

But suddenly, there was calm, as the circles began to throb and blaze. Suddenly, they felt Halloween and walking down the streets of Edward's neighborhood with pillowcases full of candy. Renee felt Edward secreted in the audience of childhood piano recitals and watching the videos from the video store that she had rented only minutes before him. Those weekends were unruined, those last chocolate chip muffins at the Dunkin Donuts that she had once snatched up were uneaten or shared. They sat together and marveled at how strange their absences from each other's lives actually were. They could not help but fall asleep on the couch, full of wine, full of memories and full of perverse potential that could cost everybody a reality.

At the Zoo

The afternoon lay down and napped somewhere at the beginning of 80 degrees and stretched neither forward nor back, seeing neither seventy nine or eighty nine again. The moist little sea breeze was maybe a bit too perfect for two cynics and the absence of ominous clouds made it all too clear it was a day to be enjoyed without shame or pressure, even by the two people, who had the most reason to be ashamed of enjoying it together and were under the most pressure to separate from one another. Renee and Edward were enjoying this clear day and had gone to the zoo in order to enjoy it further.

On this Sunday afternoon, there was no better place for the two of them. The prophecies and messages and examinations of their lives had left each of them thinking about the scope of creation, the beauty and all there would be to lose. There was no better place they could think of to look at creation's splendors, the miracle of life on earth. As they walked through the zoo, the earth was no longer just the closet where they hung their clothes, the street on which their apartment buildings lie and the shaded windows behind which ex-lovers enjoyed their new relationships. This was the earth where giraffes teetered on their awkward legs and craned their long serpentine necks and stared with their strangeness out on ours, the earth where sea otters played and brightly colored birds lit up the skies. They marveled at the greatness of elephants and laughed at the pathetic, demanding roars of caged lions. There in front of the glory of nature's diversity, they held hands, drank three dollar cokes and bought bags of little plastic zoo animals like they did back when they were children.

The blue sky turned blue gray and then the blue faded turning the sky into a curtain of gray printed with clouds. Like drips of paint, the rain oozed down, slow drips, hard drips and at last a deluge. They fled from the fading of their day together and found themselves seeking refuge in Edward's apartment, since it was the closest of their two homes. They dried off and sat down on the floor, laughing at the zoo and the rain and the absurdity of their purchases. As the rain fell down on the animals at the zoo, their little plastic refugees found comfort in Edward's living room, where the two were lining up the toys like armies ready to march on one another. Looking over their collections, they traded between each other. Edward gave Renee two tigers for a polar bear and a giraffe, since Edward's bag had a glut of tigers. The two groups of animals began to look as if they hadn't been randomly assorted at all, and in spite of their military formation were filled with more fascination than violence for the other ones.

They spread their little menageries further apart and lay down on the floor between them. Edward tried to remember simple joy like this, times when the coldness of his family, the electricity of his nerves and the blandness of his surroundings didn't overwhelm and stifle and poison things. He couldn't think of many, and couldn't think of any one that served as an example of something better than this. He listened, smelled, contemplated, felt. The animals looked on as he lay his head on her chest and he listened. The circle made sounds that made him happy, he barely even needed to know what they were. There was a syncopated percussive heartbeat drum, and an ecstatic wild jazz and beyond that it was just a choir of joyful sounds. He felt like thanking the angel for letting him know that there were feelings that the senses just can't comprehend. He felt like thanking the angel for the brand and the way it felt when they got close. He wanted to feel them close together, so he got on top of her. The skin between their shirts burnt like a supernova, flared up and exploded with screams of bright joy inside them, screams that streaked like fireworks. They kissed and it defied the world of simple words and concrete feelings, it was a kiss like an atom, incredibly simple, infinitely complex and pulsing with its own special power. As they kissed, the circles shared their noise. Edward was amazed to hear beautiful music in himself, and Renee moved by the orchestral brilliance of her soul. For the first time, each heard their own music. Renee pulled her head back, moaned and stretched out her arms.

Time froze when the zoo animals fell to the floor. It seemed as if a person who listened closely enough could hear their final cries, the sounds of giraffes, monkeys, lions, tigers, grizzlies and all manner of beasts begging not be swept up into the flood outside. Renee stood up and she began to cry. No matter what happened, neither of them could be Noah and none of their little ark would be spared.

It Takes a Train to Cry

Renee and Edward, concerned about the fate of everything decided that they needed some time apart. It was not an easy decision, but it was still one they agreed upon immediately. It was the kind of thing there could be no room to argue about. So, each decided that they would try and find a long term means of making themselves feel better. Renee's friend Claire had sworn that Tristan would be the guy for her. He was nice enough, he was in a band and he was fairly attractive, so there was no reason not to give him a shot. After all, the whole end of creation of business was meant to keep Edward and her apart, not to make them inseparable. There was no reason missing somebody who it was existentially adamant that she should not have met in the first place. She repeated these mantras to herself as she sat down at her favorite little restaurant across from Tristan, the reasonably attractive musician.

"So, what do you, Tristan?" she didn't notice that her posture screamed "job interview."

"Well, I'm between things, but what I really care about is my music I guess. So, mostly , I practice my drumming, play some X-Box, play some hockey with my bros…"

It was at this point that Renee realized she had never liked Claire very much.

Unsurprisingly, Edward was not faring much better. After taking stock of his life, he realized it would not be all that effective to seek a girlfriend, since it would be a long, exhausting task and he didn't feel he had the energy for it. Besides that, he was mortally terrified of dating, which felt to him like giving a presentation in 9th grade history class. Surely something else was out there that could bring Edward some modicum of happiness, but the question was what?

Since Edward was never very good at taking stock of his life, he decided that what he most likely needed was some sort of interesting hobby. Perhaps, he reasoned, he would have something more to talk about on a date if he devoted himself to a single activity, or maybe even two activities if he got ambitious. As a kid, he had liked the idea of model trains, and it would surely be something that would take up a lot of time. So, Edward opened up his phone book and looked up hobby shops. He had forgotten that hobby shops usually don't stay open past 7 and got no answer from three of them. He regretted spending most of his day lying around trying to figure out what he could do next. Life granted him a small favor, though, and he found a place that would be open for another hour.

Wandering through the store, he was amazed to find

model railroading to be a very expensive hobby. The track was expensive, the switches were expensive, the buildings were expensive, and even the tiny people who worked near those buildings proved to be pretty damn expensive. His career as a model railroad engineer would prove to be a time consuming and expensive, but Edward still dropped twenty dollars on the engine of an HO scale locomotive. Disappointed in the little train, Edward decided to search for another hobby.

Renee found her leisure time no better occupied.

"Drums are much more complicated than people think they are," said Tristan to a fading Renee. She wished she could listen, but when he talked about drumming, all she could think about were the vibrant instrumental ecstasies of the circle, "there's tablature to learn, sticks to chose from, different kinds of drums, pads…" She disappeared from Tristan's conversation and found herself listening to the things she'd heard the night before. She could think of neither a garage band or a brilliant orchestra who could play that and who could let a person accompany on their own soul.

Leaving the hobby shop, Edward was stunned by an epiphany: model railroading was more often than not a hobby for violently antisocial dorks. Seeking a more appropriate hobby, Edward ended up in the music store. Music was also quite pricey, even moreso than model trains. Edward looked in his wallet and looked through the store, and found the two agencies to be violently opposed. Edward's seventy three dollars adamantly refused a guitar or drums and the store insisted he get something. There was a compromise, with some bloodshed at a fifty dollar purchase. Edward's wallet felt weak and the store felt embarrassed, but Edward felt triumphant, as the owner of a shiny new harmonica.

Edward's feeling of triumph was short-lived. Upon leaving the music store, he realized that much of his disposable income until his next paycheck was gone and he had bought a model train and a harmonica. He shrugged and made his way to the nearest cheap restaurant he could find. He would go, he would eat, he would take his mind off Renee and he would stop calling into work the next day, a day when he would hopefully still have his job. Yes, he would take his mind off Renee- who mocking fortune, in the form of Lucille Geary the waitress sat him at the booth directly across from. Renee was paying no attention to the goings on in the restaurant, but could feel the circle sing, transcending itself, wailing the pain of its Edwardless days.

All that Edward had felt he wanted was peace, until Renee spotted him and he spotted her spotting him. In spite of the danger and the fear and the trouble, his desire for peace drowned in his desire to be near her. It was all hunger, nothing in his stomach and spirit but the neglect native to an evening alone with a repressed, desperate self. He could feel her stifled desire to scream out for him and she could feel his stifled desire to beg her to come close. But he didn't want to make it known, since after all, she was over there on a date and it would be better to just let her finish her date and move on. Maybe he'd get better at the harmonica, maybe it would give him some kind of solace. He was not going to scream out and certainly not going to beg for her in front of her date. The guy was attractive, laid back and probably even interesting. Interested in things that would make a fondness for model trains and playing an overpriced harmonica look downright boring. He was sort of curious what those things would be, so that maybe he could develop an interest in them.

"We're kind of neogrunge emocore," Tristan explained to a less than fascinated Renee, "but we have a cello, so we're different that way. There was kind of an ethnic punk thing going on for awhile with bagpipes and shit but that didn't really work out. I don't think bagpipes are a very versatile instrument to be honest. And the guy was drunk all the time, and really full of himself. He was always asking if we could try and squeeze in another solo. And you can't really do that with the bagpipes. You can't just write a bunch of songs with big bagpipe solos, it just doesn't work. And that you know like changed EVERYTHING…"

That's when Renee decided it was a more than adequate time to acknowledge Edward and at the same time extricate herself from the tentacles of boredom that threatened to choke her to death as Tristan went on about the finer points of garage band construction and the emotional depths to which his drumming had taken him. She leapt up as she after an accidental casual glance she "saw" Edward at the next table.

"Oh my god, that's my friend Edward!" she exclaimed, "this is just too much! Yo, Edward c'mere, I've got someone for you to meet! God, this is just crazy. What are the odds?"

Edward was Mengele in Argentina, Elvis pumping gas in West Virginia or La Virgen de Guadalupe on a tortilla. Tristan couldn't help but glance over at this probability fracture. He could smell the import Renee placed on him and was curious. Curious and somewhat confused when he actually saw Edward. The puzzled blind date could be aptly called blind, because in Edward he could see nothing. This was not the sort of man he was used to competing with, and he was hoping this was not the sort of man that would prevent him from scoring with Renee.

"Hey," said Tristan, "sup?"

"Not much," Edward replied, "what's goin' on with you guys?"

Nobody bothered to answer that question.

"Why don't you sit down, Edward?" Renee asked. She patted the seat next to her. Her gaze was a baseball to the back of Edward's knees. It was blunt, the impact sudden and he went down, more falling into the seat than sitting in it. He was close enough to feel fingers of unseen radiance emanating from her circle and tickling him. It was hard to resist the temptation to just slouch down, relax and let them do their work, doing the things they did to the symbol on his chest and everything inside him. Instead, he tried to maintain some kind of decorum, sitting up as straight as he could and not daring to move closer. It would be out of the question to sit beside someone on a date with somebody else and start rubbing against their breast while squealing breathlessly. For a moment Renee was not above such temptations. Renee "ooed" and then regained the kind of composure that could only be faked, the kind of composure that the histrionically stiff Edward had been faking.

Edward breathed deeply and held on tightly to the shopping bags, which he had yet to let go of. The paper bag made an audible crinkle as the unseen fingers caressed him. The sound perked Renee up, let her try and get her mind off the pleasures of the circle and the oubliette of tedium that dating Tristan would be.

"What's in the bag?' Renee asked.

Edward reached in, pushing the little hobby shop bag with the toy train out of the way and grabbing the harmonica. He held it up, still for some reason saying, "it's a harmonica."

She couldn't help but think about how he held it like an engagement ring, like he was somehow petitioning her with it. Holding the little harmonica, he looked more like he was on the inside. He was eccentric, sort of boring, but loving, benevolent and sort of futile in a way she couldn't help but find sweet. He lost the love of his life and tried t o fill the void with a harmonica. It was the sort of gesture the Edward Renee had come to love did all the time. She was absorbed in the striking sweetness of the moment, so much so that she almost didn't cut Tristan off before he went on about his band again.

"Oh, cool, we had a harmonica guy…" Tristan began.

"I didn't know you were into music, Edward." Renee's hands were folded under her chin, fixing her face in place so her attention could be undivided.

"No," said Edward, head drooping, "I just decided to take it up. You know, as a hobby. I have a lot of free time lately so I figured I should have a hobby."

Renee nodded and gave him a sad look. "You could be like Bob Dylan. You kinda remind me of him."

Edward felt warm. He wasn't only the most interesting person in the room to her, he was actually interesting. He reached into the bag and took out the little train, holding it up almost proudly. "I also got this."

He thought about her words and the things he held in his hand and his thoughts were whispered between the circles. They glowed in his sad , eager eyes. This is how we pretend we're going somewhere when we're not. We spend our days with new people who we don't care about, go on journeys seated beside strangers. Renee was no different from Edward, a desperate young man who had bought a harmonica to play the blues and a train on which to ride out of town and never come back. But the journeys ended in the same place, at the same restaurant. They both had the same blues and the same loss and the same ideas. Tristan suddenly felt as lonely as Edward used to feel. Everybody at the restaurant felt a little lonely. Renee didn't even notice when Tristan walked out and neither did Edward, since they were the only two people in the room, seated together on a journey in a tiny empty little train.

"I want to see you again," said Edward.

"I do too," said Renee.

They still went back to separate houses and contemplated lonely journeys through life.

Origami

There was a loud hum at the core. Chanting voices united in prayer, an abbey of invisible monks that they could both hear in the circle, perhaps all pleading together for the right to be, perhaps echoing through Renee and Edward's respective souls to ease the unbearable burning, to drip away the bits of permafrost that the prophecies and the angels and the ordeal had left in their hearts. The two of them couldn't help but listen to the chanting, and as they did, they could not help but stop and reflect. It was a world of beauty and potential, with no end to its bounty. At least the chanting claimed that, at least those who chanted felt it and cried out for it. As Edward and Renee reflected, they could not help but wonder whether this was so or not. If this world sought to soothe and bring them peace, then why didn't it just let them have it? With all the strange, uneasy, cold days that the two of them had live through, and the taste of hope that they knew they could never have more of, surely it owed them that. But the chanting just said "calm down. All is well. Life is safe and beautiful and the divine is all around us."

But looking back, Edward found few rewards in life. The moments his soul wanted back, that the choir sought to give him, in defense of divinity and the great all that surrounded him were by no means numerous, by no means significant. The chanting wanted Edward to remember joy and to forget, and in truth the two things couldn't happen together. When he thought of joy, he thought first of Renee, and when he thought of Renee, the choir sang louder, sought to drown her out in the hum. But the memory of Renee was unsinkable. The drowning, and the drips of melting ice were not enough to let her sink, to leave her be. He thought instead of the ice, the oblivion and the loss and the Renee he would never have again and the Renee of the past let out a piercing scream that could not be denied even by the sounds of joy. The humble chanting of lesser angels and the mercy of divine vibrations stopped, because the two of them longed for their pain and would take it any day over that sort of bliss. Edward knew what would have to happen, and it did.

He was not surprised at all by the coming of the angel of judgment. He sat at his desk and looked upon the wings and flames and sword without fear this time. He had already begun to defy the orders given him and there could be no further harm done.

"If you've come to smite me," said Edward , "then smite

me. My life can't be right. Nothing can be right. If God sent you to kill me, then he's a hypocrite. He bothered to create me, then went and decided I can't love who I want to love, I can't have any fun and I can't feel like I have a good reason to get out of bed. Last night I bought a model train. ONE model train. And a harmonica. Are these the actions of a person who wants to live his life? If that's what life has to offer me, a model train and a harmonica, then I'll take anything else at all. Smite away."

When the angel finally spoke it was still using its mountain splitting, soul shredding voice, but there was neither fire or brimstone anywhere in its words. "I can't kill you. This is too delicate. This is a paradox, you see. I can only apologize and say that I'm afraid. There are assurances that have been made, but I have a job to do and I'm scared of never being able to do it again. I tried to stop you so that it wouldn't begin and therefore it wouldn't be the only way, but I couldn't. I can't kill you because at this point, it's more than likely that it's the only way, and I can't prevent things from happening the only way they can."

Edward was surprised to see the ice blue eyes grow wet with tears. He felt a tide coming in somewhere where it shouldn't come in and as the angel's eyes moistened, salt, shells and dead fish filled the room.

"Do you remember Sophocles in Oedipus Rex, he said "let no man be happy if he lives." That can't be. If there is no chance for joy anywhere in a life, that life can't be created. Sometimes a suicide happens because they've been placed too far from the joy to be had, but we can't create people with no potential for happiness. You, like most, can't be happy unless you love and are loved. So, if you don't have the chance, you'll be joyless. I came to tell you how much I love existence. I want you to really appreciate what you have no choice but to destroy. When I listen to that hum you heard and enjoy all the contentment of the things that get what they need, I get the only joy angels find, the hum at the center. I brought it to you both and discovered it didn't work. Joy isn't at the center for you. Incomprehensible. I can't kill you because at the center we understand that life is fair. The circle was to warn you, but it showed you instead. I wish I knew how life could be fair when it could all disappear because somebody makes a circle. I'm sorry you have to take away everything."

Edward didn't know why he felt like smiling. "I have to?"

"At the center we all know that life is fair. "

"I'm sorry," said Edward, "I really am. But why would we end the world?"

The angel just sort of floated. "Seraphim kill. Archangels explain. You'll know. Whatever happens, take a day please. The two of you should enjoy existence."

The angel disappeared leaving Edward alone and ecstatic on the beach that his living room had become. He felt like calling Renee, but realized that she was probably meeting with her angel. For some reason, Edward didn't even think about what life was like before he had to take such considerations. Heart full of relief, he let the hum play through the circle and took some joy in it. "She'll call," he said to himself, "she'll find out it's okay."

Renee too was not surprised to see her angel. She was frustrated, though. She, like Edward had had enough of nature telling her what to do, begging her not do it, and taking everything that feels good away. They told her not to see him, then inscribed her with the circle that burned for him, and made things more unfair with each passing day. Each day, it was just the pain of separation, the desire to see more of him and the knowledge that there was no way for it to happen. She wished she'd never heard of heaven or angels or tattooed circles in her life.

"Go away," she told the angel, "I'm tired of this. Thank you for letting me in on the whole inner peace thing, but inner peace doesn't mean much when the stuff outside you is a crock of shit. This world where angels can fly around telling people what to do all the time and saying who you can be with and who you can't is a crock of shit. The music is beautiful and it is clear that there are many who don't this way, but it's a crock of shit and I would like to get out of my house. God, I wish I just had a gun…what is it, silver bullets? Stake through the heart? How would I go about killing you?"

"You could try sleeping with Edward Brown," said the angel's crocodile head dryly.

"That's very funny," Renee replied, making no indication that it was at all funny. In fact, she still looked like it was quite the opposite.

"I'm here for a reason," said the angel.

"Are you going to kill me?" Renee asked. She sounded like she was asking if it wanted more tea.

"Seraphim kill. Archangels explain."

"Then explain. You might not remember, but you didn't give me that luxury."

Seemingly from nowhere, the angel produced a sheet of paper.

"There are all kinds of symmetry in this world. Everything has something of a perfect other half. But the symmetry isn't always perfect, and the souls are pressed closer together, created with spiritual proximity to their other half. These souls are usually created with other prospects, chances of deep happiness to be found in their environment and conditions. Sometimes there aren't, but usually there are. But, we messed up with you and Edward. You were perfect halves. There were no other things that really filled you. You two make a circle."

"So what's the problem with that?"

The angel held up the piece of paper. "Your symmetry is too perfect. We failed to give the world something better for you two to have. And when the folds touch…" the angel folded the paper vertically, aligning the halves perfectly, "what happens to the things along the crease?"

"They're still there."

"Flattened out, hidden, folded over and then creased. Crushed by the perfect alignment of the halves. Everything is along the crease and the two of you are prepared to make the fold. The paper won't be what it was, not at all. It will be changed and undone."

"Not if I don't see Edward again." Renee didn't feel like that was an option, but she felt like saying it anyway. She was confused and infuriated by this mistake that was made, by the fact that what her soul needed was the other end of the paper, which wanted nothing from the middle either.

"That's the way it will have to be. That's the only rightness. We can't stop the perfect symmetry and all the things at the center are scared of what will happen when the edges meet there. But I came here to tell you, that in all actuality, there is nothing better to do. In the center we know that life is fair, the same game with players positioned differently. I'm sorry we put you on the edge. It must have made you wonder sometimes."

The angel left, and Renee picked up the phone eager to meet in the center.

Neither Bang Nor Whimper

Leon had been selling people newspapers for forty five years. Old people, young people, cops, hookers, soldiers and priests all came to Leon. There were days when he would say to them "don't miss tomorrow's" because he had a feeling that something big would be in it. Over time, the people learned to heed that warning. It made them call loved ones, take the day off work and on some occasions update their insurance. Something big in the paper usually meant something bad. The day after Leon's warnings there were always dead movie stars, poor countries at war and all kinds of new worlds happening all around them.

As he did every morning before work, Lieutenant Quinn bought a paper.

"What's in tomorrow's news, Leon?" he asked, half joking.

"Damnedest thing," said Leon, "I close my eyes and look and I try to figure it out and all I see is "no news is good news"."

This was enough to make Quinn call in for the day. Jenny Quinn, age four was a bit confused that her daddy would let the bad guys go free and roam the city just so he could stay home and play Candyland with her. She consoled herself with the thought that she was much safer with her daddy at home and there was no need for her to worry about the bad guys because her father was, after all , right there. The Quinns felt okay, certain that for once no disasters, real or imaginary could come about and tear them apart for awhile.

Kelly Hutchinson had been teaching English for twenty seven years and had been buying the paper off Leon for just as long. As she tended too, she got her paper at six am sharp and asked Leon the same thing everybody else would today.

"Funny thing," said Leon, "I think about it and I look ahead and you know what I see?"

Kelly shook her head.

"I see no news is good news."

They laughed together, somehow knowing they were sharing a truly big joke.

Kelly's students, who had been indifferent and a bit bored with the works of the English Romantics were surprised when instead of a paper, their teacher walked them down to a pond a quarter mile from the school. The whole procession looked a lot like of the mother duck who was bringing her ducklings back there as well. The class sat down and they looked out at the water and up at the sky and then they looked into themselves. They saw that there was a lot of import and no small modicum of truth to be found in the words of Wordsworth and Blake. Maybe more importantly, they saw that Hutch the tyrant, Hutch the bitch, Hutch of the 8 page paper due Monday felt and thought and experienced most of the same things they did. And many of those things were things that Blake and Wordsworth thought, things about man and nature and symmetry.

Patron after patron came to Leon with the same question, until finally, around noon, Leon hung a sign up that said "Leon the psychic news dealer says no news is good news." It was an odd thing that Leon himself for some reason decided to join the throngs of people going to the zoo. Perhaps, like Mrs. Hutchinson they all had a desire to get to know nature a little better. Like Lieutenant Quinn, he decided that he would spend time with family as well. He called his daughter, Jill at work and asked her if maybe her kids would like to spend some time with their grandfather. The babysitter was tipped and the two three old girls "oohed" and "ahhd" their way through a makeshift Serengeti. Leon marveled at how his day had been more full of surprises than ever.

There, at the zoo was the one client he had ever lost. In Leon's mind, something had to be wrong with somebody who stopped buying the paper, and Edward was the only man Leon knew who suddenly stopped buying the paper. The dour young man who Leon assumed had simply committed suicide was at the zoo with a beautiful young woman who for some reason was happy to see him. Leon was even more surprised when Edward walked up to him and said hi.

"Hey, what's goin' on, Leon?" Edward smiled.

"All I can feel or see is that no news is good news. I think the world's gonna end. But, I don't feel like it's all that bad. There ain't any Russian nukes or terrorists or martians, so I guess we can still rest easy."

Edward nodded, bearing a quiet confidence that surprised both Leon and himself. "That's good to know," said Edward, "cute kids by the way."

"They're my granddaughters I took the day off to take em hear. Everybody seems to have gotten the same idea."

"It's a gorgeous day, even if it's the last one."

Leon nodded. "You two look good together," he said and then went on his way.

Edward smiled again, brimming with new confidence. He wrapped his arms around Renee and they embraced and kissed in front of the tiger cage. The tigers watched and understood. The patrons watched and understood and for reasons unknown to them were mesmerized. None could account for why the kiss seemed like history. None could tell why they all felt like smiling at and waving goodbye to these two people or why they all felt as happy at the zoo as they had anywhere else in their lives.

When Edward and Renee went home and they shed their clothes, the two shared skin and eyes and muscles and wisdom. The circles didn't just touch, they combined and they blazed like a new sun with fresh unfathomable light. As they moved and loved and lived as one, existence could feel it.

Once angry and idle angels felt it as they took the wheels from God's chariot. The ophanim spun on their own, feeling what it was to be their own circle to spin into motion, to spin into creation, to fly and move and burn paths across the cosmos. The once angry seraphim had no jealousy for the newfound freedom of their brothers and rejoiced as they shattered their dull swords and cool breezes put out their unrelenting flames. They listened as it rang through heaven, the truth they had to remember: "if being cannot let men be, than life is the failure, not man. An earth that cannot satisfy is not the earth."

The devils in arrogant hell thought to laugh at first. The damned all gathered at the gates and wondered if they could escape, but there was nothing to run to for them. The stayed where they were and felt the ecstasy reach down. As the folds came together, the damned could feel the joy of living and the chance they had at heaven and felt a hell where the flames had burnt out. They looked up and saw the morning star, the angel of light that once was floating up through the void toward bits of a broken heaven. He reached up his hand like the painting by Michelangelo and found it taken by God whose eyes were humble, tearful and understanding.

"Both of us were wrong," he said, "I should have let you be happy."

As Leon the newsdealer went home, all he could think was what the headline would say. It would probably say Mideast peace talks still failing or Iranian nuclear program progressing, or train crash kills fifty. This wouldn't be in the headlines and it made him happy to know that. People wouldn't have to read the bad news, they could go outside and feel the good, the delight of two lovers doing what they needed to do to be their fullest. "Not with a bang, but a whimper" he remembered from a poem he'd once heard. He laughed his way out of creation, as did the president, the pope, every house cat and every wicker rocking chair.

Renee and Edward floated in nothingness and still they couldn't stop themselves, their joy and love uncontainable. They laughed and wept and touched each other, understanding what it was to be every inch of being, to be a circle. The new Sun cut, squeezed and kissed delicious new experiences , bursting forth joy and power in spasms both embarrassing and beautiful. They didn't even notice the Creamsicle sky that built around them and the trees in shapes unbeknownst to them, they knew nothing of the strange animals and oceans of inexplicable colors. Enormous eyes seemed to open as planets came into light and being. There was Edward, there was Renee and there was life; life that sought to explore new symmetries.

Brian's Girl

I can believe it, actually. The look on your face says it all, that dirty, special "Dear Penthouse" look that guarantees us an unparalleled entertainment. You let one of the priestesses in, didn't you? You don't let in the priestesses. Never let in the priestesses. You treat them like Jehovah's Witnesses, aluminum siding salesmen or housewives collecting for the Friends of Nyarlathotep. But, of course it's easier with the Jehovah's Witnesses. I mean…Jesus, Jehovah's Witnesses never look anywhere near that good.

Two weeks ago, one of them comes to my door. She's wearing little jean shorts and a red leather bustier and she's carrying a Hello Kitty backpack. She's got her hair up in pig tails to look about twelve. But, obviously, considering the assets that bustier is holding up, she sure as hell isn't twelve. Of course, I answer my door. Everybody probably does. It's the first step.

"Are you Brian?" she asks me.

"No," I reply, deeply disappointed in myself for neither being this guy or lying about it. She doesn't seem at all fazed.

"Would you mind taking some pictures of me?" she asks. She smiles widely and innocently and sort of bounces in place as she waits for me to answer. It takes me a second to answer. I have to wonder if this is some kind of weird and very unfair sting operation. But when I answer, I tell her yes. Of course I tell her yes. It almost ceases to matter for me that she might somehow be a cop. Nothing ventured, nothing gained. The credo of the successful single American male. She mutely hands me a cellphone and points out the camera button.

She goes in, and the moment she walks in the door, she

begins posing. She gets up on all fours and presents herself like a cat.

"I love my ass," she says, as casually as she would "Big Mac and a small Coke", "make sure to really accentuate it."

"Got it," was the only response I could muster. What else do you say to a request like that?

It wasn't a hard one to fulfill, that's for sure. Here was a girl who definitely ate her Special K in the morning and then high-tailed it to the gym. It was round, smooth, eye-catching and obscene. It was a Magic 8-ball of an ass, and there I was, on my hands and knees taking pictures of it. How can you describe the feeling of knowing someone for all of a minute and a half and kneeling behind them with a camera? Maybe it wasn't a conventional relationship, but I felt that maybe it could be a good start. You want to call me naive don't you. It's eating you up. But you're starting to feel stupid, too. Judge not lest ye be judged.

After I snap a few pictures, she looks at me and she says in that same "Big Mac and a small Coke" tone "it looks better when it's a little pinker. Spank it awhile. Give it a few pinches." It's exciting, because a little scrap of interest slips past her puzzlingly professional demeanor.

I was right about the girl. I was right about her ass. What? You were gonna talk dirty, you were gonna talk smut. So, I'm talking smut, I'm talking details. It's soft and firm at the same time, sorta like a basketball feels. I actually had to spank pretty hard to make a mark or to get her to make a sound. The pinching might have drawn blood from a less fit, less muscular girl. I snapped a few more shots, suddenly feeling artistic, kind of free. I worked the angles, zoomed in the ripe-looking reds and pinks. The shots were really something.

After I've taken about twenty or so pictures, she turns to face me, and she takes her top off. They're largish B-cups, pretty spherical, and there's a ring in each nipple. More than nice. She smiles, licks her lips and then she takes one of them in her hand and runs her tongue along the nipple. I feel so envious. Finally, instead of smiling at the cellphone, she smiles at me. She reaches into the Hello Kitty handbag and takes out a boxy little webcam. Expensive stuff. It's wireless.

"You wanna fuck me?" she asks, making sure to turn on the webcam first, "you wanna fuck me, Brian?"

I didn't know who the hell this Brian guy was, but I did want to fuck her. I answered as much of the question I could truthfully. Within seconds, her panties hit the floor and she's on her knees, quickly and desperately opening my zipper. She pulls my pants and my boxers down and grabs my balls, squeezing, massaging them. She kisses the shaft of my cock over and over again, before she opens her mouth. She gives me a slow, deep, skillful blowjob. She makes sure to keep her eyes wide, to stay in the frame and makes seductive little pouts with her mouth as she sucks. I was in a show that days before I might have been embarrassed to jerk off to. Showy, sorta inorganic to an observer.

She takes me out of her mouth, revealing to the camera that I'm rock hard, like a magician showing that the sword he's plunging into the magic box is sharp. Well, then again… She stands up and slowly, teasingly, cinematically she lowers herself onto me. She rides my cock as if it's going to take her to the next town if she just keeps on moving. She gyrates, dances, bounces and works it like it's nobody's business. Then, she gets down on her knees again and she lets me…yup, you know. Not on the best day of my life do I have the privilege with most girls, but this time I get to. And it lasts.. As those muscles squeeze around in this tight, sacred, profane place, I forget that I don't know her at all. I forget that during the photo shoot she acts like she knows me and I do this for her every day. I forget everything but this doorway to warmth and bliss shutting me in. When she turns off the camera, I'm almost can't pull out.

At this point, it would have made sense for her to gather up her clothes and leave. But, not much about the encounter made sense, so I shouldn't have felt so relieved when she didn't. I wondered whether it could be like this every day. Maybe I could call her sometime and actually converse. Maybe she would show me her place. The fact that she stayed and let me watch as she cleaned the fluids from her body, and thought about the experience made me feel good. Yet, still I wondered just what she thought about it and why she had even come to the house to begin with.

"Can I use your computer?" she asks. There was something odd about the way she asked, though. Like computer was a substitute for bathroom and was something as normal and utilitarian as one.

"Sure," I answer her, "upstairs in my room, first door on the right."

So, she goes up there and she doesn't come back for like twenty minutes. I'm starting to get sort of tired and hungry. I need to get this energy back, you know? And I figure maybe I could learn something about this girl if we go out together and have a meal. I head to the room to ask her, and there she is on MySpace, just pondering a sentence with this bomb squad look on her face, like everything will go up in smoke if this sentence doesn't turn out right.

And there, at the top of the screen, I see the most confusing of several confusing things that happened that day. It said, "I think I love Brian. Today when we made love again, it felt different, special, savage, loving and brutal." I remembered those words perfectly because the last thing I expected was to see her writing them on her MySpace page, twenty minutes after sex, when she doesn't even give me her name.

"Umm, I don't know what this is," I say to her, "but my name isn't Brian and if you haven't gotten my name wrong, I'd kinda like to know about this Brian guy."

"Oh, you're Brian," she says, "you know who Brian is? Brian is anybody that I fuck then talk about in my blog, that's who Brian is. It's too much to keep up a relationship, but I need somebody to write about, so there's five Brians a week. Brian's actually my dog's name. Like on Family Guy."

I don't know what to do. I feel like crying or yelling, but all I could really come out with was "Why? Who are you?"

She just laughs. "What am I? What do names matter? You can take any one you want. You can call me BludKitty88 if you like. I'm a priestess."

"A priestess?" I ask her, "a priestess of what?"

"I gotta go," she says, "I need to edit that video."

So, I figure that that's it, but the next day, there's a cute brunette at my door, wearing a bustier, green fishnets and she asks if I'm Jake and if I would like to take some pictures. This is when I figured I would say no, but I don't say no. There's some strange cloud of "fuck me" that I just can't ignore coming off of her. With her there, there's no decency, no social contract, no need for affection. There's just me and my dick and my need for excitement and relevance. We go in and she lets me tie her up. Her breasts look huge, spilling out of the bustier and propped up by the ropes. I take a whole bunch of pictures and I know immediately to take the webcam from her big, black Gucci purse and start it up. She spreads her legs, but keeps her ankles together and it feels so good to be in charge and taking advantage of this filthy, dirty damsel in distress. She calls me Master, as I bend her into all the positions I want her in, and have my fill. We fuck until we're both good and exhausted and the ropes are starting to chafe her and then she goes upstairs and starts writing on her MySpace page. On the way out, she introduces herself as MystressTenebre, with a "Y."

So, the next day, I take a look at the MySpace pages, and I'm kinda flattered that I'm better in the bed than the last three Brians and Jakes were. On the MySpace page there's a link to something called SAW. Of course, I click on it, and there's a psychedelic background, droning technomusic and a big Andy Warhol face. The only words on the page are "have your 15 minutes", as well as links to all of the videos. They range from hours of people standing in the mirror making funny faces to fake snuff films, to what might be real snuff films. I'm pretty certain they are, since the users who put them up never seem to post again. I go the bathroom and I throw up. I take a long shower and I tell myself that today I'm not going to be a part of this madness. I beg a God I haven't prayed to since I was six to give me the strength and resolve to resist this shit.

But there's this tall voluptuous redhead in a tight tank top and Daisy Dukes waiting at the door with a great big smile and the promise of another day of wild, sexual misconduct and voyeurism. I just can't shut the door in her face. It's not weakness, it's something else entirely. I need this. I need her today. When the pictures and the sex are done, I go up to see her and I have to ask, because I really need to know.

"What is SAW? What are you guys about?"

"Servitors of Ascendant Warhol. Don't get all Ira Levin on my ass, okay? We're just helping to make things just right for when he comes back. You should be grateful! People will see you. If nobody sees you and nobody reads about you, you're nothing. I've helped you gain some relevance. Be grateful and take the new Gospel to heart."

In a way, she's sorta right. If a guy pumps gas all day, the only people that know about it are the people who get gas, but he makes a video of himself pumping gas, then it's possible that a thousand people will see it. He writes in his blog "still pumpin' gas" and it becomes important and after that go around with this priestess, people all over the internet will think I'm somebody because I'm fucking this gorgeous chick and she's going wild. I start to like the idea a little and I start to hate this girl so much that it doesn't matter at all when she leaves. She's just a tramp who's part of some scary cult. The guy says "everybody gets their fifteen minutes of fame" and these girls give it and these girls get it.

It starts to happen every other day with these girls. Lingerie, big heels, tight little t-shirts and the wrong name. It's too much for a guy to take, the sex and the little bit of anonymous stardom. The more I fuck, the more people see it and the more guys out there wish they were me. But what really gets to me are the blogs. I think I love Jake, I think I love Harry, I think I love Jamal, I think I love Lorenzo, I think I love Raphael. I've been Jamal, I've been Roger, I've been Lorenzo, and I start to realize that it isn't fame, It's not fame if it's not you. When Marilyn Monroe's on a coffee mug, it's not Marilyn. It's a mug. I started to lock my door after that, and I haven't really seen anyone until you.

They don't leave you the same these girls, because I see. You'll see too. Every night I have the same dream, every goddamn night and someday everybody will have that dream and when the plague of dreams comes down the whole earth will be nothing but that dream. That's why you don't let in the priestesses, you poor son of a bitch. They're the marching band in the parade, accompanied by elephants, transvestites, fireeaters and clowns, and when they're done, Uncle Andy will be back, proven right. Covered in gaudy jewelry, his hair shining blinding white hot, he'll look invincible with his black turtleneck and superior smirk. He will turn the sun into a disco ball that calls the dead to dance the night away. Riding in James Dean's Porsche with Marilyn and Elvis and Jayne Mansfield, he will cross the sea and turn the Vatican into Caesar's palace, boxing a hundred rounds with L. Ron Hubbard to see who inherits the earth. There will be no winners, although Brian does well for himself.

About the Stories

Re-Mancipator

Never, ever, ever, ever, ever, ever, ever, ever, ever, ever, ever, ever try to make your other ideas sound good by coming up with what you think is a really shitty idea. I made this mistake by presenting Jeff Burk, my editor at Eraserhead with a bunch of pitches including one that I thought was so goddamn lazy, nobody would possibly want to read it. "Zombie…Lincoln." Years before Seth Grahame Owes Me Millions of Dollars wrote Abraham Lincoln, Vampire Hunter, I had an idea for zombie Lincolns. Of course, Jeff and Eraserhead were all "FUCK YEAH, ZOMBIE LINCOLNS!" So, I had to write a zombie Lincoln story. Since I hated this idea, I had to put as many things in it as possible that had nothing the fuck to do with it at all. Absinthe helped. Thanks, Absinthe! You the man now, dawg!

Assorted Salesmen at the Birth at the Antichrist

I was thinking about the Magi and how amazing they seemed to be. Jesus had a great crowd around him. But what about the Antichrist? Salesmen. Sorry. Too bad you already bought this book.

The Adventures of Blackmetal Bjorn and Accomplice Boy

Varg Vikernes is a figure that fascinates me. He's a Black Metal legend who can't seem to stay out of jail for burning churches and for stabbing a guy who was enough of a pretentious twat to call himself Euronymos. Varg is kind of hilarious for a murderer and a pyromaniac. He's the world's silliest hatemonger, which is quite an honor to have. I wondered what it would be like to

247

have Varg as your Tyler Durden or Puff the Magic Dragon. Wouldn't it be weird to have Varg Vikernes as your conscience? But then the story got serious. My book *Murderland* predicted that with bullying reaching epidemic levels and Civil Rights becoming once more a social battleground, we would have a new rash of school shootings. None of these have been a young gay man picking up a gun but if you push people hard enough, they push back and in a world where might makes right that will often be done at gunpoint. I hope at some point you stopped laughing or that you didn't start.

An Author is a Beagle as a Flying Ace

Julie Newmar was where I discovered women. I am very much a man who loves women, as complicated as my feelings toward the individual women in my life are. These are stories about our complicated relationship with the goddess told in drabble form. She's a hell of a woman, Julie Newmar.

Hit and Fun

Sometimes objects just feel alien to me and I look at them and I see their textures and structures and how confusing they really are. Traffic lights look like weird rectangular faces of something otherworldly. I don't like or trust them. They creep me out. Then I thought of how much power and influence they have, wondered how our brains got hot-wired in this way. My musical project, Sad Monster Party featuring musician Mike Bibby, did an album whose centerpiece is a song inspired by the Trikloptikon myth and it has been mentioned in a few of my performances. Check out Seeds from the Bloody Rise of the Elder God Trikloptikon to hear me screaming metal vocals about the traffic light god. It's pretty cool. There's also a song on there called "Spooky Roller Disco" that I am immensely fucking proud of.

'

Beast with Two Back
Terror of intimacy is a common theme in my work. I like intimacy. I hate the nightmare of our separation from other human beings. But there's this thing that happens in relationships that gets scary, when you start to move in tandem and you start to think in tandem and the concept of sex becomes dominate by a single person in your imagination and they start to own it and they start to own the potential of what your body can do. Is it a kind of Nirvanaphobia, a kind of fear of unity with the Brahmin that prompts our strange terror of invasion and the death of self? I don't know. But it's a shitty feeling that prompted a dream which featured the central image of the story. This story has been good to me. It was selected not just for Cameron Pierce's anthology *In Heaven, Everything is Fine* but was also as an honorable mention in *Best Horror of the Year* by Ellen Datlow

The Man in the Film Noir Hat
This piece is made of jazz and exuberant noise. I wrote it when I was a senior in high school and it made me really happy. I liked the idea of an encounter with the angel of bad ideas. I liked the way I told this story in sound and poetry. I like this story. This story got me one of the rejections that kept me writing. Andrei Codrescu from *Exquisite Corpse* glibly said to a professor who ended up in the same rejection bracket as me "Maybe you should give Garrett Cook a scholarship." I had come close. It would not be impossible…though it would take another seven years and it would be *Exquisite Corpse* to publish me, ironically in the same issue with Tom Bradley, who would be instrumental in building *Imperial Youth Review*.

All About the Sheriff
This story is about the world ending around you. It's about thinking love doesn't come back. I was at the tail end of a relationship, around the same time I had just finished "Beast

249

With Two Backs." And I was hurting and afraid of freezing up. Have I? Maybe. But sometimes in the deepest parts of winter, it warms up and we let ourselves flow down, we let ourselves become fresh, crystal clean snowfall. I feel this story, cold as I was, is me doing that some.

Octopus

I had a dream senior year of high school, sitting in a wheelchair, high on Valium and Codeine and waiting to find out if I had a tumor on a bone in my leg. I didn't have the cancer, which was nice. But I'd rather not have had the dream of bonelessness, floating around in a sea of despair. I later revisited this image years later as I was thinking about masculinity and what it means. Masculinity is something I think about a lot because I never got to see how it was done. This story was picked up by Jeremy Needle of Evil Nerd Empire for the anthology *Hatter Bones*. It was one of my first three sales.

Having Set Out to Be Vanquished

I had not read too much by Clark Ashton Smith but when Cody Goodfellow says you could do cool stuff with an author's world and there will be a spot in his antho set in said world, you give it a shot. And I did. I wanted to take cosmic horror and fantasy into a more intimate, visceral and human place and to deal with my anxieties about never being loved again after that relationship. I was loved again. And maybe I'll stop being loved and then get loved again. It's more organic now than I thought it was. It will be okay. This story hurts like hell.

Dieselpig

This was meant to be an introduction to Wake at the House of Butchered Hogs. It's the most political thing I've ever written in a lot of ways. Drone warfare is very disconcerting to me. The news media is very disconcerting to me. The idea that there will come a time when we as a culture will be lionizing soldiers that go out there to be less human than they are inhuman is disconcerting to me. Dieselpig is a sad, over the top manic piece.

The Wake at the House of Butchered Hogs
This was going to be the centerpiece of a book, with the high concept being a trip out to the most fucked up silent film ever made but we couldn't quite make it work and having this piece as the main selling point for a book is box office poison. Heinrich Pseudonym, the director of the piece has been referenced in other work I'm working on and in my Ultimate Bizarro Showdown pieces as the author of the reprehensible *The Magic Sorority House*. This story is Bunuel doing straight porn with cosmic horror infused in it. It combines Chambers and Dali and Rollin and things like The Gorilla with straight up neurosis and existential terror. I'm glad I get to share this with you.

Coathanger
Speaking of things that hurt like hell, here's one of them. I've never felt quite welcome on this planet. Illegitimate, body dysmorphia, bipolar and god knows what the fuck else, I spent a great deal of my life believing that the Earth was going to simply spit me out or revoke my right to live or some sort of retroactive abortion could happen. Probably just me. Probably. This one comes from a dream springing from that place. I have some awful dreams.

The Granny Crunchbones
I think faeries should be terrifying. They've always been referred to as alien, older than man and sinister in their ideologies and motives. Faeries are meant to represent the shit we are encroaching upon at our own idiot risk. I wanted to take that to a modern place and still make it scary, merging it with traditional urban legend. This is the most meat-and-potatoes horror story in here but I'm okay with that.

251

The Donor

Men expect a great deal of women. We want them to be saints and saviours and objects of worship. We project a lot and their worth is so often derived in their minds from the things men have projected. That makes me feel bad. I wanted to tell a story here that salutes an act of passion and enthusiasm by somebody who thought she was nothing special but turned out to be a huge boon and load off my soul. She did something really beautiful and saved a bit of my sanity and this story, in my own dark, perverse idiom salutes her for being her. She'll never know just how cool she is.

And You Told Me Again, You Prefer Handsome Men

This was for an anthology about queefing. I did not know if I wanted to submit to an anthology about queefing. It seems like a bad idea to submit to an anthology about queefing. What kind of idiot submits to an anthology about queefing? Well, this idiot. I had to try and make queefing into something intense. One of the things about Bizarro writing I love is that I am extremely competitive and Bizarro has a tendency to provide you with fantastic straightjackets to escape from. You get more and more flamboyant public deathtraps to wriggle your mind out of. And this one was irresistible. So I wrote a story about queefing. I'm sure Ray Bradbury had dozens of fucking queef stories in his drawer that he just didn't have the stones to share. What's up now, old man? Something gaseous this way comes, Ray Ray!

Yeah, sorry. I'm not actually like that at all.

Along the Crease

Dante and Blake left me obsessed with the idea of divine symmetry, the thought that maybe somewhere out there was a perfect other half. I now think that maybe we are more awkward shapes than circles and maybe there are corners and angles found in a lot of people, not just the one. Anyway, I was then drawn to the idea of perfect symmetries being too much for the world to bear and forcing a couple to create their own world. This does turn out to be painfully true as I discuss in "Beast With Two Backs" but in this case, I look at it from a more positive perspective and bask in the elegance and wonder of a symmetrical world. Part of me still believes in symmetries, though if they are so, then they are surely catastrophic in their way. I like the Sundance channel aesthetic of this and the narration. It was a departure during the time when I was discovering me but I'm happy about it.

Garrrett Cook is an author of bizarro. horror and mythos fiction. He is a two time winner of the Ultimate Bizarro Showdown and a winner of the Wonderland Award for his book *Time Pimp*. He works as a freelance editor and teaches workshops on writing in the Bizarro genre. He finally resides in Portland, Oregon.

www.ingramcontent.com/pod-product-compliance
Lightning Source LLC
Chambersburg PA
CBHW020652030726
47498CB00002B/474